ONE WRONG TURN

M. A. HUNTER

Boldw⦾d

First published in 2023 as *The Trail* by Boldwood Books Ltd. This edition first published in Great Britain in 2024 by Boldwood Books Ltd.

Copyright © M. A. Hunter, 2023

Cover Design by Head Design Ltd

Cover Photography: Shutterstock and iStock

A CIP catalogue record for this book is available from the British Library.
Paperback ISBN 978-1-80549-552-9

Large Print ISBN 978-1-80549-551-2

Hardback ISBN 978-1-80549-550-5

Ebook ISBN 978-1-80549-553-6

Kindle ISBN 978-1-80549-554-3

Audio CD ISBN 978-1-80549-545-1

MP3 CD ISBN 978-1-80549-546-8

Digital audio download ISBN 978-1-80549-547-5

Boldwood Books Ltd
23 Bowerdean Street
London SW6 3TN
www.boldwoodbooks.com

To all those who've underestimated me all my life:
The joke is on you!

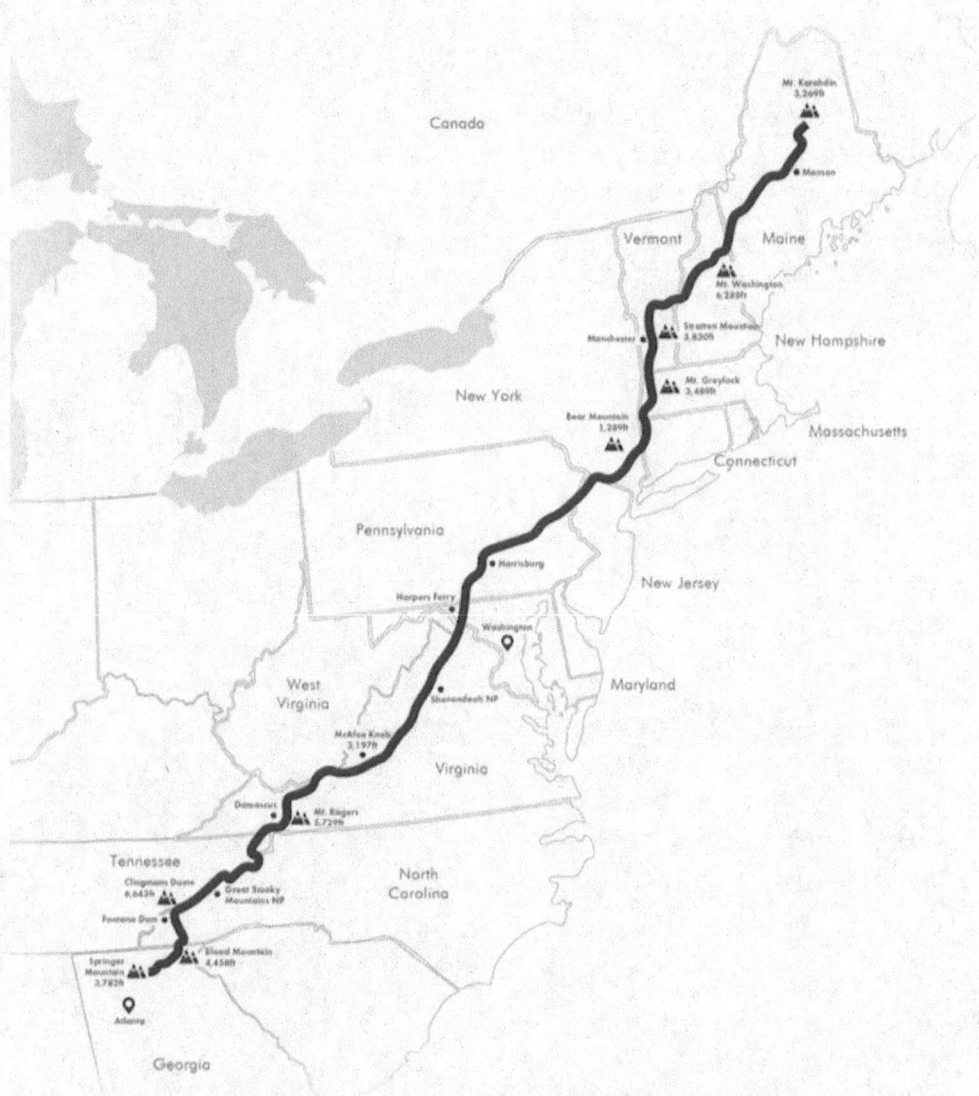

APPALACHIAN TRAIL

·UNITED STATES·

If you see something, no you didn't.

If you hear something, no you didn't.

If someone calls your name – don't look, run.

1

JESS

April 2023, Brighton, East Sussex

It's been years since I had a formal job interview, but ultimately the role is to answer customers' queries about their insurance policies. How hard can it be really? Ashley's already warned me that there's four weeks of classroom training before I'll be unleashed into a live environment, so they can't be too choosy about who they're looking for. So long as I don't drop an F-bomb halfway through the conversation, I should be fine.

The bus terminates at the station, and it takes me

a moment to get my bearings, before I spot the large branded sign beyond the Jury's Inn hotel. I'm just flattening out where my skirt has risen from being seated when a car bombs past, sending a tidal wave of puddle water over where I'm standing. I don't move for what feels like an age.

This can't be happening!

I hear a couple of faceless sniggers over my shoulder, and will myself to open my eyes and survey the damage. I can feel water dripping from my hair, and when I look at my salmon-coloured blouse I want to cry. The material is sodden with giant patches of mud stained through.

The car that caused this damage is nowhere in sight, but I silently offer a curse on their life, as I search for a window to assess my reflection. Noticing a hotel, I stop and head inside, making my way to the ladies' toilets, but what I see is far worse than I imagined. The face looking back at me is older than I remember. The dark rings beneath the eyes, the crow's feet pinching near the temple, and the chapped lips belong more to someone nearing middle age, instead of the sprightly woman struggling to find her place in the world. I pluck a grey hair which stands out against the backdrop of my otherwise darker mane. When did I get so old? Why do I feel as though half my life is already over?

When I picture myself, I'm still the awkward teenager who dreamed of writing Pulitzer material, thriving on a diet of coffee and intrigue. I've always been drawn to writing, even when it was only scribbled musings on Post-it notes, or embarrassing confessions in the diary I kept as a teenager. Writing is when I feel most like my true self. Growing up, Lois Lane was my hero, but where were the warnings about how tough it is to make it in the world of journalism? I interned for three whole years, waiting for my chance, only to lose out to a twenty-year-old former reality star. I've been writing freelance ever since, but editors aren't interested in my theories on the parliamentary scandals. And to be honest, my heart isn't in writing basic fluff pieces about local dog shows and art exhibitions. I want to use my natural investigative instinct to dig out hard truths and dark secrets, but I'm yet to stumble on anything I can get my teeth into.

At what point should one accept that the dream they've been striving for will permanently remain out of reach? How many times does 'one more throw of the dice' become flogging a dead horse?

Setting up the website seemed a good way of

keeping myself writing amidst the slew of bar jobs, but unfortunately it doesn't generate any money and almost as few stories. The contact form automatically pops up within fifteen seconds of the homepage being pinged, and doesn't even require the user to leave their contact details, so they don't feel scared to reach out. I clearly state I will protect the identity of my sources, as any good journalist would, but if I can't lure readers to the site, how am I going to get any stories worth writing?

The last story I managed to get published involved a scandal at the town council where I was able to prove a string of backhanders had resulted in contracts being handed to out-of-town builders, but as soon as the story was printed, the newspaper was forced to print a retraction when my only source got cold feet. That particular editor has stopped responding to my emails. For all I know he's shared his views with other editors and that's why nobody wants to publish me now.

And that's why I am standing in a bathroom, staring back at my dripping wet reflection. I don't have time to go home to Hove and change and get back before the interview starts, and I don't want to let Ashley down, so I'm just going to have to grin and bear it. With some dampened paper towels, I do my best to pick off the bits of leaves and twigs that have lodged themselves in the material of the jacket and in my hair.

Outside the hotel, a black cat scurries past, pausing momentarily to stare up at me with judgemental eyes, before hurrying away. I can never remember if black cats mean good luck or bad, not that I believe in such superstitions anyway. I still look like a drowned rat, but make my way towards the building, and try to ignore the curious look the guy behind the reception desk gives me when I tell him my name. I'll just explain what happened to the interviewer, and that my decision to still turn up shows my resilience and good character. Let's hope he believes me.

I take a seat in the waiting area, and have never felt so old. I'm one of six wearing guest passes, but the nervous expressions, acne breakouts, and expensive colognes scream of college graduation. When Ashley said the contact centre was packed with young minds, I didn't realise she meant literally. But what I lack in youthful enthusiasm, I more than make up for in life experience (comparatively).

I type out a quick message to Ashley to thank her for everything and to reassure her that I've arrived and I'm ready to give it my all. She's the only family I have left, and I won't let her down. I know she's due at the hospital for her six-month scan mid-morning so I'm not surprised when she doesn't respond immediately. I know how lucky I am to have her on my side, even if boring accountant Roy thinks I'm taking advantage of his pregnant wife's good nature. Overhearing them arguing this morning was cringe, and I hate that my staying at theirs last night has caused more trouble. Overdue rent: another reason why I *need* to get this job.

Where would I be if Ashley hadn't offered me these clothes and cash for the bus? I owe her so much, and I know I need to start returning the kindness she's shown me since...

I quickly shake my head to clear my mind: I can't think about any of that now. For all his complaining, I know Roy had a point when he said it's time I stopped focusing on the past, but it's tough when I don't have closure. I could have kissed Ashley when she said as much and reminded him how lucky they both are to have both parents alive and well. What do I have? An ex-husband who wilfully cheated on me and then filed for divorce last year, citing *me* as the problem; a landlord who calls round when he suspects I will be in pyjamas; and a website which costs more to run than generates any actual stories worth chasing. Most of the time the only messages I receive through the site are from spam bots offering to promote my site on their sites at a cost I can't afford.

Ashley never knew what she wanted to do when we were growing up, and when she decided she wanted to move out of her parents' bungalow she kind of fell into her position at the insurance company. Credit to her, she has earned three promotions in the last ten years and is highly regarded from what I understand. She's right: twenty grand a year to answer the phone is twenty thousand reasons to make the most of the interview, and if I play it smart, I might be able to continue writing freelance in my spare time.

My phone pings with a notification, and I am grateful as it serves as a reminder to silence it before I'm called in. Expecting to see Ashley's response to my own message, I'm confused when I see it's actually a new anonymous message from my website, but it's the subject line that leaves my mouth on the floor:

BODY FOUND IN THE APPALACHIANS

2

JESS

April 2023, Brighton, East Sussex

There is no text accompanying the note, save for a link to a website, which I eagerly click. My eyes skim the words of the article, already recognising what each means. It's what I've been waiting to read for the last thirty years, and even though it's what I've been anticipating, I still can't believe that they're there, laid out in text.

'Jess Grogan?'

I can't tear my eyes from my phone's screen, even though I hear my name being called.

'Miss Jess Grogan?' the voice calls again, and this time I force my eyes towards the sound.

'Uh, yes,' I say, searching for the person calling out to me. 'I'm Jess Grogan.'

The young man in white shirt and navy tie is standing beyond the security barrier, glancing at the clipboard in his hand. 'You're Jess Grogan?' he asks, catching my stare.

I stand, and nod, pocketing my phone in a swift action. He seems relieved to have found me, and strains a smile, nodding for me to approach the barrier, before stooping and scanning the security pass hanging from his neck. The machine beeps and he ushers me through. I oblige and the arm of the barrier drops beneath the weight of my thighs. My skirt has adhered itself to my legs, making walking more difficult.

He opens the large fire door through to the bank of lifts, and I catch the puzzled expression as I cross in front of him.

Ordinarily I'd try to crack a joke about swimming to the office to break the ice, but my head is all over the place. It can't be a coincidence that a body has been discovered in the same region *she* went missing from. I need to read the article in full.

His brow furrows with empathy, and he calls for a lift.

'Interviews are taking place on floor five,' he tells me as the doors part and we step inside. 'Would you like me to show you where you can... freshen up?'

I quickly shake my head, as there's no saving the outfit now. It'll cost a fortune to have it dry-cleaned.

I want to turn and bolt from the carriage, but as I'm about to step forward I picture Ashley's face when she mentioned the bonus she'd receive for referring me for a role. The doors close, and the carriage begins to ascend. It isn't too late to tell this guy I've made a mistake and need to leave, but I sense it won't reflect well if I ask them to postpone the interview.

My choice is simple: hurry through it, or walk away and snub my best friend's efforts.

It isn't even a choice.

The doors part and I exit first. I spot a woman in a tabard emerging from what must be the ladies' toilet, and I tell my escort I've changed my mind and will freshen up, ducking in through the door before he has a chance to argue. The doors to the two cubicles are both open and I'm relieved to be alone. I drop my bag on the counter beside the basins, and flatten my palms on the smooth ceramic, allowing my head to dip while I try to take calming breaths. The scent of disinfectant fills my nostrils, but beggars can't be choosers. I need to get my shit together. If only I hadn't checked my email.

I raise my eyes and stare back at the tired reflection of a woman who just needs a lucky break.

'You can do this,' I tell her quietly. She nods back at me, but I can see the doubt in the wrinkles of flesh above her nose.

My phone feels like it's burning a hole in my pocket, and I cave, yanking it open, and unlock the screen. The bold letters of the headline stare back at me.

BODY FOUND IN THE APPALACHIANS

I spy today's date in the top right-hand corner of the screen, but I don't recognise the news outlet reporting the discovery. Must be some local East-Coast publication. There isn't a great deal of detail, save for the fact that the discovery was made by a couple of thru-hikers who'd lost their bearings and inadvertently left the trail path. A mountain rescue team has been called to navigate the logistics of extracting the remains from the cavern where they were discovered.

I'm reading too much into it. The Appalachian Trail extends over two thousand miles from Georgia to Maine, crossing through fourteen states in all. Being such a vast area, people must go missing all the time.

It doesn't mean it's her.

My head snaps back up and I stare at the terrified woman facing me. There hasn't been a single day when I haven't imagined the moment I'd finally have closure, but I never pictured myself receiving the news in a musty toilet.

I flick back to the email message, looking for any clue as to who sent the link, but they've chosen not to reveal their identity. It was Bruce's idea to include a bit about my mum's disappearance on my website, but it's been years since the site generated anything valuable. And why now, when I'm about to turn my back on journalism for the last time? I can't help but feel the hand of fate – or something else – dragging me back to where I'm supposed to be.

Get your shit together!

I take a deep breath, and run the tap until the water warms, and then splash handfuls onto my cheeks, dabbing them with a paper towel.

It's just an hour, and then I'll be free.

I discard the damp paper towel in the bin, grab my bag and pull open the door. The floor I am then led to is open plan with pods of six desks where staff members are busy chatting into headsets. A rhythmic beat is drummed on keyboards as we move along the floor towards two closed doors at the end of the room. The blinds are drawn on the floor-to-ceiling windows, as if some great secret is hidden beyond.

'This is your eleven o'clock,' I hear, the words announced to those beyond the doors, before my name is added.

The room is about three metres wide and a couple of metres long, with a table in the centre, behind which sits a woman with a pointy nose and half-rimmed spectacles. She instantly reminds me of the school librarian who used to take pleasure in shushing me and my friends.

I smile as I force eye contact, but she doesn't reciprocate. Instead, her gaze takes in my sodden appearance, but I don't even try to explain. The guy beside her must be in his early fifties, his head shaved to hide the rapidly receding hairline. He nods for me to sit at the single chair across from them, a pen poised in his hand.

The guy clears his throat. 'Welcome... Jessica, is it?'

'Jess,' I correct, but smile to show I'm used to the slip.

'Ah, Jess, thank you,' he says, scribbling a note on

the pad before him. 'I'm Mike, and this is my colleague, Sharon. We're Recruitment Managers for the company, and the plan today is to ask you several competency-based questions to help us get an idea of who you are, and how you might fit in to the operation.'

Corporate speak – I detest it.

'Can I get you something to drink before we begin?' he asks.

The last thing I want is to drag this out any longer than necessary.

'I'm not thirsty,' I say, glancing up at the clock that hangs on the wall behind them. Frustratingly the hands don't appear to be moving.

He glances at his colleague who offers a short nod, and then fixes me with a hard stare.

'We'll begin by looking at the CV you sent in with your application,' she says, her accent a thick, nasal Northern Irish. 'It says your current employer is the *Sussex Express*. Can you elaborate on what you do for them?'

Surely if they've read my CV they'd know the answer to that question, but I grind my teeth rather than react. 'I'm a writer... well, a journalist. I write stories and articles for the newspaper.'

Her eyebrows rise. 'Full-time?'

'Freelance. I get paid by the word.'

'Oh, I see. So, what's inspired your sudden change of direction? Big change from reporting the news to manning the phones in a contact centre.'

It was a mistake coming in. If I'm honest, I only agreed to the interview because Ashley persuaded me, but this Sharon woman is right: this isn't the role for me, and I'm too old to start over.

'I'm looking for something more stable, with a regular income, and more sociable working hours,' I reply.

'Still a pretty major change, though, no? How do you think you'll cope with adjusting to a more... regimented working pattern?'

I picture the headline again.

What am I doing here? My place in the world isn't to be tied to a desk. I'm an investigator. I can already smell blood in the air, and all I want is to get the hell out of here and find out more about what they've discovered in Maine.

'Can you describe a time when you faced a difficult problem and how you managed to overcome it?' Mike asks, and it's like I'm instantly transported back to that day when I woke to find a host of familiar faces in my childhood home.

I couldn't understand what they were all doing

there on a Tuesday morning. I couldn't find my dad anywhere, and everyone kept touching my head and stroking my hair as if I was some prize pet in a show. Hushed conversations everywhere I turned, and then eventually I found my dad on the swing seat in the back garden, a glass of what I now know to be Scotch in his hand, even though it was still early morning.

I asked him what was going on, and why all the people were gathered. I knew it wasn't mine or his birthday, but couldn't imagine any other reason why so many people would be in our home. Every time he tried to speak his eyes would screw up and he'd end up burying his face in his free hand.

I was only five years old, so I didn't immediately understand what they meant when they said I'd never see her again. And the truth is, I don't think I've ever overcome that.

'We can return to the question if you need time to think about it?' Mike offers reassuringly. 'In fact, if there are any questions you'd rather return to, you just have to say. It won't count against you.'

I nod, but the truth is I just want to bail. If it wasn't for Ashley, I'd already be on my way. She looked so pleased when she'd got me dressed this morning, her maternal instinct in full force even though I'm the elder. Would she expect me to stay if she'd seen what I have? A break in thirty years of radio silence is more significant than an interview, surely?

'Okay, how about this one,' Mike says, turning the page of the pad. 'Can you describe a time when you had to make a difficult decision? Explain what made it difficult, what your considerations were, and what you learned from the experience.'

I look at Mike and then at Sharon, and my lips part but no words emerge. I'm wasting everybody's time here. I don't want to work for this company, and as much as I'm grateful to Ashley for trying to help me, what this morning has driven home is that I will never lose my investigative instinct. Ashley is going to be angry, but I think she'd understand if she'd seen that article too. The truth is, my mind won't rest until I have answers, and Bruce is the only one who might be able to provide them.

I push back my chair and stand. 'I need to go,' I say quietly.

Mike frowns and Sharon's chin practically hits the table.

'I'm sorry, but I have a personal matter I need to attend to,' I add.

3

NORA

September 1993, Hanover, New Hampshire, USA

Straightening, Nora counts the items on the bed for a third time, comparing the list with the one in her head. Pack, tent, thermal sleeping bag, foam sleeping pad, food supplies including granola bars, water-resistant trousers, spare hiking boots, water bottle, water purification tablets, compass, map, underwear, spare polyester tops, diary, waterproof wallet, small first aid kit, and torch.

Seventeen items. She's sure the list she wrote before leaving the UK had twenty items on it. She steps back and allows her eyes to slowly move around the interior of the small motel room. The beige drapes are pulled closed, but there is golden sunshine streaming through regardless, so there's no need to switch on the light. The chest of drawers with the box television standing on top remains untouched. She knew there was no point in putting anything in the drawers for the sake of one night.

Her gaze continues to move around the room, until it falls on the large round mirror on the wall above the basin. The light above the mirror is switched on, creating an angelic glow on the toothbrush and toothpaste on the counter beside the basin. She snaps her fingers together and crosses the room, collecting both items, dropping them on the bed beside the other objects, and beginning the count once again.

Nineteen. Still something missing.

She tries to recall the book she read by someone who had completed a thru-hike of the Appalachian Trail. He described multiple events on his excursion, and what items he wished he'd had with him, and what he ultimately used to survive. The book detailed several towns a short walk from the AT where fresh supplies and equipment could be purchased in an emergency, so if there is something missing, she should theoretically be able to replace it, but the fact that she can't remember what it is will play on her mind.

She counts the items again a final time, before she begins to pack them into the large pack recommended yesterday by the man at the equipment store. He'd looked at her with a frown, as if her slight frame was a flaw. She didn't waste her breath telling him that she's as capable as any man attempting the month-long hike from Hanover to Mount Katahdin. She purchased the 60-litre pack he suggested, and spent last night pacing the room wearing it fully packed to acclimatise to the weight.

She carries the pack to the door of the room, before returning to make the bed, even though she knows the motel maid will be in to change the bedding at some point. That's when she spots the Polaroid image of Jess on the floor and immediately scoops it up.

Twenty.

She kisses her daughter's face and presses it to her heart. The one item she brought with her that can't be replaced, and she almost left it behind. She must have fallen asleep holding it. Just seeing the green eyes with hazel centres tugs at her heartstrings. She recalls the last time she got to breathe in the divine scent of her daughter's skin, how her beautiful smile had been replaced by an angry scowl, and how those eyes had spilled tears of disappointment.

Her heart breaks again as she recalls the venomous words Jess snarled as Nora headed out to the waiting minicab.

'I promise I'll be back before you know it,' she'd called over her shoulder. 'I love you, my angel.'

Not for the first time, she questions whether she made the right decision in adding her name to the list at the PTA evening and signing up to this adventure. But what choice did she really have? Without an urgent heart transplant, four-year-old Ashley Torrance won't live to see her next birthday, and the poor mite has already spent too many hours stuck in hospital being poked and prodded, and wired up to machines. What kind of existence is that for a child? Bake sales and raffles are all well and good, but they won't make the kind of money that will make a difference. And it's not like she's the only parent risking their child's wrath to complete the challenge. Twelve other volunteers have already flown back after completing their sections, and in a couple of hours, Nora and her team will swap places with the next four.

One day, she'll make sure Jess understands why

she felt it necessary to volunteer. And she will do everything in her power to make it up to her.

She glances at her watch. Eight, which means it will be 1 p.m. back in Brighton, so Jess won't be home from school yet, and Frank will still be at work. There's no phone in the room, so even if she wanted to call and leave a message, she'd have to go searching for a payphone in a town she's unfamiliar with.

She looks at the photograph again and zips it into a small pocket deep inside the pack where it will stay dry.

She starts at a knock on the door. Opening it, she sees Bruce, strapped into his pack, smiling back at her. His hair is perfectly combed to the side as always, and his colour-coordinated ski jacket and backpack make him look as though he's just stepped out of a catalogue.

'The others have headed to the diner down the street for breakfast. I said I'd come and get you,' he says.

She leaves the door open and heads to the bathroom to switch off the light above the mirror. 'I'm not hungry.'

Bruce steps into the room, and lowers his pack to the floor. 'Are you okay?'

She offers a nod of reassurance she isn't feeling. 'I'm fine.'

'Well, that's good, because I'm bricking it.' His face softens into a smile. 'It's okay to be nervous about what's to come, but this might be the last cooked breakfast we have for a few days. Better to leave with a full tummy.'

She doubts his concern would extend to the others, but returns the smile.

'I just keep thinking what is a girl from Lancashire doing here, pretending to be... I don't know... Indiana Jones.'

Bruce chuckles, rubbing his temple. 'What about me? I'm a forty-year-old primary school teacher from Kent. If my university friends could see what I'm attempting, they'd have me committed.'

Nora shakes her head. 'At least you're in shape. You've run marathons and spend hours at the gym. This is the most exercise I've had since giving birth!'

'I've run one half marathon, and that was years ago when my midlife crisis first started. If I could go back in time and meet the version of me that ever thought this was a good idea, I'd give him a good talking to. At least you're younger and not overweight like me. And I can't bench-press to save my life! You should see some of the guys there, now they're real pros. I'm just a guy who gets hot and sweaty without really achieving any muscle gain.'

'Let's just agree that we're both crazy, and that it's too late to do bugger all about it, and go, shall we?'

He lifts and passes her pack to her, before securing his own. 'Sounds like a plan.'

The diner is a five-minute walk from the hotel, and although the sun is bright, there's a crisp bite to the breeze, so Nora has no regrets about opting for the green fleece-lined jacket. They pass signs advertising free lodgings to hikers, discounted camping equipment, and refreshments. This town is clearly one that embraces its place in the Appalachians, and welcomes hikers of the AT with open arms. Even so, she can't escape the feeling that they're being watched, and keeps her eyes glued to the sidewalk.

It feels in stark contrast to the mining town she grew up in. If her parents could see her now, would they feel proud of the choice she's made, or criticise her for abandoning her husband and daughter? She honestly doesn't know. Her father never approved of her marrying Frank, the ten-year age gap between them not helping, and they'd made less effort to stay in touch when she agreed to move to the south coast with him. Even when Jess was born, she'd expected her widowed father to embrace grandparenthood, but she now buys an extra birthday card for Jess in case he forgets.

The others are already seated in a booth when they arrive, and judging by the mound of packs sitting just inside the doors of the diner, they're not the only group heading for the AT today.

'Finally,' Charlie says, instantly raising his hand to flag down the waitress.

'Sleep well?' Ken asks, handing them both laminated menus.

'Like a baby,' Bruce says, sliding in beside Charlie. 'You?'

'Didn't want to get out of bed this morning,' Ken replies, his Swansea roots more apparent in contrast to Charlie's Californian twang. 'Do you realise it'll be days before we get to enjoy such luxuries as mattresses and pillows again? How are you doing, Nora?'

She nods, and tries to smile through her anxiety.

A woman with a light grey perm sidles over, her tabard smeared with something red that Nora assumes is ketchup. 'What can I get for you fine folks this morning?'

'I'll have the Yankee Breakfast, with coffee and OJ on the side,' Charlie says, without hesitation.

'Pancakes or biscuits?'

'Pancakes. Oh, and extra syrup.'

She jots down his order, and turns to Bruce, who quickly looks at the menu, before answering. 'I'll have the same as him. Thank you.'

She scribbles the order and fixes her eyes on Ken.

'I'll have the patty melt and a tea, please?'

She finally looks to Nora, and despite her lack of appetite, she knows that a few miles into today's trek her stomach will be grumbling if she doesn't fill it. 'Can I have the blueberry waffles, please, and just a glass of tap water.'

'Can we get a plate of fries for the table, too?' Charlie adds as the waitress collects the menus, and heads out to relay their order to the kitchen. He turns back to Nora. 'Ken and I were just talking about the possibility of running into some black bears on the hike. You ever come face to face with a black bear back where you're from?'

Nora only met Charlie last night, and she has already taken a dislike to his misogynistic view of the world. If she'd known he was the distant cousin of Ashley's dad, she would have had second thoughts about signing up to join the final section of the trek. He was already at the motel when they arrived late last night and she prefers not to think about the way he was leering when she got out of the taxi.

Nora looks back to him, biting her tongue to resist

the urge to rise to the bait. 'There were one or two Neanderthals where I grew up, yeah. Don't imagine you'd see many in LA, though.'

He narrows his eyes. 'We've got far worse where I'm from, little lady, and I'll let you in on a secret: they're far scarier than you could ever imagine. In fact, if you spot one, you shouldn't think twice about getting outta the way. Don't look, run!' He narrows his eyes, and leans closer. 'Reckon you're quick enough to outrun a black bear?'

She sees him grinning at the other two, but sits on her hand so she can't be tempted to slap the smirk from his face. Instead, she fixes him with a firm stare, and recalls what she read before her flight.

'Actually, in the event that a bear wanders into our camp, the correct procedure is to make ourselves as large and frightening as possible. If it remains unfazed, that's the point to beat a hasty retreat.' She reaches over and takes a napkin and uses it to wipe a smear from the plastic table. 'And I don't have any worries about being able to outrun a bear,' she adds. 'In fact, I don't need to be able to outrun a bear, as like most predators it will target the weakest in our group. All I have to do is outrun one of *you*, and by the looks of it, I don't imagine that being much of a problem.'

Bruce howls with laughter as the waitress arrives

with their drinks, and Nora's nerves about the trip finally begin to settle. In a world where chivalry is AWOL, she has no doubt that Charlie will be the first to quit if the going gets tough. And based on what she's read, they're unlikely to run into a bear in the tail section of the trail anyway.

No, the biggest threat she's identified is Charlie himself, and she feels pretty sure she's already got the making of him.

4

JESS

April 2023, Brighton, East Sussex

I should phone Ashley and tell her what's happened, but if she's in the middle of her ultrasound, I don't want to disturb what should be a tender moment between mother and child-to-be. The truth is, I'm using that as an excuse because I know she won't react well to news that I bailed on the interview, but once I sit her down, show her the article and explain what it means, hopefully she'll forgive me. Right now, I have bigger fish to fry.

I haven't messaged Bruce to tell him I'm on my

way over, and for all I know he could be away, but I'm sure he'll want to hear the news as much as me.

Passing the Grand Hotel, I continue along the front, inhaling the fresh sea air. There was a time when coming in to Brighton for rock and ice cream was a treat I savoured, but Dad wasn't the same after she disappeared. I know he tried his best to keep my upbringing as 'normal' as he could, but I can't re-member seeing him away from work without a drink in his hand. It wasn't a surprise when his liver gave up, and in many ways, it was a kindness to him.

Losing both parents before my seventeenth birthday was less kind on me.

And if it hadn't been for Bruce, God knows where I would have ended up. He insisted I move in with him after Dad passed. Bruce used to say it was what my mum would have wanted, but I only had his word for it. And because I was sixteen, social services had little power to argue with my choice.

I reach the seafront apartment building, and press the buzzer for Bruce's flat. There's a long pause before the crackle of static is followed by Bruce singing a greeting.

'Hi, it's Jess,' I say into the intercom. 'Can I come up?'

There's a buzz and I push through the door,

mounting the stairs up to the first floor, two at a time. Bruce is standing in his doorway when I arrive, breathless on his floor. He's wearing a garish leopard print Hawaiian shirt, the top three buttons unfastened, revealing a perfectly tanned chest. He's wearing three-quarter length khaki trousers, despite the mild temperature, and is barefoot.

The bracelets on his arms rattle as he pulls me into a warm embrace. 'I thought you were Paolo returning with our fish supper. To what do I owe this pleasure?'

I wait until he's pulled me inside the two-bedroom apartment and closed the door before I drop the bombshell. 'I think they've found Mum.'

His eyes widen, and his mouth hangs open, but he doesn't speak.

'Someone sent me a link to a Maine website running the story,' I continue, slipping off the still-damp suit jacket, and hanging it on the back of one of the dining chairs in the corner of the room. The doors to the balcony are open, and the gentle breeze should help to dry out the material.

'I don't know what to say,' he says eventually, his eyes shimmering. 'Can I see it?'

I unlock my phone and hand it to him, watching his reaction as he scrolls through the limited detail.

He drops to the wicker sofa across from me, and offers the phone back. 'There's no mention of Nora. It doesn't say for certain that it's her.'

I lean across and take the phone, skimming the words again to check that I haven't imagined the whole thing.

'True, but given where you all reported last seeing her...' I leave the sentence hanging.

He presses a hand to his mouth in shock. 'Have the police been in touch with you yet?'

I shake my head. 'No, I literally received the email half an hour ago. I came straight here.'

He smiles warmly. 'I appreciate you letting me know. I hope for your sake – for all our sakes – that you're right.'

It's a strange situation to be in. For any normal person, hearing that a loved one's remains may have been found would be treated as a tragedy. But when that loved one has been missing with no explanation for thirty years, the prospect of closure feels like a blessing.

He points at my outfit, brow furrowed.

'I'm almost reluctant to ask. Have you been working undercover in a mud-wrestling operation?'

I feel the corners of my mouth lift; he always knew how to lighten the mood.

'I had a job interview down the road when Mother Nature decided to conspire against me.'

He sits forward, legs and arms apart. 'An interview? For another periodical?'

'I wish! No, at a call centre.'

He can't keep the surprise from his tone. 'Oh. I thought you were going to tell me one of those broadsheets finally realised your quality and had come begging for your services. Your talent is wasted down these parts.'

Bruce has been my biggest cheerleader for the last nineteen years. Even when he was coming to terms with his own identity, he has always championed my desire to write. And together, he and Paolo have reminded me that even in grief, the world keeps spinning.

He sits back in the chair, and pulls one of the brightly coloured cushions across his chest. His tan, which covers every inch of skin from the top of his clean-shaved head to his toes, is far too golden to be natural. The three days of heatwave last week wouldn't have been enough to create such an even glow. I still remember a time when the thought of sunbeds, lurid shirts, and pierced ears would have felt alien to him. He's come a long way since he returned from that trip to the States. Why haven't I?

He purses his lips together. 'I sense you're waiting to ask me something. Don't be shy. You know we have no secrets.'

I exhale sharply. 'Tell me again the last thing you remember about her.'

He cocks his head and smiles empathetically. 'I remember Nora was a funny, adventurous, and kind woman who loved you to pieces.'

Here we go again: always the same answer.

'Then why, when I was only five, did she willingly leave me behind to go off gallivanting on some hike?'

I don't mean to shout, but it still bothers me that she was prepared to go travelling for a month when I was at home and needed her. I've heard Bruce justify her actions countless times, but it isn't good enough. I should have been her whole world.

He takes a minute before responding. 'Your mum made an incredible sacrifice to help a family in desperate need. She didn't take the decision lightly, and I can tell you she regretted not having you with her every step of that hike.'

'Then why didn't she take me out of school to go with her? It's not like I wouldn't have been able to catch up.'

'She wanted to. Believe me! But your dad wouldn't have it. He was the pragmatist in their relationship, and he knew Nora wouldn't have been able to focus on the challenge *and* take care of you, which would have meant him flying over too, and there was no way he would have got time off work to do that.'

'For years I hated her for going,' I say, lowering my eyes. 'It wasn't fair that so many of you went over and she was the only one who didn't return.'

Bruce doesn't answer, but he stands and crosses the room, wrapping his thin arms around me, holding me close. 'I can see how that wouldn't have been easy for you. The whole community was desperate to help Ashley and her family; and you know your mum would've done anything for anyone, especially her goddaughter. I'm not exaggerating when I say Ashley wouldn't have seen her fifth birthday if it wasn't for that hike.'

'I said some awful things to her the day she left.'

He kisses the top of my head. 'I know, but she knew you didn't mean any of it. You were upset because you were going to miss her, and I don't think many moments passed when she wasn't thinking or talking about you. She was so proud, and it's only because she believed you were strong enough that she even contemplated going through with the challenge. You shouldn't beat yourself up over words spoken in the heat of the moment. She knew you loved her, and she cherished you.'

'Tell me what you remember about the days before you last saw her,' I say, holding him tight so he can't break free and avoid the subject.

'Do we really need to go over this again? She was in a bad way; can't we just leave it at that?'

I shake my head, my nose brushing against his shaved chest.

He sighs and I feel his frame slump. 'We were nearing the end of our hike; we were only days away from ascending Mount Katahdin in Baxter National Park. We could almost see the peak from our camp; that's how close we were.'

'Was she excited about the hike ending?'

'Of course she was. She was desperate for it to be over so she could get back to you and your dad. By that point, we'd all had to overcome various ailments: the norovirus, dehydration, swollen muscles and tick bites. Not to mention our encounters with wolves, and other wild animals. We were all ready for it to be over. Believe me, I could see how keen she was for it to be over.'

I pull myself away so I can look into his eyes. 'You told the police that Mum went crazy in the days before she abandoned the camp.'

Regret fills his eyes. 'Those weren't my exact words. But, yes, something changed in her. At the time, I put it down to a negative experience with drugs.'

That's something that's never sat right with me. 'Mum wouldn't willingly take drugs. She was fervently against that kind of thing.'

'As was I. But you have to bear in mind that we were all away from our everyday lives, and some of the group – Charlie in particular – were determined to make the most of it. We ended up at this festival in Darby, one of the towns near the AT, and it wasn't until the day after that we realised that some of the food and drink there had been spiked. I never got to ask what your mum saw, but I've never forgotten the trippy shit I hallucinated. To this day, I wonder if it triggered something in her head, and that's why she behaved the way she did.' He sighs. 'I shouldn't have let her out of my sight.'

I know he blames himself for her disappearance, and I didn't come here to try to make him feel bad. The love and support he's shown me since more than clears his debt as far as I'm concerned.

'Do you think they're her remains?' I ask.

He looks down at me, and I can see how torn he is. 'I just don't know. Would I like it for you to get the closure you need? Absolutely. But wanting something to be true, and it *being* true are different things, Jess. I'm sorry, but I wouldn't pin your hopes on it being her. Can I be honest with you right now?'

I recognise the serious tone; it's the same one he used when he broke the news that my dad had died. I nod, even though I'm already dreading what's to follow.

'You know how much I care for you, and so I say this out of love: stop chasing ghosts, Jess. You'll never be able to move on with the future if you don't let go of the past.'

I know he's right, but the truth is, I can't embrace the future until I know what happened to my mother.

5

NORA

September 1993, Hanover, New Hampshire, USA

While the others are arguing over how to divide the diner bill, Nora quietly leaves the table and settles with the waitress, leaving her a generous tip as a thank you. Then the four of them strap on their packs and head to the waiting taxi. It feels like cheating to hitch a ride to the handover point on the AT, but as Bruce is quick to remind them, given the mileage that is to come, there is no point adding bonus steps.

Nora can't ignore the feeling of dread slowly spreading like the shadows overhead. The single-track road, which the taxi bounces along, is lined with the tallest trees she's ever seen – maples, firs and spruces – and beyond the first three or four rows of trees there's only darkness. She's read up on the type of wildlife they should expect to see once the hike starts proper, but looking into the void, she can't imagine how anything could survive out here.

'Cheer up,' Bruce whispers beside her.

She meets his stare and forces herself to smile thinly. 'I'm fine.'

He maintains eye contact. 'Can I let you in on a secret?'

She nods.

'I'm desperate for a wee.'

She chuckles at this, her shoulders relaxing fractionally. 'I warned you not to drink all that coffee!'

He crosses one leg over the other. 'I was going to go when we'd paid the bill, but then—'

She pats his knee gently. 'I'm sure we'll be there soon enough.'

He pulls a face, and nods at a sign declaring the entrance to the trail in a mile, and then the reality of what they've agreed to do drops like a tonne of bricks. She pictures Jess sobbing and her heart breaks.

They are meeting the other group at the Lafayette Campground parking lot with the intention of following the trail up to Lonesome Lake. The other group will use the taxi to get back to Hanover and get cleaned up before catching their flights home. Nora's never envied anyone as much. She reminds herself to think of Ashley, and the reason she agreed to this lunacy in the first place, but now that she's reached this point of no return, she desperately wishes someone would give her the chance to bow out. If one of the others would just insist on continuing their hike, she could give up her place. A proverbial win-win. But she knows the chances of such a miracle are second to none.

The taxi parks, and the driver helps Charlie lift the enormous packs onto the rough, dusty ground while Bruce goes searching for a restroom.

Nora notices the drop in temperature the moment she opens the door. The sky is a quilt of mid-grey, and the earlier heat they experienced in the town centre has been replaced by a much cooler climate.

'We need to get to some hut on the trail,' Charlie states. 'That's where we're supposed to be meeting the others. I don't know about you guys, but I hope they're not running late; I can't wait to get started.'

Bruce secures his own pack, before helping Nora lift and secure hers. Despite the extensive training she undertook back in the UK, the bag feels heavier now, as if the weight of expectation and burden are sitting there along with her provisions.

'You okay?' Bruce checks.

She desperately wants to tell him how she's anything but okay, but instead thinks about Ashley in the hospital bed, plastic tubes poking out in every direction. She nods.

'The sooner we start, the sooner it will be done,' she says.

The path up to the trail is lined with knobbly stones, and the cool breeze whips the dust around their feet, as if somehow trying to warn them of the dangers ahead.

At least it isn't raining, Nora tells herself, more than aware of how much heavier their packs will become when soaked through. Small groups of hikers are gathered to their left and right, some exchanging stories about what they've faced, others excitedly chatting about what they're anticipating.

This is like nothing Nora has done before, but she shares none of the excitement. Of the thousands of hikers who visit this part of the world every year, there can't have been many Brits who've attempted to hike the trail. Sixteen other residents of Brighton and Hove have already completed their sections of the route, and now they will be the final four. What seemed like a crazy idea – a venture that Nora never believed would happen – is now upon them, and none of them can truly comprehend what the next month will bring.

The pathway is lined with wooden signs explaining where they are, what's ahead, and statistics on the number of hikers who've trodden this same path. How many of those felt this level of dread?

A large sign hangs from a birch tree at the end of the pathway, declaring they are now officially entering the Appalachian Trail, and Nora is certain the temperature just dropped another degree. The knobbly rocks marking the defined pathway disappear, and she spots a white-painted rectangle on the bark at the end of the path.

'Those are white blazes,' Ken comments, pointing at the strange marking as he reads from the glossy pamphlet he's been holding since the cab. 'It's to help hikers stay on the correct trail. These six-inch by two-inch markers have been painted onto trees every couple of metres in case one becomes disoriented.'

Nora and Bruce exchange looks, but don't interrupt him. On the flight over, Ken told her he is a Scout leader and a master with a map and compass.

'A team of volunteers freshen them on an annual basis, and there are literally tens of thousands of such markings on trees from Springer Mountain in Georgia, all the way to the top of Mount Katahdin.'

'At least we won't get lost,' Charlie scoffs.

Famous last words, Nora thinks.

'Here they are,' a voice roars from somewhere ahead, though Nora doesn't at first recognise the owner of the voice.

They're due to be meeting Andy, Max, Simeon, and Joanna, but the four people sitting on the edge of a giant boulder look nothing like the people she met with at the multiple events leading up to this.

Bruce and Ken approach, while the group tentatively hops down from the boulder they were sitting on and limp over. Joanna Kocienski was already athletic-looking but the woman with the bandana tied around her muddy face is practically gaunt. Gone are the gold hooped earrings and long plastic nails. It seems an effort for her to raise an arm and wrap it around Nora's neck.

'Hello, stranger,' she says, and Nora instantly recognises her working-class accent.

Nora returns the hug, but there's nothing of her. Joanna looks as though she's been held in segregation on basic rations for the last four weeks. The transformation is unbelievable. Surely this can't be the same woman with whom she shared a bottle of chardonnay two months ago. Her daughter Becky is slightly older than Jess, and Nora can't bring herself to ask how much she's missed her.

'Are you a sight for sore eyes,' Joanna says, releasing her grip and studying Nora's face.

'Likewise. You look so... so different.'

Joanna lifts a clump of her mud-spattered fleece and says, 'Reckon I've dropped a couple of dress sizes.' She smiles. 'How are you feeling about the hike?'

'Can't wait,' Nora lies.

'Believe me when I tell you it's going to be nothing like you expect. Oh, and whatever you do with your food, make sure you keep some chocolate back. Over the coming days, there will come a point where you ask yourself exactly what you're doing here.'

'Think I'm already there,' Nora quips.

'No, I'm talking like *seriously*, you're going to reach a point where you just want to give up and turn back. It happened to all of us, and no matter the cajoling you'll just want to sit down and let nature decide your future. *That's* the point when you need to pull out your secret stash of chocolate. You'll need something to force you back to your feet.'

Nora gulps audibly. 'Here I was hoping you'd tell me what a wonderful time we have in store.'

'Oh, you'll have a blast,' Joanna quickly assures.

'To leave everything behind and get back in touch with Mother Nature is so worth it. I think I was ready to give up after day three, but the chocolate and the others managed to get me straight. This has to be one of the toughest things I've ever done, but the sense of achievement is... it's just...'

She can't finish the sentence as her eyes fill and a sob catches in her throat.

Nora pulls her closer again and holds her as the tears flow.

'I thought I was going to have to fight you off trying to take my place,' Nora quips again.

Joanna shakes her head and composes herself. 'You're going to have such an amazing experience. Life changing!'

I'd rather not.

'Any last-minute hints or tips you care to share?'

Joanna takes a step back and considers the rest of her group, who all appear to be swapping war stories with Bruce and the others.

'When it feels like the worst it's ever going to get, just remember you don't know what's around the corner.'

If the words were supposed to offer reassurance, they failed.

Andy, the tallest of the group, joins them, and beams. 'I bet you can't wait to get started.'

The first time Nora met this man from Johannesburg, she thought he introduced himself as 'Indy' as in Indiana Jones, but it wasn't until several weeks later – and after she'd called him Indy multiple times – that she was corrected. He told her he was flattered by the comparison to the whip-cracking hero and the irony of how he now looks isn't lost on her. No coat, despite the chill to the air, the chequered shirt is only fastened halfway, and his chin is coated in a thick band of salt and pepper stubble. With the beer belly significantly flattened, and the tortoise-shell glasses gone, he looks every inch the Hollywood action hero.

'Have you warned her to steer clear of Snake and Weasel yet?' he asks Joanna.

'I was just about to,' she replies, wrapping a skinny arm around his middle in a friendly embrace, before turning back to face Nora. 'You'll come across all kinds of hikers on the AT. Some are day hikers who will want to hurry past, and you'll probably only see once. Others are thru-hikers, the pros. They're the ones who are doing this from end to end and tend to treat the whole experience as some professional accomplishment, which I suppose in a way it is. And then there are section hikers like us, and they generally seem to be quite an amiable bunch. Anyway, Snake and Weasel are section hikers. We managed to ditch them a couple of days ago, but they did say they were heading to the summit of Katahdin, so they might catch up to you guys.'

'And that's a bad thing because...?'

Andy and Joanna exchange glances, before Joanna replies. 'We came across them in one of the hostels, and... I don't know... you know when you just get a bad vibe about people? They kept pestering those of us in the hostel for any food or clothing we could spare, even though they seemed to have packs full of gear themselves.'

'Stank of weed too,' Andy chimes in.

'We're all for helping out a fellow hiker,' Joanna concludes, 'as are so many of the awesome people we've come across, but this was just something else. Someone I spoke to reckoned they scrounge stuff that they then sell to pay for their drugs.'

Nora makes a mental note to share the observation with the others.

Max is next over, bringing with him Charlie, Bruce and Ken. 'We heard snow is expected north of here over the next week, so you guys should tread carefully and wrap up warm. You need to be averaging eight to ten miles a day to stay on course for reaching the summit by the end of the month, but some days of that will be easier than others. When the ground is even and fairly flat, make the most of it and clock up the extra miles, because when you hit some of the ascents, you'll never maintain that pace.'

Nora's bones freeze at the mention of the snow and colder temperatures to come, and in that moment, she wants to suggest that they all take a few days in Hanover until the weather improves, but the rest of her group aren't on the same wavelength. Even less so when Max pulls the stuffed lion from his pack and hands it to Bruce.

'Lest we forget why we agreed to this madness,' he says sombrely. 'This is Rex – Ashley's favourite toy. You need to take a picture of you and him each day so that a scrap book can be put together when we're all back in England.'

Nora stares at the lion's ungroomed mane and knows she can't possibly bail out.

Bruce stuffs the toy into his pack, and then proceeds to follow Ken and Charlie further into the forest, leaving Nora staring after the four who look so relieved that their adventure is over. She's never felt more envious in her entire life.

6

JESS

April 2023, Hove, East Sussex

The walk back to Hove has done little to temper my certainty. I am confident that the remains alluded to in the news article belong to my missing mother. Thirty years of waiting for news, not knowing whether she'd ever be found, or whether she would one day show up with some crazy story about where she's been and why she couldn't let me know she was safe.

There's also a part of me that thinks Bruce hasn't

been totally open about what happened in those days before her disappearance. My dad would tell me how level-headed and careful Mum was about everything she did. In the weeks leading up to the trip, she read every book she could find about surviving in the wilderness, and specifically about the hike they were about to attempt. She became obsessed with being fully prepared for any kind of hindrance. She knew how to survive wild animal attacks, how to treat blisters and callouses to avoid infection, and what kind of plants and berries were edible. Even if she'd become temporarily waylaid, or stumbled off the trail, she'd have found a way to get back.

For me, there's only one reason my mum never returned from that adventure: someone or something stopped her.

The case remains open in the US, and there is a police team in the UK who contact me once every couple of years to advise there have been no updates from their US counterparts. Because she fled the camp, there was no physical evidence that she was attacked. No blood or sign of disturbance. Apparently, some tracking expert managed to follow her for up to half a mile, but then it was as if she vanished into thin air.

I don't yet know exactly where these remains have been discovered, but I'll be interested to see if they're in the same sort of vicinity as where the trace was lost.

I can do nothing from here.

After my father passed, Bruce was kind enough to introduce me to Charlie and Ken who were the other members of her troop, but neither provided anything more than Bruce did. Their stories all had the same ring, which means either they're all telling the truth, or they've all agreed on a *version* of the truth. The issue is I have no way to disprove what they've said.

As far as the world is concerned, my mum went crazy and wandered off the trail, never to be heard from again. Unfortunately, it wasn't the first – and may not be the last – time it has happened. It's a plausible story, and that appears to have been enough for the Maine sheriff department who was investigating.

I have researched every reported disappearance from the Appalachian Trail – or 'AT' as it's known by those who've hiked it – and there have been a dozen murders committed. The majority have been solved and the perpetrators locked up, but one or two remain unsolved. I've looked for patterns, locations, and anything that might help shed light on what really happened three decades ago, but there's no commonality between any of the killings. I don't want to think that Mum suffered in her final hours on this earth, but it would make it easier if I had someone else to blame.

If it is her they've found, then I hope swift justice will follow.

I'm assuming Ashley has now heard about my fleeing the interview as she's already sent messages via text, Facebook, and WhatsApp, demanding answers. I know it's not easy to read someone's tone in a written message but based on the increasing number of exclamation marks, I'm sensing she's growing angrier by the second. Probably best if I don't head back to hers tonight. The last thing I need is for her to throw me out.

I love Ashley to bits, and I know I'm culpable for her current state of frustration, but I also know that giving her space to vent will make my eventual apology more palatable.

That leaves me with little choice but to head back to my flat and hope I can sneak in without Mr Popovich spotting me. I empty my bank account at an ATM, ready to hand it over to him as a down payment towards what I owe. If I'm lucky, I might be able to get a couple more shifts at the bar, and if that fails, I'll have to tout my extensive waitressing experience at other pubs and restaurants in the county. I know Bruce would be more than happy to offer me help, but he's already done too much for me, and I can't take advantage of his generosity.

I reach the end of the street, but don't head straight up it. Popovich owns three of the blocks of flats, which he rents out, but lives in one of the few detached houses on the hill. If I head up the road and he happens to be looking out of his front window, he'll see me, or his barking Alsatian will. That dog goes ballistic whenever anyone walks past the front window if she happens to be inside. She's actually very friendly once Popovich has invited you into his house, but until that point, his dog's temperament is set to vicious.

Rather than risk such an encounter, I continue on to the next road which runs parallel to ours, and head to the top, before circling back. It would be sod's law that he happens to be at the block, but as I head up the garden path and in through the old oak door, I'm relieved when he doesn't spring out.

I'm exhausted when I make it to the fourth floor and freeze when I see the sheet of A4 paper crudely taped to my front door. The words EVICTION NO-TICE loom large in bold font. I pull it down, and screw it up, slotting my key into the door, but it doesn't turn. I pull it out, blow on the metal ridges as if this might somehow fix the issue that is starting to become more apparent. I slide the key in again, but it jars rather than twists.

'Son of a...' I mutter under my breath.

I can't believe he's changed the locks. I've been a loyal tenant for two years, and it's only the last three months that have seen me late paying the rent. I told him I would get the money to him. Can he even do this? He's not warned that he plans to evict me, nor that he'd access my home and change the locks.

My phone vibrates with a voicemail as I miss another call from Ashley. I brace myself and listen, but delete the message when she gets to her second expletive.

I flatten out the eviction notice and study the content. It says I am evicted on account of not paying rent arrears, that he is keeping my initial deposit to cover the cost of replacing the locks and cleaning the property in order to let it again. Apparently, he has gathered up my possessions, and is storing them at his home address.

I'm no expert, but I'm sure he's not legally allowed to remove my possessions or change the locks, especially without notice, and given I'm working my socks off to get him the money I owe.

My instinct is to phone Ashley and ask her opinion but given the stream of messages, I don't think I should push my luck. I stuff the piece of paper into the pocket of my still-damp suit jacket and make my way back down the stairs. Stomping from the building, I am ready to give him both barrels and to demand he provide new keys to the property, but as soon as I reach his house, I can see the driveway is empty.

I jab at the doorbell, and thump my fist against the wooden door.

When Popovich doesn't come to the door, I drop to my knees, and lift the flap of the letterbox.

'Mr Popovich? It's Jess Grogan. I've come about your eviction notice. Can you let me in?'

I listen for the sound of movement, but there isn't a peep. Certainly no sound of barking, which must mean wherever he's gone, he's taken the angry dog with him.

The cloud overhead is darkening, and I have no doubt that it won't be long before rain arrives. I shout through the letterbox again, but Popovich isn't home. I do, however, spot several large black sacks just inside the door. It has to be my stuff: clothes and the few keepsakes I felt compelled to hang on to. It seems so little for a life already half-lived. By this age, I'd always assumed I'd be settled in a relationship, maybe married, with a home to truly call my own. That's how grown-ups are supposed to conform, but I just haven't yet.

I stand and straighten, considering my options. I don't have any friends in a legal capacity to check my rights with, but even if I did, I won't gain access to my flat until Popovich returns, whenever that might be. He shouldn't have taken my things, though, and it's galling that they're so close, but there's no way my hand will fit through the letter box.

Stepping back, I almost trip over the large plant pot that separates the overgrown lawn from the paved driveway. It looks so odd, with no sign of plant life, and essentially just a ceramic pot of earth.

I wonder...

Despite myself, I attempt to lift and move the pot, half-expecting to find a key beneath it, but no matter how much I strain and gurn, it doesn't budge. It seems unlikely in this day and age that Popovich would keep a spare key beneath something as obvious as a flowerpot.

But that doesn't mean he might not absent-mindedly leave a back door or window unlocked.

I move further down the drive until I reach the garage. There are more ceramic pots here, and a gate into the garden, but when I try the handle, it doesn't budge. Frustrated, but not perturbed, I wheel over the recycle bin and position it against the gate, jiggling it to check it won't topple under my weight, before hoisting myself up onto it. I look back to the main road, but my position is partially obscured by the property's chimney breast.

I've done nothing wrong yet, I remind myself, but the truth is I've done far worse in search of a good story, including rooting through people's discarded rubbish. If I suspected Popovich of wrongdoing, I wouldn't think twice about trespassing on his property, so why am I fearing the worst about what I'm about to do?

I lift myself up onto the upper rim of the wooden gate, swinging one leg over, and wincing when an errant splinter breaks the skin of my right calf. If Popovich returned right now, I don't imagine he'd think twice before phoning the police.

But then isn't what he's done far worse? He entered my flat without permission or notice, stole my property, and changed the locks.

Screw it! If the police turn up, I'll just tell them I'm running a story on landlords illegally evicting tenants.

I swing my other leg over the gate, and drop, relieved when the heels of my ankle boots don't crumble. Flattening my skirt, I take several breaths, before trying the handle of the patio door immediately to my right. It doesn't budge. Staring through the glass, I can see that this door leads to Popovich's kitchen. It's the only access point as the double-glazed windows further along the wall don't appear capable of opening.

I'm about to accept that fate doesn't want me to take any further risks, when I eye the dog flap cut into the wall beside the door. I instantly dismiss the idea as ridiculous, but then I think about Ashley's voicemail, and the truth is I have no choice but to get what I need.

I push the flap with my foot and it goes in, and I quickly drop to my knees, kicking off my boots. I manage to squeeze myself through the thick piece of rubber. It's a tighter squash than I'm anticipating, but suddenly I'm flat out on Popovich's linoleum floor.

I scrabble to my knees, then race through to the black sacks, lifting them up, before reconsidering. If I take all the bags, he'll know I've been in here, and then he might report me to the police. The truth is: my curiosity won't be sated if I hang around and wait for the truth. I need to know how and why my mum died, and if I can find the answers to both questions, then maybe I can write and sell the story and make enough money to clear my debts once and for all.

Opening each bag, I rummage through until I locate my all-weather jacket, walking boots, jeans, a couple of sweaters, and all my underwear. I throw the items into a holdall that also topples out of one of the bags, along with my passport. Unlocking my phone, I pull up a flight schedule.

7

NORA

September 1993, Appalachian Trail, New Hampshire, USA

They've been walking for hours, like a herd of elephants, one following another, with Ken the Scout leader at the front, map and compass held out in front of him. Nora thinks about the white blazes painted on the trees. She'd started to count them originally, almost as a measure to validate that Ken hadn't taken them off course, but as boredom took hold, she'd stopped at 184.

Research into the AT promised spectacular views, encounters with wild animals, and vistas incomparable with the rest of the world. What she probably hadn't appreciated then was just how many trees they would walk past, and just how tough the terrain would be. There's no let up to the rises and dips with each footstep.

Impossible to find a steady rhythm, and despite the never-ending incline they seem to have been on, Ken has already repeatedly pointed out that steeper climbs lie further ahead.

She can't yet comprehend how tough repeating this level of travel over consecutive days and weeks is going to be, but she's already certain that she never could have completed a full thru-hike from Springer Mountain down in Georgia. Credit to those who've managed it, but five to six months of endless walking – feeling as though no progress has been made – would be just too much for her psyche to handle.

Joanna warned her that there would come a time when she'll have had enough and would want to pack it all in, but she suggested that that would be after three or four days, rather than three or four *hours*.

For the first hour, Charlie had appointed himself as narrator to their journey, sharing his experiences of hikes along the Pacific Crest Trail, and through Yosemite, both on the west coast. Listening to him talk had certainly helped pass the time, even if she sensed he had embellished on more than one occasion. But the words dried up as the strain of walking *and* talking had taken a toll, and now they're moving in virtual silence, interspersed with grunts as each of them take a turn to stumble along the route, littered with unwieldly rocks and thickets.

Nora can feel blisters forming where the hard soles of her walking boots rub against her heels. She tried breaking them in before they left England, wearing them on the school run, on trips to Safeway, and while running the vacuum around their two-bed mid-terrace, but clearly her efforts were in vain. She'd give anything right now to remove them and soak her feet in the foot spa Frank gave her last Christmas. She'd only had it out of the box once since she'd been given it, and now realises what a mistake that was.

As she continues to follow the back of Bruce's bright orange pack, she pictures life at home. She tries to imagine what Jess would be up to at this moment. It's just after 2 p.m. locally, which means it will be just after 7 p.m. in the UK, so Frank has probably already put her to bed. Hopefully he's keeping his promise to read to her every night. Jess has such a vivid imagination that Nora wouldn't be surprised if she one day became a writer herself. She loves hearing Jess' stories, how she takes well-known fairy tales and adds her own twists. Like when Goldilocks is fleeing the three bears' house and stumbles upon the wolf from Little Red Riding Hood, and stops him from eating the grandma.

Nora smiles now at the memory, the first inkling of joy in several hours, if not days. She can't wait for them to next get to a town where she can phone home and just hear her daughter's angelic voice. It's all the motivation she needs to continue putting one foot in front of the other.

'You doing okay?' Bruce calls back over his shoulder, his voice hoarse with the effort.

'I'm still here if that's what you're checking,' she shouts back.

'You can forgive me for checking,' he says, this time adding a glance, before raising an arm into the air and demanding they all stop.

Nora manages to prevent herself from crashing into his bag, her legs operating on some kind of autopilot. But it's the look of concern in Bruce's eyes that troubles her most.

'We need to take a break,' he declares, another nervous glance at Nora, as if she's been taken over by an evil spirit and he wants to avoid eye contact so he, too, doesn't become infected.

Ken and Charlie walk slowly back to the group. To

the right of the path there is a small stream, leading to a circle of water about the same size as the paddling pool in Nora's garden.

'Too many rest stops and we won't make it to the campsite by nightfall,' Ken warns.

'And if we don't rest and recover occasionally, we won't make it at all,' Bruce fires back, lowering his pack to the floor and promptly sitting on a tree stump near the pond. He unfastens his boots, slips off his thick woollen socks, and dips his feet into the water. 'Son of a bitch, that's good! We should get a photo with Rex while we're here.'

Nora is grateful for the break in the monotony, but not as grateful as she is for not being the first to ask for the stop. She is determined to prove to them that she's just as capable as they are, though it's taken considerable willpower not to ask for a rest.

Shuffling over to the stump beside Bruce, she slips the pack from her shoulders, removes her boots and socks, and screeches uncontrollably as the soles of her feet make contact with the cool water.

Bruce opens the top of his pack and reaches in, rummaging about until he finds his water bottle and two granola bars, one of which he offers to Nora. She accepts it gratefully and welcomes the sweetness as she bites into it. Charlie keeps his pack on, but crouches down beside the stream, and dips his neck scarf into the water, before tying it around his forehead in an effort to be macho. He's clearly decided to try to live up to some kind of Rambo-type persona, and Nora bites her tongue to keep her laugh at bay.

Ken is the last to sit down, and when he does, he compares his watch to the map.

'Actually, we're making good progress so far,' he admits. 'We can afford a ten-minute rest stop.'

When he's not taking on insane treks across states, Ken is an actuary for an insurance company. Nora doesn't know what that entails, but Ken's wife describes him as a man obsessed with calculations and logic. He seems to be in his element with the task of bearing the map and compass, not a role Nora was keen on.

They all start at the snapping of a twig close by, Bruce placing a protective arm across Nora's front, as if that would be enough to prevent a savage attack from a bear or wolf. A moment later, a tall man with long blond hair framing his face, wearing a fitted Yankees cap, appears through a gap in the trees, quickly tucking his shirt into his three-quarter length trousers.

His eyes widen as they fall on the group.

'Oh, hi,' he says nervously, with a strong northern

European accent. He's carrying his pack in front of his body, and as he's emerging from a thicket of trees, it's clear that wherever he's been, he hasn't been following the marked trail.

He steps out, and behind him, a shorter woman, also in three-quarter length trousers and adjusting her bra strap, appears. She also has long blonde hair, but hers looks as though it hasn't been brushed in several days, and is poking out in all directions as if she's literally been dragged backwards through a bush.

'Um, this is Inga,' the man says, holding out a splayed hand towards the woman, who takes it and moves out from behind the trees, also carrying her pack in front of her body. 'And I'm Brynjar.'

Charlie, Ken, and Bruce still look wary, but Nora can't keep the awkward smile from her face. 'Hello, I'm Nora, where are you guys from?'

Brynjar seems to relax, and moves closer to the stream, crouching down beside it, running his hand through the water and then pressing it to his mouth, drinking the contents.

'We're from Norway. Have you been on the AT long?'

'First day,' Nora replies. 'I presume you two were just...' she can't bring herself to say it, 'taking a rest? Like us.'

Brynjar and Inga swap anxious glances and then quickly nod. 'Yeah, we were just... resting.'

Bruce looks from Nora to the couple and then back again before the penny drops. Charlie and Ken still frown with confusion.

'We're thru-hiking,' Brynjar says, leading Inga down to kneel beside him, 'and then when we're done, we're flying to Canada to hike the Continental Divide Trail, starting at Waterton Lakes National Park. We've already climbed Kilimanjaro and Ben Nevis.'

'Oh, wow, that's pretty impressive,' Nora says. 'You must love hiking.'

'When you grow up in the Fjords, it's in the DNA. It was nice to meet you, but we should be going.'

Nora wants to stop them, to ask if they want to join their group. Hearing from someone who's *actually* completed a hike, as opposed to someone who just *claims* to have done, would make a welcome change.

'Best of luck with your adventure,' Brynjar says as he helps Inga secure her pack, before fixing his own, 'and remember to stay on the trail. Straying from the white blazes only leads to trouble.'

Nora stands swiftly, pulling her arms across her middle, suddenly aware of their surroundings. 'Trouble?'

'I'm sure you'll be fine,' he says, offering a reassuring smile, 'so long as you remember that nature eats what it wants to eat; it doesn't differentiate.'

He turns and departs without another word, Inga hurrying after him, and it's like someone just walked over Nora's grave.

8

JESS

April 2023, Bangor, Maine, USA

An eleven-hour flight from Heathrow later, and with my credit card now maxed out, I find myself at Bangor International Airport in southern Maine, a short drive from the infamous Appalachian Trail. The flight included a two-hour layover at JFK in New York, but there wasn't time to visit the city. It's 1 a.m. here, which means it's 6 a.m. back home. I struggled to sleep on the plane and I feel exhausted.

The flight steward eventually took pity on me and slipped me an extra mini-bottle of chardonnay, but by the time I was finally drifting off, the captain was announcing our approach to JFK. I long for a bed and a hot shower, but I haven't yet booked accommodation as this trip was more than a little rushed. The last thing I did before boarding was to send Ashley a message apologising for what happened in the interview, and promising to explain when I see her next.

The flight wasn't full, but people barge past as we disembark the plane, and hurry across the concrete towards the open doors where airport staff wait to greet us.

'Welcome to Bangor,' one says as I slope past. I nod in her direction, but my eyes are watering with fatigue.

It's a mild morning, and the air is filled with the smell of burning rubber and exhaust fumes. I hear American accents left and right. Most chatter excitedly as we head in through the doors and climb the carpeted stairs towards the Immigration Control signs.

Switching on my phone, I am alerted to multiple voicemail messages, and step out of the tidal wave of travellers, dropping onto a hard plastic bench that's as uncomfortable as it looks. I'm genuinely tempted to use my holdall as a pillow and just crash here for a few hours, but I'm pretty sure airport security might have a thing or two to say about that.

I listen to the messages. All are from Ashley. She's still angry in the first, disappointed that I left the interview before the end. There's still bitterness in the second message as she demands I phone her with an explanation. But the third message, left just as I was landing, is a plea that I phone and let her know where I am. I can hear the pained concern in her voice, and it reminds me of the way my dad spoke when the police asked him to do a public appeal for information about Mum.

I can't not think about him as I sit here, in this foreign land. I don't remember a lot about that time because I was only five. I remember my grandma – his mum – breaking the news, and not immediately understanding what she meant. How do you tell a child that they'll never get to speak to or cuddle their mum again? I must have processed the information at some point, as I recall lots of dark moments where I'd sit in my room crying and talking to her ghost.

If he were still alive today, would he have come across with me? I'm not sure. He'd have been in his seventies, and given his alcoholism, probably wouldn't have been in any shape to travel and chase down leads as I know I'm going to have to do over the coming days.

She disappeared from this state thirty years ago, but there must still be people around the area who were here back then. I have pictures of her, scanned to my phone, that I'd like to show around – see if anyone recalls seeing her at that time. Somebody knows what really happened to her, of that I'm certain, and I know I won't rest until I find out the truth.

I locate Ashley's number and dial. She answers immediately.

'Oh, thank God, you're alive. Where are you, Jess?'

Did she think I was in danger? Or did she think I'd harmed myself? She should know me better than that.

'I'm sorry about the interview,' I say, determined to show my remorse. 'I appreciate how much effort you put in to secure it for me, and I'm sorry that I couldn't go through with it.'

She exhales sharply. 'I just wish you'd been honest with me about not wanting to go for the job.'

'I did want to go for it... I mean, I know you're right, and that I need to find a steady wage before I go into total financial meltdown—'

'There are other jobs out there that you can go for,' she counters, cutting me off. 'Having worked in the contact centre, I know how straightforward – and, actually fun – it can be. Twenty grand a year is not a lot, but it would cover your rent and an occasional takeaway; that was all I was thinking.'

I want to jump in and tell her that my ducking out had nothing to do with the nature of the job, but she's not even paused for breath yet.

'I was speaking to Roy about it last night, and he told me I shouldn't have pushed you towards a job interview that you clearly didn't want and wouldn't suit your laidback approach to life anyway.'

Roy's never been my biggest fan, but he's been worse since Ashley fell pregnant for the second time. He sees me as a bad influence because I've not sold out and settled. But I can't imagine school-aged Roy longed to work as a tax accountant, live in a three-bedroom semi in the suburbs, and drive a Volvo. Ashley's dream was to be an actress, but failing to get into drama school put an end to that. I know she loves Roy, and she couldn't be a better mum to Daisy, so I'd argue she's found her calling, but even she'd admit she never saw herself where she is now, working as a Risk Manager for an insurance company.

'I'm sorry I put that pressure on you,' she concludes, with a sigh.

'That's not what this is. I am truly grateful that

you've tried to help, honestly, Ash, but it's just... Right before the interview I saw something about Mum, and it threw me. I'm not ready to give up on her yet.'

There's a pause that lasts so long that for a moment I think we've been disconnected. I check the signal in the top corner of my screen, but I have three bars.

'Ash? You there?'

'Yeah,' she says eventually. 'Listen, I know I've told you before, but I feel like you need to hear it again: I'm sorry for being the reason you lost your mum—'

'What happened to Mum isn't your fault,' I interrupt firmly. 'I don't blame you for her choosing to take on the hiking challenge, and I won't have you blaming yourself. It was *her* choice to go. None of this is *your* fault, Ash.'

There's another pause on the line, and I use the break to share my news.

'I didn't leave the interview out of spite, I think I have a clue now as to what happened, and,' I take a deep breath, 'that's why I've flown to the States.'

'You're... you're in America now? As in I'm speaking to you and you're in another country?'

I can't help chuckling at her disbelief. 'Yep, I maxed out my credit card and I've literally just landed in Maine. It's just coming up to 1 a.m. over here.'

'You left the interview to fly to America?'

'Kind of, yeah. I know it sounds mental, but I received a tip-off that remains have been found not far from where she disappeared. I'm never going to be happy until I find out the truth, so I've come over and that's what I intend to do.'

I wait for the inevitable Roy-inspired lecture about how I refuse to accept reality and that this jaunt is just another example of me running away from my problems. I can picture him belittling me, the moment she shares this update with him. He'll gloat about how he'd told her so, and that I'm the waster he always said I was.

I'm thrown when she responds with something completely different.

'What can I do to help?'

'You've already done too much,' I say evenly.

'I don't like the thought of you being over there on your own. I should come and join you.'

'Um, no, Ash, I genuinely appreciate the offer, and there's nobody I'd rather have with me. But you're six months pregnant for one thing, and you have to take care of little Daisy. Just tell her that her legendary godmother will be back to see her again soon enough.'

'You can't do this by yourself, Jess. The Appalachians are not safe for a woman on her own.'

'Of course they are. Thousands of women travel the AT every year. I've read up on it. There's a greater chance of me getting harmed in Brighton on a Friday night than there is of some harm coming to me out here. Besides which, I'm not planning on hiking the actual trail.'

'Does Bruce know you're there?'

'Not yet, but I'll let him know, I promise. He knows how important it is for me to find out what happened.'

She sighs again. 'All right, but I'm going to transfer £500 into your account.'

'No, Ash, you can't—'

'Yes, I can, and I don't care what you say, the decision is made. If I know you as I think I do, then you've probably not even packed spare shoes.'

I think about the suit and heels I borrowed from her for the interview, which are now in the holdall, after I changed into something more comfortable at Heathrow.

'There, it's done. I know you'll pay me back when you can, and I trust you to spend it wisely. It's the least I can do. I wouldn't be here today if it wasn't for the efforts of Nora and the others.'

'Roy will be pissed off.'

'Let me handle my husband. If he thinks it's okay to invest in his brother's stupid inventions, then it's fine for me to invest in my friend's future.'

I wish she was here so I could hug her.

'Keep me posted,' she says before disconnecting, and I tell her to give Daisy the biggest hug and kiss from me.

The river of passengers from my flight has dispersed, and so I make my way along to immigration and passport control, feeling as though I'm finally on the right course of my destiny.

9

NORA

September 1993, Appalachian Trail, New Hampshire, USA

It's so quiet in the thick woods that there isn't even the sound of birds cooing in the distance. And where once there were spotlights of sunshine lighting the rocky and leaf-strewn muddy ground, now there is only darkness. Stopping and slowly spinning on the spot, Nora can make out no discernible hint of direction. Everything looks the same and, whilst there are white blazes on trees, it would be easy to become disoriented and follow the blazes already passed.

It's been five days since they met Brynjar and Inga.

Nora never thought she'd miss the hum of traffic so much, but she'd now give anything for a sign of life. Back home, she can't walk anywhere without bumping into someone she knows – even if just a friend of a friend – but here there is literally nobody. They passed a couple of southern hikers an hour or so ago but nobody since. She's never felt so small, so isolated; so insignificant.

Recording details of their journey in her diary is the only thing keeping her tied to the past. One day, she hopes to be able to share details of her hike with Jess, and help her understand how tough it was.

It isn't just tall and spiky trees that cut them off from the rest of civilisation. Wild plants with daggers for leaves scratch and threaten, unperturbed by the mammals daring to intrude on their habitat. Nora has never been particularly green-fingered – further rebellion from an estranged mother who cared more for the wellbeing of the plants in her greenhouse than the troublesome teen who craved attention – and she has no clue which of her surroundings constitute plants and which would be classified as a weed. The whole area is overgrown with indistinguishable foliage.

And she never expected to see so many enormous craters of earth where mighty red oaks once stood before falling. Like graves unable to keep hold of escaping decomposing carcasses. Then, just as she rises over a solidified mound of earth, gravity is suddenly pushing her down a dry and sloping ravine. She struggles to maintain her footing as the loose ground beneath her feet carries her. If she stops for just a moment of rest, and loses sight of Bruce's orange pack, she's certain she'll be lost in these woods forever with no chance of escape.

She has no sense of direction, as the sun is long since hidden by the canopy of dark green leaves and branches that stretch as far as the eye can see. It's as if this place is hidden from heaven, a charred heart beating in the void.

It's after six and Ken has informed them that the sun will set before seven.

Nora ducks beneath a low-hanging branch, and her foot catches on a root poking out of the ground. She crashes to her knees, not for the first time. Her splayed fingers break her fall, palms scraping across the rough and ruddy terrain. She winces at the bite of broken skin, defeated. It would be so easy just to stay here and offer up a white flag, and God knows she's now less fearful of the shame and embarrassment that would come with quitting this ridiculous expedition.

As she forces herself to her haunches, there's no sign of the orange pack, and fear slices at her throat. Snapping her head left and right, she's no longer sure which direction she was facing when she fell. Did she roll? Is straight ahead the right way, or should she be following the white blaze on the trunk to her left?

She tries to call out for Bruce, but it's been more than an hour since her water bottle ran out and her throat is thick with earth and dust.

'Bruce,' she croaks, trying to cough to generate enough saliva for a second effort.

The trail seems to bend to the left up ahead, but she can't recall if that's a bend she's already overcome or one she's yet to encounter. Closer to the ground, she searches for boot prints to indicate recent disturbance to the undergrowth, but all this waiting around is only putting greater distance between her and the others.

Why haven't they noticed she's become separated? Why did she have to be so blasé about going at the back of the line? Bruce offered to bring up the rear, but she insisted that she didn't need mollycoddling.

What happens when they realise she's not there? Will they even be able to retrace their steps in the darkness and come looking for her? Will they realise how far back she is?

Straightening, she listens for any sound of their movement, and hearing nothing, she charges forwards, following the bend around the trees, before realising a giant boulder is blocking the path. She doesn't recall seeing anything this size before, so she isn't retracing her steps, but it isn't obvious where the others have gone, until a hand appears out of the sky. Looking up, relief floods her body as she meets Bruce's eyes.

'There you are,' he declares with more than a hint of relief. 'Figured you'd gone for a pee, but when you didn't come back... I was beginning to think I'd have to get back down and form a search party. Here, grab my hand, and I'll help hoist you up. Watch, though, the surface is smooth. Place your feet carefully.'

She ignores the stubborn voice in the back of her head, telling her that she doesn't need his advice, and grabs on to the warm hand, planting her feet where Bruce indicates, and allowing him to help. As she pulls herself up and over the edge, she realises that it isn't a boulder, and in fact a small cliff face, which is why she'd lost track of the bright glow of Bruce's pack.

Ken and Charlie are standing further back, in a heated conversation, and as she approaches, she can hear they're arguing over a change in plans. The temperature feels like it has dropped again: she can see clouds of condensation billowing from their mouths, and there is a low-hanging mist just above eye level. She recalls Max's warning about approaching worse weather and the threat of snow, and now understands Ken's urgency to set up camp sooner rather than later.

'We agreed to camp at Breakers Point tonight,' Charlie challenges.

'And that's at least another mile away and there's no guarantee that we'll make it to Breakers Point before the snow starts.' He looks at Bruce and Nora, before fixing Charlie with a softer stare. 'We're all exhausted, and could do with sustenance and rest.'

Charlie looks at the others. 'What do you two think? Keep going or stay here?'

'I'm fine with here,' Nora says without missing a beat, and is relieved when Bruce sides with Ken's logic.

Charlie looks disappointed, and exhales loudly, before unfastening his pack and slipping it from his shoulders.

The clearing Ken was referring to is another thirty yards along the pathway, and the ground is pitted with stones, so Nora uses her rolled sponge mat to clear away some of the debris, before unfastening her pack to locate her tent apparatus. The wind has picked up here, with less foliage offering protection, and she can't wait to lie down flat in the comfort of her sleeping bag.

Flakes of snow land on the ground and blot on the dark, compacted soil as she begins to set up.

'Do you want me to give you a hand?' Bruce offers.

'That's kind of you, but I've had plenty of practice.'

'Once the tents are up, we should try and light a fire,' Ken says, nodding at the pit marked by a circle of rocks in the centre of the clearing.

Bruce and Nora agree, but start when Charlie screams out in frustration. Head snapping up, Nora sees the shell of his tent lift in the wind and tumble away from the clearing and along the path away from them. Charlie doesn't think twice, charging after it into the darkness, leaving the others screaming after him.

10

JESS

April 2023, Bangor, Maine, USA

It takes me an hour to pass through immigration, and in my head it's now after breakfast, but the lack of sleep means I can't stop yawning. I've adjusted my watch to Maine time, which means it's still only two in the morning. My body clock doesn't know if it's coming or going.

Despite the ungodly hour of the day, three of the five car rental agencies are manned, presumably to accommodate the fact that flights into the international airport don't stop just because most normal people would be asleep at this time of the day. With Ashley's money in my account, I approach the first with renewed optimism, but the only vehicle available is an eight-seater motorhome. At this point I'd hire a bicycle, but 150 bucks a day for something I could live in with a small family is overly excessive, given I don't know how many days it will take for me to recover my mum's remains.

'Is there seriously nothing smaller?' I ask the girl, who looks as though she'd be happier attending a goth event. Her hair is matte black, her black eye makeup must be weighing her eyelids down, and I lose count of the number of piercings that adorn her face and neck.

'No.'

I move to the next desk, where an equally lifeless guy stares back at me. He is slumped on the desk, head propped up by both arms crooked at the elbows. I think I actually wake him when I approach. Again, no small compacts available. This is how my journey continues, and I'm more than a little frustrated by the time I'm rejected for a third time.

'If you give me your number, I can call you if we have a cancellation,' the final woman suggests. I scribble it down.

'Are there any cheap hotels or motels within

walking distance from here?' I ask with hope in my eyes and voice.

She laughs out loud and wishes me good luck in my quest.

It's just after half past two, and I'm having serious regrets about my decision to come over here. I should have gone to Ashley's house, explained what I'd been sent, apologised for screwing up the interview, allowed her to vent, and then waited for her to help me formulate a plan. She'd have probably helped me find a cheaper flight, booked accommodation and a rental car. I'm certain with her pragmatism and organisational skills I wouldn't be wandering the threadbare carpet at the airport with no idea what to do next.

I'm hungry, but there are no restaurants or cafés in the arrivals terminal, so I carry my bag out of the airport into the cooler-than-expected dark night air, and cross the road to departures. It's much busier over here with excited travellers wheeling cases and trollies, gathering parties together and looking for screens to check gate numbers. Heading away from the check-in desks, I board an escalator to the second floor. Most of the shops – selling the usual array of handbags, stationery, and gifts – have their shutters down, and most of the restaurants and cafés have cordons over their entrances.

I do, however, spot a tavern at the far end, which appears to still be operating.

Surrounded by varnished, wooden partitions, it smells of stale, sweet alcohol. Two older men with large bellies prop up the bar on stools, while the tired woman behind the counter wipes small glasses with a towel before holding each up to the light as if checking for smears.

'What can I get you?' she asks without meeting my stare.

'Are you able to rustle up any food?' I ask, pulling a face ready for yet more rejection.

She drops the towel on the shiny bar, and slides across a laminated menu. 'We've not got any salmon, lamb, or lasagne. Otherwise, what'll you have?'

I'd been expecting to have to choose between salt and vinegar or cheese and onion. Dropping my bag, I quickly skim read the menu and settle for a cheeseburger and fries, and a diet cola. She rings up the order and I keep my fingers crossed as I tap my debit card against the machine, but Ashley's money must definitely be in my account, as the transaction is approved.

She hands me a plastic pyramid-shaped marker with the number three on it and tells me my food will be out in ten minutes. I should challenge how a cheeseburger and fries can be prepared so quickly, but I'm too tired.

One of the men at the bar tips his glass in my direction, but I'm in no mood to be chatted up by some wino, so I ignore him and head to the furthest corner and slide into a booth, standing the marker on the edge of the table. Connecting to the airport's free Wi-Fi, I check for emails and see one from the insurance company advising me I've been unsuccessful in my application for a job. It's not surprising but feels like a further blow I didn't need today.

'Spare change?' a voice asks quietly.

Looking up from my phone, I see a slight man in a flat cap, his navy coat worn thin at the elbows and shoulders. The wispy beard and mane of grey hair poking out at the sides is unkempt. He's holding out a small, bashed metal pot, and the skin around his fingertips is dry and cracked. My heart goes out to him.

'I don't have any American cash on me yet, but I'll buy you a meal if you'd care to join me?'

He looks up and I see the surprise and doubt in his deep-set brown eyes. His cheek bones are so prominent, and if I had to guess, I'd say it has been years since he had three square meals a day.

'Please join me,' I say, waving my hand towards the bench across the table from me.

He removes his cap, and clutches it to his chest as he slides into the booth eagerly.

I locate a menu at the far side of the table and push it across to him. 'Apparently they have no salmon, lamb or lasagne. If you order a burger and fries, it comes with a free soft drink.'

His eyes light up as if it's Christmas, and when the lady from behind the bar brings over my food, and he asks her to bring the same for him.

She looks at him with a steely gaze.

'Is there a problem with my friend?' I challenge her, and she looks as if she wants to say something, but thinks better of it, and instead heads back to the bar to ring up the order.

'I'm Jess,' I say, extending my hand towards him.

His handshake is cold and limp when he returns it. 'Isaac. Where you headed today?'

'Well, actually I've only just arrived. I flew in from England, and I've yet to sort out a motel for the night.'

'You don't wanna be sleeping on those streets. Damned cold for this time of year. That's why I come here; at least it's warm.'

I don't want to pry, but given his worn attire, and virtually empty begging pot, I'm of the opinion that Isaac is homeless. I wonder what else we have in common.

'Most of the time the security guards will throw out any of us who try to sleep, but we can get a couple of hours of warmth before they turf us out. You look like you could do with a couple of hours' shut-eye yourself.'

I cover my mouth as the uncontrollable yawn escapes.

'So what brings you to the single largest producer of blueberries in the United States?'

I smile. 'Is that a fact? I didn't know that.'

He smiles back, his shoulders relaxing. 'It's also well-known for its lobsters, lighthouses, and moose.'

'And the Appalachian Trail, of course.'

His smile drops at this. 'Less said about those mountains the better. I'd steer well clear of them if I were you.'

My interest is piqued. 'Why do you say that? I heard the Appalachian Trail was one of the best hiking spots in the world, let alone the country.'

'If people in this country really wanted exercise, they'd ditch their enormous cars and walk to work and the malls. Why go and do something stupid like hike up mountains, destroying natural beauty spots when they've already done so much damage down here?'

I shake a bottle of ketchup and drown my fries in

it. 'I had a friend who hiked the Appalachians once.' I pause. 'Well, in fact it was my mother. She came here thirty years ago.'

He cocks an eyebrow. 'Not safe to be going in those parts these days. There's more of a "them and us" culture than there's ever been, especially after the pandemic.'

'Them and us?'

'Them that live off the grid. Did you know in this country there's an estimated 180,000 thousand families who live disconnected from the rest of the world? And there's a belief by some in the bigger towns that those who've spent their lives living up in those mountains have medicines and potions that prevent and cure illnesses. But they won't share this ancient knowledge with the rest of the world.'

I'm reminded of the Eloi and Morlocks from H. G. Wells's *The Time Machine*. 'But surely you don't believe that, though?'

He looks at me warily. 'There's all manner of strange goings-on in those parts, you mark my words. I've heard stories of people feeling like they're being hunted, hearing strange whispers amongst the trees, even people vanishing.' He reaches slowly across the table and rests his hand on mine. 'A word of advice: if you see something, no you didn't. If you hear something, no you didn't. If someone calls your name – don't look, run.'

His food arrives and we both tuck in while I try to get him to expand on the stories, but he's either been exaggerating or doesn't want to frighten me further.

The cheeseburger is like manna from heaven, and I devour the lot, and am tempted to order dessert, but the woman at the bar hasn't stopped firing daggers at the two of us the whole time we've been here. As we're leaving, Isaac tells me that the diner at the opposite end of the terminal will be closed until six, and if I duck beneath the cordon, I should be able to sleep on a soft bench for a few hours.

I thank him for the tip and offer to withdraw some money from an ATM for him, but he pats my arm and declines.

'You've already shown me more kindness than half the strangers I meet. I wish you well in your quest. May God keep you safe.'

Those are his final words, but what he's told me about the mountain people has me questioning: was it one of them who killed my mum?

11

NORA

September 1993, Appalachian Trail, New Hampshire, USA

The light is already fading so quickly that Nora can no longer see the spot where Charlie tore off into the woods. A spotlight suddenly appears and she can now see that Bruce has fastened and switched on his head lamp. She searches through her pack until she finds her own and pulls the elastic strap as wide as she can before slipping it over her head. The strap squashes the top of her hair bun, but she resists the urge to adjust it. Both lights shine towards the small opening in the wall of trees around them, but there's no sign of Charlie returning.

'Where is he?' Bruce asks rhetorically. 'Surely someone as experienced as he claims he is would have got hold of the tent and been back here?'

Nora doesn't want to share her own scepticism about some of Charlie's claimed skills.

'This is why you need to secure the ropes first,' Bruce continues, looking down at his own poles and canopy.

'I can't hear anything,' Nora says. 'Wherever he is, he isn't close.'

'One of us needs to go and find him,' Bruce declares, kicking up a cloud of dust as he gets to his feet.

'We need to wait here until he comes back,' Ken counters, moving closer to join them. 'We stick to the plan: set up camp and start a fire. It's the best way to help Charlie find his way back to us.'

Nora can see the logic, and a roaring campfire would be the best way to cut through the ever-growing blanket of ice enveloping them, but what if Charlie fell? What if he's injured and can't get back without help? It's getting colder by the second, and exposed he'll surely freeze to death.

'And what if he's fallen and hurt?' Bruce snaps back, as if reading her mind.

Ken opens his mouth to respond, but no words come out.

Bruce glances back at the opening before looking down at them both. 'You two stay here and set up your tents. If you get a chance, set up mine too. I'll go and look for Charlie.'

Ken's head bobs as he cleans snowflakes from his glasses and considers the suggestion, before shrugging in resignation.

'And what if something happens to you, too?' Nora says. 'The safest thing is for us to pack up and *all* go looking for Charlie, *together*. Separating the group further is just madness.'

'And if Charlie returns and sees we've abandoned camp?' Ken sniffs.

Nora looks around the opening. 'This site's not going anywhere. We'll build the fire, and then head out, taking Charlie's pack with us. If he returns while we're gone, the fire will keep him warm until we get back.'

'And if he doesn't return?' Bruce whispers, but neither Nora nor Ken are prepared to answer the question.

While Nora packs up the tent gear, Bruce and Ken set the wood Bruce has gathered in a pyramid shape before lighting the kindling with a cigarette lighter.

There's still no sight or sound of Charlie, and his absence is doing little to ease their fears. The snow has begun to settle on the ground around them too, and as they once again wearily strap on their packs, Nora is certain the snowflakes in the air are thicker.

Ken switches on his head lamp and unsteadily they move towards the break in the trees. Although the lamps provide decent coverage of their surroundings, there are just so many trees that it's still impossible to see beyond two metres in front. This is not the trail path marked with blazes, so it's hard to determine which direction Charlie headed when he left the trail. Maybe if they had an experienced tracker with them it would be feasible to follow in his footsteps, but tracking people is not a skill any of them possess, even Scout leader Ken.

'Charlie,' Nora calls out, hoping the sound of her voice will carry on the wind that's whipping at their faces.

At least the canopy overhead is offering some shelter from the snow.

'Charlie,' Bruce calls out next, but there's no sound of anyone shouting back.

The last thing Nora wants is to be stumbling through the darkness and into the unknown, especially after ten hours of uncomfortable hiking. But the ground is so uneven that it's impossible to keep from slipping. Nora is the first to feel her foot skidding on loose earth, and suddenly her left side is sliding away from the group. It's only Bruce's quick hands that stop her from falling, grabbing her and pulling her back up.

'Are you okay?'

She nods, despite the racing of her heart and the growing ache in her sinuses.

'We need to be careful,' Ken warns. 'The ground here is slick with ice.'

The trees block their path ahead, leading them into another opening which makes it seem as if another trail once existed. A faded blaze marker is visible on one of the trees, but it's more red than white. Nora doesn't want to tell them about the warnings racing through her mind.

'M-maybe we should turn back,' she ventures, but Ken yanks at a piece of cloth hanging from a pointy branch ahead.

'I'm sure the tent must have come this way.'

So they continue further off track, with Brynjar's words echoing in Nora's mind: *nature eats what it wants; it doesn't differentiate.*

Without the protection from the trees, the wind blows the snow in from all directions until it feels as though they're in a shaken snow globe, but the storm is relentless.

'Charlie,' Nora calls out again, but her voice is blown back at her, pellets of ice pelting her teeth.

Bruce puts out his arm to stop the group, shielding his eyes with the other. 'We should go back,' he says, his voice barely a whisper over the howling. 'We can't see a thing out here, and it's too dangerous to continue.'

'We have to find Charlie,' Ken shouts back, but if there's any aggression in his voice it is muffled.

He doesn't wait for Bruce or Nora to counter, pulling the collar of his coat tighter around his chin, before bending into the onslaught. He charges forwards, but within seconds he disappears from view with barely a smothered shriek.

Nora's mouth drops but the terrified scream she's feeling doesn't escape.

Bruce takes her hand and signals for them to move forward carefully. Legs apart, head lamps directed at the ice-white ground, they take one step at a time until they see the large round void in the floor.

Bruce helps Nora down to her knees, before joining her and then they slowly crawl forwards on all fours, carefully placing each hand, testing for stability.

At the edge, they stop, peering in where Ken lies in a heap, shielding his eyes from the beam of their head lamps. He's about six feet down and despite the presence of six wooden spears buried at the bottom, he's miraculously avoided puncture.

'Must be some kind of animal trap.' Bruce's voice echoes against the rounded sides of the hole. 'Looks like the trap was covered in branches and leaves. Can you stand?'

Ken winces as he twists onto his knees, and places his hands on the ground. 'My wrist,' he hollers back up. 'I think it's sprained or broken.'

He raises his arm to show them, but there's no sign of protruding bones, much to Nora's relief. She can handle grazes and burns but limbs at unnatural angles and bone poking through skin turns her stomach.

Bruce pulls back from the edge of the hole. 'We need something we can use as a rope to tie round him and hoist. Any ideas?'

Her mind goes blank, as she tries to recall the twenty items on her list.

'Hello?' Ken calls, panicked. 'I'm on my feet, can you pull me up?'

Bruce flattens himself on the ice, and stretches out his arm. Ken grabs hold of it, but his gloved hand slips almost immediately.

'I need you to lie flat and grab hold of his elbow,' Bruce instructs Nora.

She obliges, feeling every jagged stone and twig cutting into her padded coat.

'Now Ken, grab my hand as tight as you can, and I'll pull while Nora tugs on your injured arm. I need you to put your feet flat against the wall and try to walk up it.' He pauses and tucks his head towards Nora, his voice much quieter. 'We need to be quick because if we drop him, he'll be impaled on those spikes.'

Nora's stare falls on the sculpted point, and a thought freezes her already chilled bones: who set this trap, and what were they hoping to catch?

Ken passes up his pack first, at Nora's request, and this time when he reaches for Bruce's gloved hand, the grip holds. Nora strains to pull up Ken's left arm, until his elbows are astride the rim of the hole, and he's able to drag himself clear.

He thanks them profusely, and once his pack is back on, he gingerly tucks his hand into his coat pocket, grimacing as he does.

Nora can't stop her teeth from chattering, struggling back to her feet. 'We need to go back,' she tries to say, but the message is incomprehensible.

'He might have continued down the hill,' Ken says,

throwing his good arm towards where the trees de-scend. 'There are bound to be cave openings nearby. He might have taken shelter in one.'

Nora looks to Bruce, but he's already looking for a route around the trap. 'I think we should head for the tree line over there,' he says, pointing. 'It should pro-vide some shelter from the falling snow, and we can use the lower branches like handrails.'

He heads towards the spruces, his footprints now visible in the snow. Nora stumbles forwards, planting each foot, her legs apart for stability, but is grateful to reach the first of the branches, grabbing on for dear life. There are no white blazes, and she doesn't want to think about how far they've already deviated from the official trail. She wants to turn back. To hell with Charlie for chasing after his tent and putting himself – and consequently them – in danger. If he was half the explorer he claimed to be, he'd have known just how idiotic it was to tear off into the darkness with no torch or clue where he was going. And she was certain that if she, Bruce or Ken had acted so rashly, Charlie would be the last to join a rescue mission.

But Bruce's orange pack is already several metres ahead, and even if she tried to shout her objection, he probably wouldn't be able to hear it over the buffeting wind. He's descending the slope much quicker than she is, and all but disappears when it levels out and continues further into the tree line. She tries to call out to him, but if he hears, he ignores her.

She dares to take a look back up the slope, trying to determine whether they'll ever make it back to the campfire, but the incline is far steeper than she'd realised, and even their footprints are rapidly disappearing, almost as if they've never been here.

Giving way to her need to catch up with the others, she lets go of the branches and races forwards, careening downwards, with no obvious means of stopping, and when she gratefully reaches the flat, she almost topples over. She runs into Ken as she rounds the bend, his statuesque frame planted as he stares into the darkness. She's about to ask him what he's doing when her eyes fall on what's on the white-dusted ground ahead of them.

Two dozen handcrafted wooden crosses.

12

JESS

April 2023, Bangor, Maine, USA

I'm woken by a strange poking, and as I open my eyes, I'm repulsed by the spotty teenager staring down at me.

'You can't sleep here,' he says, his voice a strange mixture of high and low pitch as if he's in the throes of puberty. When he speaks, I can see morsels of undigested food scraps in the metal braces covering his teeth.

I force myself to sit up, rolling the ache from the muscles in my neck and shoulders. Isaac was right;

the cushioned benches in the diner did allow for some sleep, though I've no idea what time it is, until I stare up at the large 1950s-style clock hanging above the diner counter.

I stretch and stifle a yawn.

'I tell you what,' I say to the kid, taking a punt. 'I won't tell your boss you rocked up half an hour late if you don't mention you caught me sleeping here.'

His freckled cheeks glow, and he spins on his heel and heads over to the counter. I grab my bag and peel myself from the faux-leather-covered bench, and head back out into the departures terminal. The shutters are starting to rise on several of the stores, but it doesn't look as though they're officially open yet. I could murder a coffee, needing to shake the last of the drowsiness from my sleepy brain, but I can't afford to waste Ashley's money; I don't know how long I need to make the £500 last.

I find a row of seats and plonk myself down while I try to work out my next move. According to the news article, the nearest town to the discovery of Mum's remains is several miles north of my present location. I've never heard of Rockston before, but it appears to border the Appalachian Trail. I can't help but think of what Isaac told me about the dangers of mountain towns. Given that Bruce said Mum ran from their camp without her pack, maybe she made it to a town in search of help. Could that town have been Rockston? I'm taking a big leap of faith, but chasing down leads is the only way to properly dismiss the false ones. I've dug out stories with far less before.

My phone pings with a voicemail message. When I play it, I'm expecting to hear Ashley's voice so am quite thrown when I hear a more nasal tone. I can't quite decide whether it belongs to a man or a woman.

'This is a message for Jess Grogan. I'm calling from the Prism Car Rental service. We've had a cancellation on an economy compact if you're still looking for a vehicle? The rental price is fifteen dollars a day. Can you give us a call back if you want to reserve it?'

I end the voicemail, grab my bag and tear out of the terminal, racing back across the road to the sound of blaring car horns. The message was left two hours ago, and I don't want to miss out. I'm panting when I make it to the Prism Car Rental desk, and find a man in a rainbow-coloured waistcoat and tie smiling back at me. His eyes are so wide and cheery that he must be on something to be this chipper so early in the day.

'Good morning, ma'am, and how can I help you on this beautiful morning?'

I take several breaths to compose myself. 'I had an answerphone message,' I say, sweat pooling at my hairline. 'Apparently you had a cancellation on an economy compact. I'd like to hire it.'

He beams back at me. 'Well, let me take a few details and I'll see what I can find. Name?'

I relay all the information he asks for, and am relieved when he confirms the vehicle is still available. He recites information about great fuel economy, as if he's a salesman in a showroom. I should just tell him I am a woman without options, but I don't want to bring down his mood.

I book the car for a provisional three days, and he advises I can simply phone to extend if I need to. He prints off the paperwork, passes it to me to sign, and within twenty minutes I'm headed out of the door with a confirmation note to hand to the driver at the vehicle collection point. The valet is over six feet tall and frowns when I hand over the note, but he tells me to wait by his small plastic hut while he hops onto an electric scooter and heads out into the vast car park.

He returns a few minutes later, his knees pressed up to the steering wheel of the Smart car, and I now understand his dismay when he saw the rental agreement. Luckily, my five-foot-two height should have no problem fitting in to the tiny car. And still, it fulfils my needs perfectly.

For the first time in days, I feel like things are

going my way. I've yet to secure accommodation, but hopefully I'll find somewhere closer to Rockston with a bed and shower.

Frustratingly, the car is low on fuel when I get in, but the valet informs me there is a gas station a few minutes up the road. He gives me directions, which I follow, and although it's going to take some time to get used to driving on the wrong side of the road, I pull away with a feeling of giddy excitement.

I'm not hungry thanks to the early morning cheeseburger and fries, but my need for caffeine is unrelenting, and so, barely an hour into my journey, I pull into a fast-food forecourt. The car park is divided into spaces with electric charging points, spaces for SUVs, and spaces for compacts. I have no issue parking, which I guess is another benefit of the car I've been given. Locking up, I cross the walkway and head in through the swing doors. The automated ordering stations all bear 'Out of Order' notices so there is a long queue up to the counter, but I don't mind waiting. The reward of caffeine will make it all worth it.

I connect to the free Wi-Fi and send Ashley a message to thank her again for her help and to advise that I'm on my way to Rockston. She immediately responds with a thumbs up emoji and a good luck message. I should probably check in with Bruce as well. I know had I told him I was coming over here to check the remains he would have insisted on coming too, but I can't ask him to do that. Whilst he's also looking for closure, this is my fight.

I'm next in line, and I've been studying the menu above the counter to work out what I want when I suddenly sense somebody in my periphery. I gradually turn and see a guy in a red and white striped skin-tight sweater stomping towards me. His head is shaved on one side, but the other is wild and blue. A nose ring hangs between his nostrils, and as he comes closer he starts to wave his arms in a windmill effect. It's the most bizarre thing I've ever seen, and I dart behind one of the automated ordering terminals, fearing for my safety.

'Those who seek a stranger will forever be in danger,' he yells at the top of his voice. 'The truth you seek will bring nothing but trouble. Your life out here is trapped in a bubble. If you see a gun, run, run, run.'

The staff behind the counter stand watching, open-mouthed, while the woman who was in front of me in the queue is hovering behind me now.

The guy is clearly delusional, but his mention of a gun has me now thinking he may be armed and that I'm about to become embroiled in another of America's tragic stories.

'Oh, thank God. Chester!' a woman cries out as she hurtles in through the swing doors, and immediately approaches the man. 'What did I tell you about not leaving the car?' She turns to me apologetically. 'I am so sorry, did he strike you?'

Even though she's now holding his arms in place, I stay shielded by the terminal. 'Um, no he didn't. A little scary, but no, he wasn't violent.'

'Forgive me. Chester is... we're on our way to a mental health facility. He's on day release, but they mixed up his meds. I am so sorry. Please, allow me to pay for your coffee.'

She leads Chester to the counter where the three members of staff take tentative steps back. She fiddles with her purse and extracts a fifty-dollar bill, which she slaps down on the counter. 'Please, use this to buy everyone in the place a hot drink, and whatever's left can go in the charity box. Okay?' She turns to face the rest of the seated public. 'I am so sorry to all of you.'

She then proceeds to lead Chester out through the swing doors and over to one of the giant SUVs in the car park.

'I bet he's one of those from that place that burned down in Heaven's Gate,' the woman behind me mutters.

'Excuse me?'

'You know. That mental institution up there in the mountains. Burned down. Most of the inmates escaped and disappeared into them woods, never to be heard from again.'

She collects her drink as I approach the counter and order my own. The rest of the previously seated customers have now joined the queue behind me to take advantage of Chester's carer's generosity.

Stepping away, I turn and look back at the large SUV as it pulls away, wondering whether there was someone waiting for Mum when she ran off into the woods.

13

NORA

September 1993, Appalachian Trail, New Hampshire, USA

'Must be some kind of cemetery,' Bruce declares more casually than any of them are feeling. 'We should keep walking forwards.'

Nora can't move, though. She can't keep her eyes from the wooden crosses, counting them. There are two dozen, even though the plot of land isn't large enough to house the remains of that many people. And who would put a cemetery halfway up a mountain, a stone's throw from a national park? And why is there no sign to indicate it? No name of the cemetery?

Something doesn't feel right about this.

'We should be able to go round it.' Bruce nods to a small path through the trees, but Nora stands frozen, as if she's entranced by the plot.

'I-I wonder what happened to them?' she says. 'There are no names or dates. Do you think they've been here a while?'

'I don't think we should worry, and should forget we ever saw it,' Bruce says, tugging on her arm, and dragging her towards the pathway.

'We should pay our respects,' Nora insists, pulling back towards the graves. 'We don't want evil spirits coming after us because we didn't show humility and acknowledge their passing.'

'What are you talking about?' Bruce shouts back over the wind and snow, concern rising.

'We should say a prayer,' Ken adds, suddenly dropping to his knees and bowing his head.

Nora is about to agree when the breath catches in her throat. Nearby howling cuts through the wind's own drone. Nora counts the sound of two, no, three, different animalistic wails, and no matter whether they belong to wolves or wild dogs, she doesn't want to be anywhere near them.

Nature eats what it wants; it doesn't differentiate.

'We need to get back,' she suddenly shouts, all thoughts of deference now gone. 'It's freezing out here and if we don't set up camp, get some warmth and sustenance, Charlie won't be the only one at risk of exposure. For all we know, he's already back up there wondering where his pack is.'

She's reached the point where she no longer cares if Bruce and Ken don't agree. Getting back to the official trail is her only priority, particularly with predators lurking nearby.

She steps back from the cemetery, and back to the clearing, as if unlocked from the duty she was feeling at the graveside.

'She's right,' Bruce echoes, joining her. 'I can't see that Charlie would have followed his tent this far. He'd have written it off and thought about trying to bunk in with one of us for the night. There are no hostels in this area, so we're best finding somewhere to rest now and go looking for him at first light. If he's not back at camp, we'll just have to pray he's found somewhere to shelter.'

The sound of hungry howls sound again, closer this time, and unless Nora is mistaken, the sound came from somewhere above, which means their route back, in all likelihood, is blocked. She stares back up the hill, straining to hear any further indication of where the animals might be. Could it be the sound just echoed off the acoustics of the mountain side?

And suddenly two pairs of eyes stare back at her from the top of the hill, reflecting the full moon overhead. Nora freezes where she is, willing them to retreat. But they don't. They know their next meal is just waiting to be targeted.

'Run!' Ken yells as he stumbles into the clearing, his stare falling on the two predators. He doesn't hesitate, before racing through the makeshift cemetery and deeper into the woods.

Nora doesn't think twice, charging after him, but with her pack bouncing and grinding against every muscle of her back, her progress is slow. She can hear the smack of Bruce's boots on the ground in close proximity, but the snarl and gnashing of jaws is gaining on them.

They'll never outrun two wolves, let alone a pack, but if they could somehow get elevated, they might just survive the night. She scans the immediate area for trees with low enough branches they could climb up, but it's as if someone has shaved the lower end of the bark to prevent climbing.

She'd glibly told them in the diner that she'd only

need to be able to outrun the weakest in the group, but now that their lives are in danger, both Bruce and Ken are showing themselves to be more athletic than she gave them credit for.

'Faster!' Bruce encourages from just beyond her shoulder, but her legs are heavy, muscles bogged down with fatigue. She doesn't know how much further she can go.

She's genuinely tempted to release her pack and leave the wolves to scavenge through her rations, but valuable seconds will be lost if she has to fiddle with the buckle around her midriff.

Still the chomping and snarling follows closely behind, and Nora now regrets not bringing any kind of weapon. She can't remember what they're supposed to do in this situation. What did the books say about wolf attacks?

She tries to sneak a glance back over her shoulder, to see how close they might be, but all she sees is Bruce's red cheeks puffing.

'Don't look, run!'

But her foot lands awkwardly, she goes over on her ankle, and her momentum sends her crashing towards a mound of snow. Her face disappears into the ice, which brings momentary relief to her burning cheeks, but with it comes the inevitability that her race is run, and her fate is up to nature.

Bruce skids to a halt, and grabs for one of her arms, but she's already resigned herself to what will follow, and she fights him.

'You go. Forget about me. Get to safety.'

'Don't be stupid. Get up, and keep running.'

Suddenly, a loud explosion cracks above their heads, and they both instantly duck, Bruce joining Nora on the ground.

Surely it wasn't thunder.

A second explosion breaks the rhythmic gasping of their breaths, and this time it's followed by a pained whine.

Nora can no longer hear the racing paws and snarling jaws of the chasing pack.

'G-gunfire,' she whispers, and is disappointed when Bruce nods his agreement.

She looks ahead and can see Ken's terrified eyes staring back at her. He dived to the ground at the first gunshot too.

They're both thinking the same thing: who brings a gun on a hike?

While it is legal to carry a gun through national parks in the United States, with the correct permits, those that run the AT discourage carrying firearms on the trail. Not only does a weapon inhibit peace, there's also the matter of having the correct permits for all the states.

The other possibility is that the shooter isn't a hiker, but a local who lives near the trail, though Nora has heard the horror stories about such people, and would rather take her chances with the wolves.

Ken begins to crawl through the snow towards them. 'I think it came from ahead of us,' he whispers, keeping his head as low as possible.

It's all the encouragement Bruce and Nora need, turning, and sliding on their bellies back the way they came. After five metres of painful crawling, they come across a slain wolf, a hole in its side and blood pumping from its panting mouth as death nears.

In that moment, Nora no longer sees the hungry predator that would have happily torn her limb from limb. This creature is suffering and the pained expression in its eyes suggests it doesn't understand why.

'We can't just leave it like this,' she says, but neither Bruce nor Ken are listening as they continue to slide back in the direction of the small cemetery.

But then a branch cracks from behind them, and a rifle-toting moonlit shadow falls across the three of them. They freeze, Nora unwilling to turn and look at whoever was shooting. But then she hears a familiar voice.

'We ought to get out of here before the other one returns with the rest of their pack.'

She dares to turn, but can't decide if she's pleased or repulsed to see Charlie standing there, the barrel of the rifle resting against his shoulder.

Ken is first to his feet, brushing the snow from his jacket, and quickly patting Charlie on the back. 'Am I pleased to see you!'

Bruce helps Nora to her feet, but her legs are like jelly: a cocktail of lactic acid, adrenaline, and terror.

'Where'd you find the gun?' she asks, glaring at Charlie.

He narrows his eyes as he returns the stare. 'I found a lodge back along this way. I was coming back to find you guys when I heard the wolves. Figured a little firepower wouldn't go amiss.' He smiles malevolently, revelling in his role as saviour, before turning and heading back the way he'd come.

Bruce and Ken turn to follow, but Nora remains where she is.

'We can't just leave this creature to bleed to death,' she says firmly.

'He wouldn't have shown you any mercy,' Charlie hollers back without stopping.

Ken keeps stride with him, but Bruce hangs back.

'Maybe if we can find a rock or something,' he says, kicking at clumps of snow. 'It'll be the quickest way.'

Nora falls back to her knees, brings her hand up to the poor creature, and runs a gentle hand over its head and along its back. And in that moment, they share an unspeakable connection: on different paths, but both ultimately headed towards death's door.

Bruce offers a large, jagged rock he's recovered from his search, but as he hands it to Nora, the wolf breathes its last, and goes still. Nora continues to stroke it until Bruce pulls her away.

'Charlie's right: the rest of their pack will be back. We should go.'

She allows him to drag her to her feet, and then she falls in line with him. The snow fall has now stopped, and it's easy to follow Charlie's and Ken's footprints. After a hundred yards through the woods, they reach a wooden cabin surrounded by a small picket fence, as white as the snow around it.

'There's nobody home,' Charlie tells them confidently, 'and there was no sign of any tracks, so we should be okay to rest here for the night.'

Charlie holds the door open, and Ken proceeds in, but Nora plants her feet on the ground.

'We don't know whose house this is,' she says. 'We can't just break in and spend the night in some stranger's home.'

'Sure we can. We'll leave a note in the morning explaining who we are, and I'll leave my contact details so they can send an invoice for the broken window. Relax.'

Bruce seems convinced and begins to move towards the door.

'And what if the owner returns while we're in there?' Nora persists.

'I don't think that's gonna happen,' Charlie fires back, rolling his eyes. 'I've taken a look around and there's no sign of life. Okay? It's just for one night. There's a fireplace and wood, and it'll be far warmer than camping.' He pats Bruce on the back as he enters and continues to look Nora in the eye. 'Listen, princess, it's up to you what you do. The three of us are crashing in here for the night. You wanna pitch your tent outside? That's fine. Do what you want. Just don't come crying to me when you've got frostbite or there's a wolf stalking your tent.'

He steps in through the door, allowing it to close on her. Nora takes a moment, and looks up at the sky. The full moon shines back down at her as distant howling starts up again, and in that moment, she chooses to swallow her pride, and thumps her fist against the door.

Charlie opens it and leers at her. 'Ah, shit, I had three minutes in the sweepstake. What did you fellas have?' He roars with laughter, before stepping aside and allowing her in.

With only splinters of moonlight breaking through the shutters over the windows, it's difficult to see too much inside the cabin. No obvious switch for a light, so Nora assumes there's no electricity. The cabin appears to be open plan, with a wicker sofa and dining table separating the main room from the kitchen. There are two closed doors beyond the space, one presumably a bedroom, and the other a bathroom.

Ken is over at the fireplace, busy building logs, while Bruce pushes the sofa to one side, creating a larger space on the wooden floor. 'I figured we could sleep on our sponge mats here,' he says.

'Screw that,' Charlie retorts, grabbing his pack from the corner. 'I found this place so I'm calling shotgun on the master bedroom. You ladies can share the floor out here.'

With that, he heads past the kitchen, and in through the door at the rear of the property. Ken manages to get the fire lit, and within minutes, the three of them are ready to strip out of their coats. Bruce lays out the mats and sleeping bags, and for the first time all day, Nora allows herself to relax a little. Grabbing a granola bar from her pack, she excuses herself to use the bathroom.

She screams when she opens the door and sees a face staring back at her.

14

JESS

April 2023, Rockston, Maine, USA

I stay at the fast-food restaurant to take advantage of the free Wi-Fi, and to drink my coffee, but no matter how much I search for it, I can't find any details of a mental health facility burning down in the area, so I can't make sense of the woman's disdainful comments. I regret now not standing up for Chester. If he was off his medication like his carer suggested, then it's no wonder he had a bad reaction. Despite the explanation, it still sends a shiver down my spine, thinking of him targeting me with his ranting and waving arms. For the briefest of moments, I allow myself to think it had something to do with Mum's remains, but it can't be anything more than coincidental.

I continue to follow the Smart car's satnav directions until I pass a welcoming wooden sign which tells me I'm now entering Rockston, Maine (population 7,350). Fields of corn border the single lane road into the town, but traffic is fairly light. In fact, in the last thirty minutes I don't think I've seen more than five other vehicles headed towards, or coming from, the area. There are no road signs to advise me where to park, but as a strip of shops appear on both sides of the road, I see now there are marked bays on the road in front of the shopfronts.

I turn left and follow the trail of stores, eventually arriving at a large white stone courthouse that seems to be the heart of the town. A large patch of grass separates the courthouse from the road, and I can see children running about playing tag on it. Across the road there is a drug store, a saloon bar, a library and a bakery. The shops continue around the block, and I end up finding a parking bay outside a jewellery store, and across from the sheriff's office.

And there are flowers everywhere. The sidewalks are cut off from the road by raised flowerbeds filled with vibrant reds, blues, yellows, whites, greens and purples. Spring has definitely arrived in Rockston. This really could be the prettiest town I've ever been to; unspoilt by chain stores and franchises, somewhere nature is allowed to thrive.

The article said Rockston Sheriff Randy Whitaker is overseeing recovery of the remains, so he seems a good place to start. The sun is shining, and so when I get out of the car, I strip off my jumper and throw it on the passenger seat, before crossing the road. The sweet smell of caramel fills the air, emanating from the bakery on the corner, and my stomach reminds me that it's coming up to dinner time in the UK; my body has yet to adjust to the time difference. I promise myself I'll visit the bakery before I find a motel to check into.

The sheriff's office looks like most of the other store fronts in the town. Large glass windows dominate, and from the street I can see three desks along one side of the office space, and a large barred gate leading out back to where presumably they have holding cells. The windows on the right side are frosted glass, so I don't see what is there until I enter and realise there are enclosed rooms, presumably for when they have to interrogate suspects. It's otherwise open plan, and my eyes are drawn to the filter coffee machine at the far side of the room, along with a water cooler.

'I help you?' a woman in a light-brown uniform calls to me from the nearest desk, though her tone suggests the question may be rhetorical.

Her short-sleeve shirt reveals toned biceps, and when she stands, I see it isn't just her arms that she works on. I'm pretty sure I wouldn't be able to outrun her in a race. Her blonde hair is plaited but there is a compressed ring around her forehead where her hat has been pressed at some point this morning. She's frowning as she looks at me, clearly unable to place my face.

I put on my widest and most wholesome smile.

'Good morning,' I say, heading over, keeping the smile plastered to my face. 'I was hoping to speak with Sheriff Randy Whitaker, if I may?'

She raises an eyebrow. 'Sheriff's not here. Something I can help you with?'

I don't know if she's trying to make me feel uncomfortable, but I definitely don't feel welcome; I'm certain it isn't just the air conditioning that's giving me goose bumps. Maybe I'm just misreading her stance.

'My name's Jess Grogan and I've travelled all the way from England to speak with Sheriff Whitaker. Would you be able to tell me when he'll be back?'

'England, you say? What, you don't have police over there? That's a little out of our jurisdiction.'

Sarcasm now too. That's perfect!

My cheeks are aching as I widen my smile. 'I'm not looking to report a crime. I actually think I might be able to help Sheriff Whitaker solve a crime.'

'Is that right? Well, I have several unsolved you can take a look at if you're game. The Jacksons' tractor for example. Do you happen to know who took it for a joyride and left it vandalised at the town limits? Or perhaps you could help me figure out who's been stealing old Mrs Tranton's underwear from her washing line. She suspects her neighbour, but he denies it and we've yet to find the evidence to prosecute.'

It takes all my willpower to keep my frustration in check. I don't know how I've wronged this woman, but she's clearly holding a grudge.

'Perhaps Sheriff Whitaker is currently overseeing the extraction of remains from the mountains; or attending the post-mortem on those remains? Sorry, you guys call that an autopsy, right?'

She stares back at me blankly. 'I cannot confirm or deny sheriff business with a member of the public.'

I drop the smile. 'Look, I've travelled a long way to offer my help. I believe the remains found in the mountains may belong to my mother who went missing from the Appalachian Trail thirty years ago.'

I study her face for any hint of recognition, but her poker face remains fixed. 'What remains? I have no idea what you're talking about.'

'I'll show you then.' I pull my phone from my pocket, open the email, and click on the link I was sent, but it won't open as I have no data. 'Do you happen to have Wi-Fi I can connect to?'

She shakes her head. 'The library down the road does and you can connect there for an hour for five bucks. I suggest you go there.'

She turns her back and moves to the water cooler.

'Please?' I say, surprised by the desperation in my voice. 'I just want to find out whether the remains are my mum's. She disappeared from near here in 1993, and I've had no closure. I want to know why she never returned home.'

She turns back and her stance softens fractionally. 'You staying in town?'

'I'm hoping to find a motel nearby, yes.'

'Then I will let the sheriff know you stopped by, and if he wants to speak to you, he'll find you.'

I nod in defeat and head back outside into the warmer air. That certainly didn't go as well as I'd hoped. The article said the remains were found nearby, and if they're Mum's then maybe she visited this town at some point. It's been three decades, but there might be people still here who may remember her.

I release a sigh of frustration, not ready to give up yet.

In the car, I set directions to the local motel, a two-minute drive from here, and park up. I'm one of six cars parked, but there are fifteen rooms as far as I can see, so hopefully they'll have availability. I collect my bag from the passenger seat and head inside, finding a white-haired woman who must be in her mid to late seventies standing behind the reception desk. She is staring at a spot on the wall, until I approach.

'Hi, I don't have a reservation, but I'm hoping I might be able to get a room for a couple of nights?'

Her eyes meet mine. 'I'm sorry, but we're full.'

Her manner is as frosty as the deputy's, and I'm starting to think that the welcoming appearance of the town centre is just for show.

'Oh, that's a shame. Um, are there any other motels or hotels nearby?'

'I'm afraid not. If you head back out of town, there's some hotels about an hour from here. You may have more luck there.'

It's another disappointment, but I might as well make the most of this opportunity.

'Have you lived in Rockston for a long time?' I ask.

'Born and raised.' She nods proudly.

I unlock my phone and navigate to the image of my mum, which I hold out for her to look at. 'Do you recognise the woman in this picture?'

She squints before reaching for the glasses hanging from a chain around her neck, and slides them onto her nose. She continues to squint before shaking her head.

I keep the phone screen pointed at her. 'I believe she might have come through the town thirty years ago.'

'I'm sorry, I don't have much of a mind for names and faces. We do get a lot of people pass through the motel, you understand, so I think I've trained my brain to forget them.'

Still, I keep the screen pointed at her. 'She went missing in 1993, but I believe she may have visited the town. That's why I'm here. I'm trying to find out what happened to her as I believe... I believe she died on this mountain.'

The woman looks back at me, and uncrosses her arms. 'I am sorry to hear that.' She pauses and when she speaks again, her voice is softer. 'We do keep a room spare for emergencies. I can let you have it for twenty-five a night plus taxes.'

'Thank you.'

'It is a bit of a mess, if I'm honest. We use it for storage too, but I will arrange for my grandson to clear any boxes so you can get to the bed.' She turns the guestbook on the counter to face me. 'I need your name, home address, telephone number and car registration here, please.'

I take the pen she's offering and fill in where she indicates.

She reaches under the counter and hands me a metal key on a large wooden keyring. 'Room fifteen. It's the last room on the strip. Have a pleasant stay.'

I scoop up the key and thank her again, before carrying my bag to the room and letting myself in. I'm greeted by a cloud of dust and stale air as I open the door, and it causes me to cough and splutter. She wasn't kidding about the room being used for storage. There are three stacks of cardboard boxes lined up against the wall, but it doesn't stop me getting to the bed and dropping my holdall on it. I cross the room and open the window to try to get rid of the acrid smell. I know beggars can't be choosers.

There are numbers scrawled on each of the boxes, and as I open the top one to look inside, I see now it contains old copies of the guest register I just signed in reception. I guess they must keep them for an audit trail.

Suddenly I realise that if my mum did come to Rockston, it's likely she would have stayed in this motel, as it's the only one in the town. Finding her name in one of these books would prove she was here.

I check each of the boxes until I locate the period that should contain the 1993 register, only when I open the box it isn't there. It contains registers from 1990, 1991, 1992, and 1994, but there is definitely a gap where 1993 should be. I check the other boxes in case it has been misplaced, but 1993's is the only year missing. My imagination starts to draw its own conclusions.

What if she was here and someone has taken the register to cover it up? A shadow crosses my heart.

15

NORA

September 1993, Appalachian Trail, New Hampshire, USA

The wall beyond the toilet is covered in animal skulls, each pinned in place so they stare back at you. At the sound of her terror, Bruce is immediately by Nora's side, and pulls her away, turning his nose up at the sight.

'What's with all the screaming?' Charlie asks, returning from the bedroom.

Bruce nods over to the bathroom, and Charlie pokes his head around the door. He guffaws at what he sees. 'I guess the owner of this place must be some kind of hunter,' he says nonchalantly, though he closes the door so the skulls can't keep staring.

'Let's get some fresh air,' Bruce suggests, leading a quaking Nora towards the front door, leaving it ajar while they stand taking deep breaths on the narrow porch.

Nora's breath escapes in large gusts of steam, the desire to use the bathroom suddenly dissipated. Everything she'd read about the trail warned not to stray from the main route, and yet the others didn't seem the least concerned to be breaking the golden rule.

'I know you're not keen to stay,' Bruce says, wrapping a protective arm around her shoulders, 'but I don't think we can risk heading back the way we came. We can shelter here and in the morning, we'll leave as quickly as possible. It doesn't look as though this place has been lived in for some time, so I don't reckon we'll be disturbed tonight. And as Charlie said, we can leave a note to explain the damage to the window.'

She knows he's trying to reassure her, but right now the only place she wants to be is at home, giving her little girl a kiss.

He suggests they head back in, to which she nods, but then she stops.

'Can you hear that?'

He stares blankly back at her. 'What?'

She turns and stares out at the darkness. 'I don't know, it sounds like... whistling.'

* * *

Nora starts as her nightmare drags her back to the land of the living, and it takes several moments to settle her breathing and recall why she can see the side of Ken's stubbly face so close. His chest rises and falls, a bearlike growl escaping with every intake of breath, oblivious to the terror that has haunted her sleep these past few hours. The splint that Bruce fixed for him last night hangs tight around his wrist, the only part of his body that isn't tucked in to his sleeping bag. It takes a further moment for Nora to realise that Bruce is no longer spread out on the mat between them.

Daylight is already poking through the wooden shutters over the windows, which means it must already be after seven. Her diary sits on the wooden floor beside her where she was writing in it last night. She sits up, rolling her neck and shoulders, seeking forgiveness for another punishing night on the foam mattress and inflatable pillow, with its burnt-rubber odour. They've not yet completed their first week, and already she is ready to sell her soul in exchange for a proper pillow.

Her eyes fall on the door to the room of death, as she named it last night when she mistook it for a bathroom. Charlie had later informed them all that toilet facilities were available in an outhouse behind the cabin. If she were a cynic, she'd put money on Charlie deliberately not sharing that nugget, waiting to see who stumbled into the room first.

The room itself is the size of her under-stair broom cupboard at home. Only, where she would expect to find a vacuum cleaner, feather dusters, and emergency dining chairs, instead hung deskinned animal skulls. Bruce estimated bear, deer, wolf, and horse amongst other less obvious species. Clearly, whoever uses this cabin as a base has a penchant for collecting dead animals, though no part of her mind can fathom why.

Last night, it took several minutes of focused breathing to stop her racing heart. The giant bear skull hanging where she'd expected to see a mirror and basin had seemed like it was coming out of the wall towards her, and it was only when Bruce pulled on it that she could allow herself to see that it was firmly secured. Who would keep such trophies in a room like that?

There are no photographs or documents identifying the proprietor either, but Nora would guess a man, as there are no signs of any cleaning products in the makeshift kitchen, save for a sponge and soap.

The door to the bedroom opens, and Charlie stands in the doorway wrapped in a blanket, his sock-clad feet poking out the bottom.

'Morning,' he says, annoyingly bright. 'Were you coming to keep me warm?'

She turns up her nose in disgust. 'Not even if you were the last man alive. Besides, I'm happily married.'

He smirks, and moves into the kitchen, where he reaches for the metal kettle, but when he tries the tap above the sink, although it sputters and gurgles, no water emerges.

'Pipes must be frozen,' he says matter-of-factly, and pushes past her, heading to the front door.

She watches as he slips on his boots and heads out into the crisp sunshine, stooping to collect snow from a mound and dropping it into the kettle. He then returns, leaving the door ajar, before hanging the kettle above the dwindling fire. He reaches for a poker and stokes the logs, carefully placing two more in place.

'You want tea or coffee?' he asks as he heads back

into the kitchen and selects two mugs from the only cupboard.

'We can't just help ourselves to this person's supplies,' she says.

'Why not? A little bit of coffee and a couple of tea bags isn't going to push them over the poverty line. Relax, will you?'

Ken continues to snore, oblivious to the raised voices.

'Where's Bruce?' she asks, seeking a sound mind to concur with her.

'He's outside,' Charlie snaps back, returning to his room and closing the door.

Nora nudges Ken with her foot as she passes, telling him they need to get up and moving again if they're to make it to the next checkpoint.

'Morning,' Bruce calls to her when she steps outside, rubbing her arms as she does. Despite the brightness of the sun, the ice below her booted feet seems to be sending cold waves up her.

'What are you doing?' she asks.

He lowers the map and compass he's holding, and smiles. 'I couldn't sleep, so I thought I'd try and work out where we are with regards to the trail. I was hoping we could avoid re-treading our steps and somehow link back up further along, but it doesn't look like we'll be so lucky.' His nose wrinkles in disappointment.

'Never mind. Thank you for trying. How long have you been out here?'

'I came out to watch the sunrise. Ken was sounding like a banshee, and you seemed to be talking in your sleep, so I thought I'd come out for some peace.'

She can feel the heat in her cheeks. 'What was I talking about?'

'Not a clue.' He smiles. 'It was more like muttering than talking. And whatever you were saying, it wasn't English.'

Her brow furrows. 'Not English? I don't know any other languages.'

He shrugs. 'I was half-asleep so I can't be sure what it was. Can you remember what you were dreaming about?'

She shakes her head, and doesn't admit to the night terror. 'You know, I think I ache in places I've never ached before.'

He smiles again. 'I know what you mean. I know we went for foam mats to save space and additional weight, but right now I wish I'd opted for an inflatable.'

Nora rubs at her arms again as the cold bites at her skin.

'We should go in,' he says. 'I think I've worked out where we are and where we were, so it shouldn't take too long to get back on track.'

He leads the way, and the moment he pushes open the door, they're greeted with the most amazing smell as something sizzles in the tray over the fire.

'How do you like your steak?' Ken calls out, tending to the lump of red meat in the pan.

'Steak for breakfast?' Bruce echoes. 'Now you're talking!'

'Um, where did you find that?' Nora asks, closing the door and waving her hand to clear some of the smoke that's starting to fill the room.

'Charlie found a cold store buried in the ground out back,' Ken replies.

'So, it's meat that belongs to the owner of the cabin?'

Ken nods as if there's nothing unusual about the question.

'We can't eat it then. It's one thing to take shelter from a bitter night, but quite another to steal food.'

Ken meets her stare, and looks back at the meat guiltily.

'We'll leave some money and a note explaining,'

Bruce suggests, delicately placing his hands on Nora's shoulders and leading her to the table. 'God knows we could all do with some protein after last night's horror. And besides, they've already started cooking it, so to throw it away would be just to waste good food.'

'Well, I'm not going to eat it,' she says, her own stomach starting to grumble as the smell of fried steak fills the cabin.

'Good, all the more for us,' Charlie declares, emerging from his room, now fully clothed. He takes a seat at the head of the table.

'Happy not to partake in your feast.' Nora shakes her head as she moves away from the table. She opens her pack and rummages for her oats.

'We need to get cleaned up, and then we can be on our way again,' Charlie says when they've finished eating, wiping grease from his chin with the back of his arm. 'I never did find my tent, so I'm going to need to stop at a town and buy one as soon as possible.'

'There's a town about two days' walk away,' Ken confirms, studying the map he recovered from Bruce. 'We'll need to set a good pace, and hope the snow relents, but otherwise we should make it before nightfall tomorrow.'

'And in the meantime, you can bunk up with me,' Bruce says. 'My tent's big enough for two.'

Charlie raises his thumb in acknowledgement, before standing and carrying the plates to the large ceramic sink, and filling it with water from the recently boiled kettle. He sets about scrubbing the plates, while Nora locates a tea towel, and begins to wipe.

'Listen,' Charlie says quietly, while the other two roll up the mats and sleeping bags, 'I feel like we got off on the wrong foot. I'm Ashley's uncle, and you're her godmother. We're both here because we care deeply about that little girl, and her future. Right?'

Nora nods, surprised by his candour.

'So how about we start afresh, and put any animosity behind us?'

Beware of Greeks bearing gifts, Nora thinks, but nods her acceptance of the truce.

'Good. The last thing either of us needs is anything to add to the stress of this expedition. And I think you and I could make a good team. After all, we are the strongest of the group, I'm sure you'll agree, so we should make sure we have one another's backs.'

She isn't sure how to interpret that, but before she has chance to question the validity of the statement, Ken comes over and tells them they need to get moving if they want to make it to the next checkpoint.

16

JESS

April 2023, Rockston, Maine, USA

I shouldn't have looked in the boxes, because they're none of my business, but now that I have, I need to understand why the guest register from 1993 isn't in there. I mustn't assume it's because it contains Mum's name and has been deliberately removed due to a conspiracy to cover the fact that she was here, but my imagination is already making such leaps.

There could be any number of rational explanations as to why 1993 is missing. Maybe it got damaged and had to be destroyed. Or maybe it's been requested by a member of some historical society as part of a project. Or maybe it's been misplaced in another box somewhere.

Or maybe it contains Mum's name and details, and someone doesn't want it found out that she was here.

Leaving my holdall on the bed, I exit the room and make the walk back to reception, ready to confront the woman who checked me in to the room, but when I enter, with my mind racing with thoughts and questions, she is no longer there. Instead, a guy in a luminous blue and yellow Hawaiian shirt is behind the counter drumming a beat with a pen to a song that must be playing in his head. He has light-brown hair which has been bleached blond at the tips and sticks out at various angles as if he's been electrocuted.

He drops the pen the moment he senses me approaching. 'Good morning, oh, no, wait, good afternoon,' he says, glancing at his watch. 'How can I help you?'

I offer a disarming smile, hiding my suspicion. 'I wanted to speak to the woman who checked me in a few minutes ago.'

He frowns at me. 'Woman?'

'Yeah, she was much older, hair as white as snow and glasses hanging around her neck. Sorry, I didn't catch her name.'

'Well, I'm Jarod, and I don't think I've seen anyone like that here today.'

'She was wearing a purple and blue flowery summer dress,' I add, unable to understand why he doesn't know who I'm referring to.

'Is she one of our guests?'

'No, I don't think so. She was standing where you are right now.'

The lines in his forehead deepen. 'There's nobody else working here today.'

'Don't be ridiculous. She checked me in.'

'Which room are you in?'

'Room fifteen.'

He wrinkles his nose. 'That's not possible. We don't let room fifteen unless it's an emergency.'

I sigh, feeling as though I'm once again banging my head against a brick wall. 'Yes, she told me that, but I think she must have taken pity on me and said I could have it for a few days.'

I show him the key and he turns it over in his hands, before checking under the desk and confirming it is indeed the key to room fifteen. As he stoops, I see a framed photograph on the wall behind the desk showing the face of the woman I spoke to.

I didn't imagine the whole conversation!

'There!' I shout, pointing at the frame. '*That's* who

I spoke to. If she doesn't work here, what the hell is her picture doing on the wall?'

He turns and looks at the photograph, before glancing back at me. 'But that's impossible. That's my grandma and she's been dead for twenty years.'

My eyes widen, and my heart skips a beat. I move unsteadily backwards, my gaze unable to leave those of the woman in the frame. I'm about to question everything I've ever believed when Jarod bursts out laughing and clutches his gut as he falls on the desk, slapping it with his hand.

'Oh, shit, I'm sorry, I thought I was going to be able to keep a straight face, but when the blood drained from yours... ah, shit, it was just too funny.'

He slaps the desk again, and I move back to it. I'm angry that he played a practical joke, but as I stare at the tears of laughter running down his face, I can't help but laugh myself.

'Shit, I'm sorry, I shouldn't have done that, but I couldn't resist.'

'I thought for a moment, like, I'd wandered into the Overlook Hotel from *The Shining*.'

This brings more tears to his eyes, and any residual anger I was feeling vanishes too. I can't believe I was so willing to accept I'd had a conversation with a ghost.

'Is your grandmother around so I can ask her a couple of questions?'

'I'm sorry but she's napping at the moment. She gets pretty tired these days, but she should be back out later on this afternoon. I'm happy to pass a message on; it's the least I can do.'

How do I phrase this so he doesn't kick off when I admit I've been snooping?

I take a deep breath and squint apologetically. 'Actually, there are some boxes in my room with old versions of guest registers, but the book for 1993 seems to be missing, and I wanted to have a look at your guest list for that year.'

He doesn't seem bothered by my confession, so I continue.

'My mother disappeared in 1993, and I have reason to suspect she may have visited this town around that time, and I wanted to see whether she might have stayed here.'

He pulls an awkward face. 'I'm sorry, I have no idea where that would be. I wasn't born until 2001, and I only help out here when I'm back from college. Grandma and my uncle handle the administration side of things. If you need to extend your stay, request extra towels, or need directions to a restaurant in the town then I'm your man. Anything beyond that is a little out of my remit, I'm afraid.'

Given his age, there's no point in asking whether he recognises the picture of Mum, so I turn to leave.

He clicks his fingers together. 'You know who you should speak to? Mrs Daniels. She runs the tearoom on the other side of town. She's been here since the dawn of time or some shit. She'll be able to give you a potted history of everything that's gone on in this place. Head back along the main road until you get to the town centre and then follow the road around and down towards the library, and you'll see the tearoom. It's this massive white building with fancy umbrellas over the tables out front. You can't miss it. It's like a five-minute walk, tops.'

I thank him and head out of the motel. He was right: it really is impossible to miss the Rockston Tearoom, with its bright pink parasols, potted tall fern trees, and 1920s band music. I think about how much Bruce would love this kitsch, and remember that I really should phone to tell him where I am and what I'm doing. I don't want to get his hopes up unnecessarily, so will wait until I've finally tracked down the sheriff before phoning home. My phone still doesn't appear to have a signal this high up the mountain anyway, so I'll also have to send Ashley a message when I reconnect to Wi-Fi.

Stepping inside the tearoom is like stepping back in time. The dozen or so tables inside are small and round, holding two chairs each, with pretty white tablecloths and tassels. Each tablecloth then has a large pink doily in the centre. The band music is much louder inside, and when a woman in 1920s costume approaches, I hazard a guess that she is the Mrs Daniels Jarod referred to.

'Mrs Daniels?'

'Yes, dear. Is it a table for one you're after, or will you have company?'

The tearoom is far fancier a place than I would have chosen to eat, but my stomach is grumbling and, in my experience, people are generally far more likely to speak when they're getting something from you.

'Table for one, thank you.'

She looks at me wistfully. 'Do my ears deceive me or is that a British accent?'

'It is indeed. I'm visiting from England.'

'Well, I'll be, we don't get many Brits here in Rockston. You'll be thrilled to hear that we have Earl Grey.'

The bell on the door rings as someone enters – or leaves – but I don't turn to see who. Mrs Daniels shows me to a table in the window and hands me a menu printed on an A5 piece of paper, in a cursive font which is difficult to read. She stands at the table, pen and paper in hand, ready to take my order. I skim read the menu but there are no prices listed, which again in my experience is never a good sign.

'I'm not massively hungry,' I say reluctantly, 'but I did hear wonderful things about your teas, so can I just order a pot of your finest please?'

She scribbles on the pad, smiling at the compliment before disappearing out through a door across the room into what I presume is the kitchen. She reappears a moment later, carrying a tray of tiny sandwiches and takes them to a couple sitting at the table in the other window. She then heads out the back again and returns with a tray carrying a pot of tea, cup and saucer, and a small jug of milk.

I wait until she's placed the items in front of me before unlocking my phone and holding out the picture of Mum.

'I heard you have a great head for history, and I was wondering whether you recognise the woman in this picture. She would have been here back in the early nineties.'

She takes my phone and stares at it through her thick glasses, scrutinising it for far longer than Jarod's grandmother did, but she shakes her head as she hands it back.

'You said she came to Rockston? I've never seen that face before. Did she say she came to my tearoom?'

'She didn't mention the tearoom specifically,' I ad lib, 'but I wondered whether you might have seen her around in general.'

She shakes her head again. 'I can confidently say I have never seen that woman before in my life.'

My heart sinks. 'I don't suppose you have Wi-Fi here, do you?'

'I'm afraid not. You should be able to get online at the library.'

I thank her and she heads back out to the kitchen.

A man with his back to me stands and heads for the door. He drops whatever he is carrying by my feet, before quickly picking up what I now see is a newspaper, and then he heads out of the door. I realise a piece of paper has fallen, and I bend down to it, about to hurry after him when I see what's written:

I KNOW ABOUT YOUR MOM. CAN'T TALK HERE.

MEET ME AT O'REILLY'S AT 7.15 TONIGHT.

17

NORA

September 1993, Appalachian Trail, New Hampshire, USA

Ken's suggestion that they might make the next town within two days was a tad optimistic. With relentless snow blocking their path – up to the waist in certain places – progress was slow. By nightfall on the second night, they weren't even halfway there, and even Charlie was starting to question the sanity of the hike.

'Our sponsors are certainly getting their money's worth,' he was now muttering at least once an hour as the challenge worsened.

At least there hasn't been any fresh snow today.

Most other hikers must have chosen to leave the trail and are waiting before returning, as they've only seen two other people since leaving the skull cabin. Where the snow is at its thinnest, the ground is slippery, making it difficult to gain any speed and stay upright. In other lower places it's already melted, but has left muddy streams to splash through. This isn't what any of them signed up for, and the fact that the icy wind shows no sign of abatement is adding to their frustration.

Nora is cold and exhausted, and so when Ken mentions the prospect of a hostel close by, she's the first to vote for it. She can't take another night on an uneven floor. Whilst the sponge mat is able to cushion some of the bumps and spikes, it's far from perfect, and trying to carry a pack when her back is already sore from poor sleeping conditions is just making things worse. The prospect of sleeping on a sprung mattress in a building with walls has her giddy with excitement.

At the top of the next mound, the wooden hostel looms into sight, and someone has kindly cleared a route through the snow leading to it, which is just about wide enough for a knackered hiker carrying a pack. A simple wooden affair, the hostel has seen better days. At one point, the bright yellow-painted sides would have made it stand out like a beacon or lighthouse. But the paint is chipped and faded, and now resembles something you might find at an abandoned youth centre. The steps leading to the raised platform are crumbling, and as Charlie approaches, a voice shouts to him from inside, instructing him to climb up to the platform instead.

Charlie removes his pack and throws it onto the platform, before lifting himself up. Ken follows suit, and Bruce offers Nora a bunk up, which she gratefully accepts.

Entering through a door which is hanging off its hinges, they count twelve narrow bunkbeds, half lining one wall, and half the other. At the far end of the building stands a large gas stove and table where three hikers are busy laughing and preparing food. Nora can see macaroni, potatoes, and a large block of yellow cheese, which has her instantly salivating. Having survived on a diet of oatmeal, noodles, and granola bars, the prospect of cheese has her wanting to tear through the hostel and snatch it away.

The bitter breeze still manages to penetrate the flimsy plywood walls of the large shack, where gaps exist between the boards. God knows who built it, but it has an amateur feel to it. A bunting of dripping socks and vests hangs to the side of the stove, with a trail of boots lined up by the small fireplace in one corner. The room smells like a male changing room after a sweaty gym session, and it brings tears to Nora's eyes.

'How many of you are there?' a stout woman with a head of shaved black hair asks from the bunk closest to the door.

Having dreaded the prospect of being imprisoned with only men, Nora is relieved to see at least one other woman. She is sitting cross-legged on the lower bunk, adjusting the laces of the hiking boot between her hands. A scar runs the length of her face, from eyebrow to chin, but she makes no effort to hide it, wearing it like a badge of honour.

'Um, four,' Ken replies, stepping forwards.

She considers the rest of the room, before nodding. 'Three of you will be able to take bunks, but one will have to use the floor. Okay?'

Ken looks at the group and shrugs.

'Sounds fine,' Nora replies to the woman, who stands and introduces herself as Leanne from Minnesota.

Leanne leads them through the building, pointing out the three vacant beds, and introducing them to a handful of the others.

'You're welcome to cook your own food,' she continues, 'or, if you're prepared to share some rations, you can join in the feast Jean-Claude is preparing for the rest of us.'

The tallest of the men by the stove turns at the mention of his name. 'I'm attempting mac and cheese and fries. What have you got?'

They open their packs, and empty the food contents onto one of the vacant mattresses. Jean-Claude tuts as he turns items over in his hands, before selecting some of Nora's oats, Bruce's carton of long-life milk, and two Snickers bars from Ken's supplies. He raises his eyebrows to check they're happy to surrender the items, and all nod eagerly.

'Looks like we're having flapjacks for dessert,' Jean-Claude declares to the room and a loud roar almost raises the roof.

Leanne returns to her bed, leaving the four of them to fight over the bunks. The mattresses are thin, stained, and not covered with any kind of sheet, like a walking advert for hepatitis. Each bed also contains a pillow that makes Nora's burnt-rubber smelling inflatable seem more appealing.

'Should we flip for it?' Ken asks, but Charlie shakes his head.

'Listen, I got the bed at the cabin. It's only right that the three of you get them this time. I don't mind kipping on my mat on the floor. Should still be more comfortable than where we were last night. Besides, Rex will keep me company,' he adds, lifting Ashley's stuffed dinosaur into the air.

None of them are expecting such chivalry, but none of them argues against the decision either. Bruce climbs into the bunk above Nora, while Ken takes the one above Leanne.

'Do you mind if I perch on the end of the bed until it's time to sleep?' Charlie asks Nora, and she tells him it is fine.

Nora lays out her sleeping bag, and sniffs the pillow, before offering it up to Bruce and choosing to inflate her travel pillow instead.

'I feel like I'm in one of those old POW movies,' Charlie says as he surveys the row of bunks opposite. 'Do you know what I mean? I keep expecting to see Steve McQueen appear in vest and khakis.'

The Great Escape had been Nora's dad's favourite movie and she'd been subjected to it for countless years, but looking at the rickety and forever-creaking bunks, she could see what he meant.

Bruce shuffles in the bunk over their heads, and both stare up at the thin wooden slats barely holding up the mattress. Maybe she would have been safer opting for the top bunk – better that than being crushed to death.

The smell of frying potatoes and melted cheese begins to fill the hostel, and finally the damp odour of soggy socks dissipates. When a shout goes out for more firewood, Charlie raises his hand and heads out with two others, allowing Nora the chance to spread out and determine if there's any life left in the old mattress. She eventually decides there isn't, and rolls out her sponge mat on top of it, before relaying the sleeping bag. Not perfect but better than it was.

'Do you wanna buy a charm?'

Nora opens her eyes and sees a pretty, waif-like blonde girl standing at the foot of the bed. She can't be much older than sixteen, seventeen at a push. She's wearing faded blue dungarees, a thick cardigan and a padded hot-pink ski jacket. Her hair is braided, and she's the first person Nora's seen in makeup since they joined the trail.

'What was that, sorry?' she replies, offering a placatory smile.

The girl raises the shoe box of trinkets she's carrying, before reaching inside and extracting a thin leather bracelet adorned with a rainbow of plastic-looking jewels.

'I'm selling good luck charms,' she says, offering

the bracelet to Nora to examine. 'They're handmade and each one is uniquely blessed. The one you're holding brings future prosperity.'

Nora turns the intricate band over in her hand, thinking about how much her own mother would have jumped at the chance of anything that claimed to offer good luck. Before Nora's father had his wife sectioned, she'd become convinced by the power of magic, tarot and fortune-telling. It was the beginning of the end. And whilst Nora doesn't believe in luck and magic, she knows Jess would love something so pretty.

'How much?'

'They're six dollars each, or I can give you two for ten.'

'Future prosperity for only six bucks, how can I refuse?' Nora smiles at her. 'Where are you from?'

'I'm from Rockston originally, but I go from town to town selling my charms and good fortune to those I meet.'

Nora removes a ten-dollar note from her purse and offers it out. 'Do you have change?'

The girl eyes the money, and quickly shakes her head.

'Well, it looks like I'll have to take two then. This one is for my daughter. What else have you got?'

The girl passes her the shoebox, and Nora picks through it until she finds a thin silver bracelet with an inscription in an unfamiliar language.

'What does this one represent?'

The girl's eyes narrow. 'That is the most valuable charm of them all. What drew you to it?'

Nora twists the thin bracelet between her fingers. 'I'm not sure. Is it not for sale?'

'Well, it is to the right person. It provides the wearer protection from evil spirits.'

Nora bites down on her gum to keep herself from laughing, once again thinking how much her mum would have been sold by the line. 'Well, that's the one for me then.'

She hands over the money and attempts to slide the bracelet over her hand, but it appears to be too small, and she's about to ask whether she can swap it, when the girl drops the box, grabs Nora's wrist forcefully, and wraps her hand around the bracelet. She closes her eyes and raises her head towards the ceiling, muttering something under her breath as she begins to twist the thin metal.

Disturbed, Nora tries to pull her wrist free, but the girl is stronger than she gave her credit for, and the girl's hands remain clamped around her wrist.

And then just as quickly, the girl lowers her face

and opens her eyes, letting go. Nora's mouth drops when she sees the bracelet around her wrist, the girl's finger marks remaining impressed on her skin.

'Just a little tight, but it's on now,' the girl says, smiling widely. 'So long as you wear the bracelet, no harm will come to you.'

'What's all this then?' Charlie asks, returning and nodding at the girl.

'I was just buying a couple of charms,' Nora says, showing him her purchases, but Charlie has no interest in the jewellery.

His eyes haven't left the girl's, and Nora's stomach turns as she watches Charlie place his arm around her shoulders. 'So, which bunk is yours?'

'Oh, I'm not staying here. I'm actually on my way to Darby.'

'Oh, really? That's where we're headed, too. Surely you're not hiking there tonight though?'

'Of course not. No, my car is nearby. When are you due to make it to Darby?'

'In a couple of weeks if we can make it through the snow.'

'Well, if you make it by next Saturday, the town is having its annual Festival of Light. There'll be food and drink, fireworks and live music.' She glances at Nora. 'You should come.'

'Well, I *love* a party,' Charlie continues. 'Hopefully see you there then.'

The girl nods and heads for the door, while Charlie leers after her. Nora wants to remind him that he's old enough to be her father, but she doesn't want to fracture their truce, so she lets it go.

'Be careful of that one,' Leanne says, approaching. 'She try and sell you one of her charms?' she asks, using air quotes.

Nora instinctively pulls the sleeve of her jumper over the bracelet. 'No harm, just a kid trying to make some pocket money.'

'Did she mention a party in Darby?'

'She sure did,' Charlie says. 'Happening next Saturday. Sounds like a blast.'

'I'd think twice about going if I was you,' Leanne warns. 'That festival... let's just say it's got a bad rep.'

Nora sits up. 'In what way?'

'I've never been personally, but I've heard stories. Listen, far be it for me to tell you what you should or shouldn't get involved with. All I'll say is if you're serious about reaching the summit of Mount Katahdin, I'd avoid partying in Darby.'

18

JESS

April 2023, Rockston, Maine, USA

I quickly screw up the note, hiding it in my fist as Mrs Daniels reappears from the doorway to the kitchen to check whether I require anything else. I've barely touched my tea, but I desperately want to hurry after the person who left the note, though I sense he's probably already long gone.

'The man who was here,' I say instead to her, 'he looked familiar but I couldn't place if I knew him from the television or somewhere else.'

She frowns. 'What man?'

I point at the table and chair he's just vacated. 'He was over there.'

She frowns as she turns to look. 'Oh, him? I don't know. He isn't from around here.'

'I don't suppose your tearoom has any kind of security cameras, does it?' I ask instead.

She waves away the question with a chuckle. 'What do you think this place is? Stalingrad? Rockston is hardly a hotbed of crime.'

She continues to chuckle as she goes across and collects the plate, cup and saucer from the man's table, and carries them back out towards the kitchen. The moment she's gone, I drop a ten-dollar bill on the table as I'm unsure of how much a pot of tea will be in a fancy place like this. Then I grab my bag, still squeezing the screwed-up paper in my hand.

I look left and right as I emerge, scanning the street for shifty-looking figures. I have no idea what the guy looked like, or what he was wearing, save for a porkpie hat, which I think was granite-coloured. I don't even know if he was wearing a coat or not. I close my eyes and try to think back, but the truth is I hadn't even noticed he was in the tearoom until he dropped his newspaper by my feet.

There is nobody out here looking back at me as far as I can tell, and certainly nobody that looks as though they dropped the note. The word 'Library' looms large across the street, and that's where I head next, approaching the main desk behind which a woman with cropped dark hair is scowling. At first I think she's glaring at me, but then I see the crossword on the counter before her. She's tapping a pen against her cheek.

'What's another word for eternal life? Eleven letters, ending in a Y.'

My mouth opens and closes as if I'm attempting an impression of a goldfish before inspiration strikes. 'Immortality?'

Her eyes light up, and she scribbles the word onto the page. 'So that means three down begins with an L, so I'm going to say that's probably *loss*.' She looks up, smiling broadly. 'Thank you for that. You know when the word is just on the tip of your tongue but you can't see the wood for the trees? Anyway, how can I help?'

I adopt a light-hearted smile in return. 'I'm reliably informed that you are the only public place in town with Wi-Fi. I was hoping I could pay to use it.'

She drops her pen onto the puzzle book, and shuffles along to an antique-looking cash register. 'Five bucks will buy you an hour's access. There's a filter on the router that prevents the downloading of files over 4mb, and will not allow you to access any sites identified as potentially criminal. Porn, for example,' she adds with a whisper.

I hand over the cash, and she passes me a code on a bit of paper. I take it and head over to a large sofa near the window, while she returns to her crossword. I've always loved the smell of libraries, and even though I'm halfway around the world, that smell of paper and knowledge is exactly as I remember it from home. Hundreds of years of wisdom, creativity and hard work reside within these walls. The importance of libraries is often overlooked.

I log into the Wi-Fi and my phone immediately pings with messages from Ashley. The first is an email with a file attached, but it's too large for me to download. She's also sent a WhatsApp asking whether I've seen her email. I reply telling her where I am and where I'm staying, before telling her I can only send messages when in proximity of Wi-Fi. I add that I've been unable to view the attached file.

She responds immediately.

It was a photograph from the ultrasound. Daisy is going to have a little brother! You're going to have a godson. I meant to tell you yesterday, but forgot with one thing and another.

I type back:

That's fabulous news. Congratulations to you all. I bet Roy is thrilled.

Of course he is, and it should also keep my father-in-law off my back too, now that he'll have an heir to carry on the family name. Do you need anything else?

Answers, I want to reply but don't.

I unscrew the note in my hand and read it again:

I KNOW ABOUT YOUR MOM. CAN'T TALK HERE.
MEET ME AT O'REILLY'S AT 7.15 TONIGHT.

He knows *what* about my mum? The fact that she went missing, or more than that? Does he know what happened to her, and who killed her? And why couldn't he come and talk to me face to face? Granted it's not the most pleasant of topics of conversation to be held in a 1920s-themed tearoom, but he could have just asked me to step outside.

I open an internet browser and look for O'Reilly's, learning it's a bar approximately fifteen minutes' drive south of here, back along the road towards Bangor. I save the address, before messaging Ashley to tell her about the note and the odd way it was passed to me.

No way. You cannot go to a random bar to meet a stranger. He could be the killer wanting you out of the way to stop you exposing his crime.

And I thought I was the one with an overactive imagination!

Promise me you won't go and meet him.

I don't respond as something else, at the back of the library, catches my eye.

I cross back to the librarian, who is only too happy to see me again. 'To suffer or give up.'

The statement throws me. 'Excuse me?'

'Five across: to suffer or give up. Nine letters.'

'I have no idea. Listen, um, I saw you have an archive of newspapers. I wondered if I could look at everything you have from 1993 if possible?'

She pouts. 'I'm sorry, the microfiche viewer is out of order. Damned thing is so temperamental. I don't know why they don't just scan it all and put it online. Would make my life a lot easier.'

'Any idea when it will be fixed?'

'Sorry, no. It was reported to the company we hire it from over a week ago, but still no word on when they can get an engineer.'

I show her the picture on my phone. 'This lady doesn't seem familiar to you in any way, does she?'

'Oh, sure, yeah, I know that face.'

My pulse quickens. 'You do?'

'Sure, she's that hiker from England who went missing, must be twenty or so years ago.'

'Thirty, actually.'

'Right. Yeah, I remember it being all over the news. I was just about to finish high school and my friends and I had been planning to hike a section of the AT – until the story broke. Then my parents were adamant I couldn't go, which was fine as I'd gone off the idea by then anyway.'

'She was my mum. That's why I'm here: to find out what happened to her.'

She frowns empathetically. 'I'm very sorry. You should speak to our town sheriff. He might be able to share more details with you.'

I don't tell her I've already tried.

'Thanks for your help,' I say as I'm leaving, before turning back. 'Five across: try sacrifice.'

I hear an excited yelp as I head back out into the sunshine, and proceed to visit each shop and store on my way back to the motel, asking to speak to the most senior staff member in each, showing them Mum's picture, and then leaving with my frustration building. Maybe it was too big an assumption that she ever visited Rockston. There's no evidence that she ever made it off the AT, let alone as far as this sweet little town. I call in at a few more places – the garden centre, toy shop, mechanics, electronics store, candy store, and jewellery shop – but nobody can confirm ever seeing my mum, let alone meeting her.

I'm just stepping out of the bakery with a bag of cookies when a warm voice frightens me. 'You must be the woman I've received so many calls about.'

I turn, and see a man in a light-brown uniform leaning against one of the raised flowerbeds, chewing on a cocktail stick. The skin around his face is smooth, but I'd say he's older than he looks because of the self-assured way he holds himself. There's a large golden star hanging from his short-sleeve shirt.

'You must be the sheriff.'

He tips his hat in my direction, before removing it. 'And you're the woman harassing the townspeople.' He smiles, revealing a set of pearly white teeth. 'I understand you had some questions for me?'

'I do. I tried to explain who I am to your overzealous deputy, but she—'

He holds up a hand, cutting me off. 'She's very protective of my time, but she's on lunch break so why don't you and I go over to my office, where we can talk in private?'

Finally, someone prepared to offer some help.

He leads me across the road, offering cursory acknowledgements to those who greet him as we pass. He knows everyone's names and seems so relaxed that I too feel instantly calmer, even if I am a little miffed that some of the people I've spoken to have felt obliged to phone and complain about me.

The air conditioning inside the office is welcome, and he directs me to one of the partitioned rooms to the right, so our conversation really won't be overheard. For an awkward moment, I think he might have brought me in here to chastise or threaten me, but then he offers me a drink and fetches me a beaker of ice-cold water. Then he sits down at the table beside me, rather than across.

'Why don't we start from the beginning?' he says. 'I'm Sheriff Randy Whitaker, and you are?'

'Jess Grogan.'

He smiles disarmingly. 'And what brings you to our little town?'

I tell him about the news article, and he confirms he has been overseeing the removal of remains from a cavern in one of the mountains. He also divulges that it is too early to confirm how long the bones have been buried until an autopsy is completed.

'I'm aware of your mother's case,' he says quietly. 'When I first received the call about the bones, she was one of the first people I considered. In fact, yesterday I requested I be sent the items your mom left behind when she disappeared, so we could check for anything we might use as a DNA sample for comparison. But now that you're here, a sample of your DNA would be a quicker means of confirming if... it's her.'

'I'm happy to provide anything you need.'

He stands. 'That's good. Thank you. While I go and make the necessary arrangements, would you like to see your mom's stuff?'

My mouth drops open. I hadn't even contemplated that they might have recovered anything belonging to her. The knot in my stomach tightens. 'Yes, I would.'

19

NORA

September 1993, Appalachian Trail, New Hampshire, USA

Despite her warnings about strange goings-on at the Darby Festival of Light, Leanne invites herself to accompany the group along the short trail to Heaven's Gate when the snow has begun to clear two days later. By this point, all the hikers are desperate to escape the overpowering cocktail of damp clothes and unwashed men that clings to the flimsy plywood walls of the hostel. Nora doesn't care how meagre the provisions in Heaven's Gate are, so long as there's a payphone so she can speak to Jess.

What little snow remains is largely slush as they leave the AT and follow the rocky path down to the valley beyond, where the historic town of Heaven's Gate can be found. After several days of bitter cold, the front must have moved on, because in its place is brilliant sunshine, and far warmer winds. Charlie is the first to strip out of his coat, down to a long-sleeved T-shirt. Ken promptly follows suit, and even Nora eventually discards her coat, though keeps her fleece in place. Her sunglasses are buried at the bottom of her pack and it's too much effort to get to them, so she shields her eyes with a hand until her arm tires, at which point she swaps to the other hand.

Leanne is at the front with Nora and Charlie, sharing stories she's heard over the years.

'How many times have you hiked the AT then, Leanne?' Nora asks.

'I've been hiking sections since I was eleven. My dad used to bring us away as a family, so every year we'd hike a different part. He died the year I graduated – what, twenty-odd years ago – and on his deathbed he made me swear I would continue the tradition with my own kids. I never had the heart to tell him I was gay and didn't want children, so I've made it my mission to hike at least part of it every year since. I've thru-hiked twice, south to north first, and last year I went north to south. I wouldn't say it gets any easier, but your resilience improves the more you do it. I'd say I handled last year better because I knew I'd done it once before. But it takes a helluva lot out of me, and it'll probably be a few years more before I do the full trail again.'

Nora scratches an itch on her wrist. 'And do you always hike alone?'

She nods. 'My friends and work colleagues think I'm crazy and would never willingly come with me, and I'm okay with that. Most of the time I end up meeting someone or a group that I hang out with for a few days, so it's not as isolating as some might think.' She furrows her brow as Nora continues to scratch her wrist. 'Allergic reaction?'

Nora lifts her sleeve and studies the rash that has formed beneath the metallic bracelet. 'Mm, maybe. I assumed it was made of steel or something.'

'Never trust a gift from the people of Darby,' Leanne says as if it's some well-known phrase.

'It wasn't a gift, I paid for it,' Nora corrects.

'But I bet you're wishing you hadn't now.' Leanne stops and unclips her own pack. 'I think I've got some lotion in here that might help. Slip the bracelet off, and I'll get it for you.'

Nora rolls her sleeve further up her arm, and then

attempts to slip the metal band over her wrist, but she can't get it past her thumb joint. She licks at the skin, trying to lubricate it, and tries again, but no matter how hard she pulls and twists, the metal digs into her skin, and won't come off.

'You all right?' Leanne, asks, holding out the tube of antihistamine lotion.

'It won't budge.'

Leanne hands her the tube, and tries herself, gripping the bracelet, tugging and twisting in the same manner, but again, without success.

'Jesus, how the hell did you get it on there?'

'I didn't. I mean, the girl put it on me.'

Leanne takes the tube back, removes the lid, and squirts a generous amount into her hand, before rubbing it the length of Nora's forearm, and over the thumb joint. She then washes her hand with water from her bottle and takes hold of the bracelet again, but it still won't move. When Nora begins to cry out in pain, she relents.

Bruce takes Nora's hand in his, and studies the bracelet. 'Maybe there's some kind of hidden spring that widens it?' he suggests, but he can't find anything obvious as he gently twirls it. 'Maybe your arm has swollen in the heat,' he suggests, unable to fathom a more rational explanation. 'Wait until we get to the town, and we'll try and ice your arm to reduce any swelling. I'm sure that's all it is.'

Leanne raises a sceptical eyebrow. 'It could also be Trail Magic.'

Nora stares back at her blankly. 'Magic? That's your answer?'

'*Trail* Magic,' Leanne repeats. 'You never heard of Trail Magic?'

The four of them shake their heads.

'Jeez, you guys are so uninitiated! There is a community of Trail Angels – former hikers – who make it their mission to offer support to those hiking the AT. This can range from leaving coolers of food and drink at points along the route, or offering a ride in difficult circumstances. Those who've experienced Trail Magic will tell you that when they are in desperate need of something – be it food, shelter, a ride – it appears... as if by magic; as if some greater force delivered what was needed. Of course, those of us who've completed the trail before know that there are volunteers who provide these godsends, but it's the timing of those items *appearing* that's the magic bit.'

She pauses, and takes a sip from her bottle.

'There are also those who will tell you stories about a different kind of magic that exists in these parts. It's not generally talked about because it scares some, and others believe it's just hogwash made up by locals who want to keep hikers away from their towns. But there are rumours and stories about... *other-worldly* activities in some of the towns that border the AT.'

Nora thinks about the strange incantation the girl murmured when fiddling with the bracelet, but keeps her mouth closed.

'I take it you guys have at least heard of the Bell Witch, right?' Leanne asks.

Four heads shake in unison.

'The Bell family were farmers living near Adams in Tennessee at the southern end of the Appalachians in the early nineteenth century. They claimed they were being haunted by some kind of evil apparition that claimed to be the ghost of Kate Batts, a dead witch from the area. They would hear strange noises such as scratching, knocks on the walls, and chains being dragged across the floor. The apparition could speak and move objects at the property and some-times took on animal form. People began visiting the farm and would also experience the phenomena, and then when the patriarch of the family – John Bell – died, the spirit claimed it had poisoned him. It disap-peared for several years but was said to have returned later to interfere with the children's now-adult affairs.

And that's just the best-known story of witchcraft. Now, Tennessee is a long way from here, but this mountain range has been a breeding ground for those who wish to live a different way for hundreds of years. Who's to say what other secular rituals occur?'

Charlie is the first to scoff. 'Oh, please, you'll be telling us that Bigfoot roams the mountains next.'

Leanne raises her eyebrows. 'There are various recorded sightings in Virginia of a giant creature covered in hair with beady red eyes that is said to hide in the darkest of forests and leaves footprints bigger than a bear's. Myths all start somewhere. And there are the Moon-Eyed People as well.'

She continues when she sees a wall of blank faces. 'According to legend, long before the Cherokee moved into the Smokies, there was a race of small, bearded white men who lived in the mountains. They lived in log cabins, had large blue eyes and fair white skin and were sun-blind during the day, which meant they only emerged from their homes at night to hunt, fish, and build their fortifications. Because they could only see in the dark, they inherited the name Moon-Eyed People. Legend has it they were driven from their homes, and now reside in the darkened woods.'

Nora instantly pictures the cabin with all the animal skulls, and the blood drains from her face.

'And then there's the Mothman conspiracy in Virginia from the sixties. More than a dozen people reported seeing a flying man with wings ten feet long and glowing red eyes who was capable of reaching speeds of 100 miles per hour. Doubters will just say it's folklore, but if you ask me there's more that goes on in this stretch of mountains and forests than we'll ever truly know about.'

Nora tries to remove the bracelet again, but it slips in her hands. 'The girl told me it would ward off evil spirits.'

'Well, at least you'll be safe, I suppose,' Leanne says but eyes it with concern. 'We should keep going if you want to make it before sunset.'

Little more is said of the bracelet as they continue along the minor trail. Charlie is fascinated by Leanne's tales of strange goings-on, but Nora has heard enough, and hangs back with Bruce. She doesn't want to fall into the same traps that saw her own mum's mental health questioned by all and sundry.

When they finally reach Heaven's Gate, the orange sun is low in the sky, and the temperature has dropped too. While Leanne takes Ken and Bruce on a tour of the small town, Charlie heads to a store in search of a replacement tent, and Nora hurries to the only pay phone she can find, outside the sheriff's station.

She inserts some coins then dials the number she committed to memory and waits for it to ring. It is eventually answered on the fourth chime.

'Hmm... yes?' she hears Frank say wearily.

'Hello? Frank? It's Nora.'

'Hmm? What? What time is it?'

She looks at her watch and silently reprimands herself when she does the maths. 'Oh, sorry, I forgot about the time difference. Did I wake you?'

'Hmm? Yeah. I was asleep. How are you? Are you having a good time?'

She drops another coin into the slot. 'It's definitely tougher than I was expecting, but I haven't been eaten by a wolf or bear yet, so that's a positive.' She adds a gentle laugh.

'Good,' he says, stifling a yawn.

'How's everything with you? Is Jess okay? I'm missing her so much. And you too, of course.'

'Um, yeah, Jess is fine. I think she's looking forward to getting back to school.'

'*Back* to school? Why hasn't she been *at* school?'

'The accident. But she's feeling much better and the doctors have said she should be fine to return next week.'

'*Accident?* What accident? What doctors?'

The phone peeps at her, and she drops two more coins in the slot.

'Nora? Are you still there?'

'Yes, Frank, I'm here,' she says, shovelling more coins in. 'What's happened to Jess? What accident—'

'Nora? Nora? I can't hear you. Are you still there?'

She drops her last coin in the slot. 'Frank? Can you hear me? What accident?'

The line disconnects, and she slams her hand against the box, but no refund drops into the change dispenser. She returns the phone to the receiver, and lifts it again, but there's no dial tone. Racing from the phone box, she goes in desperate search of another, her mind racing with awful possibilities.

20

JESS

April 2023, Rockston, Maine, USA

Having taken a swab from the inside of my cheek and placed the stick in an evidence bag, Sheriff Whitaker carries in a large brown cardboard box and places it on the table before me. A printed sheet of paper stuck to the side reveals it is evidence related to my mum's case, rather than items recovered with the remains.

'I'm gonna go ahead and give you a little time,' he says, sliding a box of tissues towards me. 'I'll wait outside.'

He exits the room and closes the door behind him

without another word. I can't explain why but I can feel my mother's spirit in the room with me, as if she is standing in a corner watching, but I do. I reach for a tissue and dab my eyes as they begin to fill. The fact that Sheriff Whitaker requested these items yesterday suggests he too believes the recovered remains belong to my mum.

I stand and begin to raise one of the flaps on the box, but stop. I'm not sure I'm ready for this. I thought I was. Thirty years is a long time to come to terms with never seeing a parent again, but now that the truth is staring me in the face, it's like I'm five years old all over again, unwilling to accept that she's gone.

I take a deep breath, wiping my eyes and blowing my nose. I came here to find out what happened to Mum and why she abandoned me. I can't let the opportunity to learn more about her hike pass me by. I grip hold of the flap again, and flatten it back so I can peer into the box. Each item is sealed in a transparent labelled bag. These are the items she left in her pack. After she pointed a gun at Bruce and the others and tore off into the woods. She will have touched some, if not all of these items on that fateful day.

My hands are shaking as I reach into the box and lift out the first bag. It's large, containing a pair of hiking boots. Dried and crusty mud clings to the under sole of both boots. Presumably these were a spare pair, though I'm surprised Mum hadn't tried to clean them before putting them in her pack.

I lower the bag to the table and reach for the next one, which contains a jumper. The sheriff never said whether I could open the evidence bags, but assuming the remains are Mum's, they're not going to need to check the jumper for trace evidence as she wasn't wearing it when she died.

I break the seal, pull out the jumper, and press it to my nose. I'm stunned by how fresh it smells, as if it was freshly laundered before it was packed away. I inhale deeply, and close my eyes, instantly transported back to a memory. It's Christmas Day and Mum has woken early with me so I can open presents. The air smells of pine and sugarcane, and I am so excited to be tearing through the paper. I open a large rectangular box and am thrilled to see it's the Barbie doll I was desperately hoping for. I run over to Mum and give her a big squeeze.

I haven't pictured that memory in forever, and my heart throbs with love. How can a jumper have retained the essence of Mum's scent for all these years? I don't want to let it go. I press it back to my nose again, willing time to take me back to September 1993, the last time I saw her, so I can tell her how much I love her, rather than throwing a pity tantrum as she went to get into the waiting taxi. If I had my time over again, I know I wouldn't hesitate to tell her not to go on the silly hike. I'd make my feelings better known.

Over the next twenty minutes, I find bags containing out-of-date granola bars, packets of instant noodles, underwear, a compass, a wallet, a first aid kit, and a torch. Mum was so well-prepared for the hike she was undertaking, particularly when compared to the handful of items I threw into a holdall before making the same journey overseas. Mother and daughter so different, even though I have always been so convinced about how similar we are.

There's one evidence bag left in the bottom of the box, and when I lift it out, the breath catches in my throat. I had no idea Mum was keeping a diary. I tear through the evidence bag, and lift it out, flipping through the pages of notes, doodles and scribbles Mum must have been recording while on the trail. A dog-eared photo of five-year-old me drops from the pages. That the diary is in an evidence bag will mean that investigators have accessed these private thoughts, and as I begin to read the first page, I quickly snap it shut. A diary is a personal and private journal that shouldn't be invaded.

But what if it contains a clue about what led to her racing into the woods waving a gun?

If it did then investigators would already have made a breakthrough and charged someone with a crime, I rationalise.

But what if it was written in a way that only someone close to her would understand?

There's a knock at the door, and I quickly shove the diary and evidence bag into the back of my jeans, pulling down my T-shirt to hide it.

'Are you nearly done here? I'm keen to get your DNA sample over to the hospital for comparison,' Sheriff Whitaker says quietly.

I start to put the bags back into the box.

'That's okay, I'll get one of my deputies to tidy up. Are you staying in our town motel?'

I nod. 'Yes. Room fifteen.'

'Then I'll know where to find you if I have any further information.'

I smile warmly, and thank him for letting me look through the items, before hurrying on my way out of the office and back towards the motel. I don't pull out the diary until I'm back inside my room and the curtains are closed. Stealing evidence is a felony, and when he realises I lifted the diary he may decide to prosecute, though I hope he'll understand my need to get closer to Mum. And what better way than to read her words in her voice?

I'm tempted to start at the beginning, but the diary is two-thirds full, and I'm most interested in what happened in the days before the disappearance. I turn to the final entry and begin to read:

> I don't trust Snake and Weasel. Joanna and Andy warned us to stay clear of them, but Charlie seems to have adopted them as long-lost brothers. Just because they're from the same state doesn't mean they would naturally move in the same circles. I'm desperate to tell Bruce or Ken what I saw, but the two of them won't let me anywhere near them for fear I'll catch the norovirus next. Charlie thinks it's hilarious to refer to their virus as the NORA-virus, like I'm the one responsible for all their sickness and diarrhoea. He won't find it so funny when he comes down with it.
>
> We're all doing our best to wash our hands and faces at every stop, and to their credit Ken and Bruce are hanging back so we avoid breathing the same air, and they're trying to limit how many times we stop on the hike, but our pace has definitely slowed. There's no way

we're going to make it to the top of Mount Katahdin at this rate.

I can't believe I still haven't managed to get hold of Jess. It feels like some ethereal force is preventing me from telling her how sorry I am for ever agreeing to this ludicrous expedition. My intentions were well-placed, and I don't re-gret doing everything I could to try to save little Ashley, but I never realised how much of a toll it would take on our own mother-daughter rela-tionship. I hope Frank will tell her I phoned. I can't believe he offloaded her to his parents again. He promised she would be his priority while I was away.

I can hear Snake, Weasel and Charlie laughing like school children. They're getting high again. It's as if having them around has to-tally distracted Charlie from the real reason we're doing this.

One way or another, I'm not going to let the two of them out of my sight while they remain with us. I have a bad feeling about them.

I close the diary, and place it on the bed beside me. Is that it? The last thing she wrote about was Bruce's illness and two people they met on the trail. I presume that, whoever this Snake and Weasel are, they were spoken to following her disappearance, but I note the question as one I intend to ask the sheriff when I next speak to him.

I'm moved that I was in her thoughts in her final days. Bruce has told me for years that she didn't stop thinking about me, but I'd always assumed he was just being kind.

I know I could sit here for the rest of the night, reading the rest of the diary, but I already sense it won't bring me any closer to the truth of what really happened out there. If Mum did leave the AT alive, but didn't make it as far as Rockston, then there must be other towns she might have visited.

I have several hours until I need to be at O'Reilly's and what better way to spend it than a drive around to see what else I can find?

21

NORA

September 1993, Appalachian Trail, New Hampshire, USA

'What do you mean the phones are out?' Nora demands, before catching the aggression in her tone.

The man in a pale brown shirt and darker brown trousers stares back at her, trying to keep an even tone. When he speaks, it's as if he's trying to draw out each vowel sound for comic effect. 'Like I said, there's been an incident affecting communications into Heaven's Gate. An engineer is working on it as we speak.'

'So there's no way I can get in touch with my daughter back in England?'

The deputy removes his wide-brimmed hat, and runs the back of his arm across his sweaty fringe. 'Not without driving a dozen miles to the next town and hoping they haven't been affected. I'm very sorry.'

When the phone disconnected earlier, she stalked the streets looking for another phone box, without success, eventually heading into the general store to ask if there were any more. It was only when the teller told her there wasn't that she went demanding answers at the sheriff's station.

'Did the engineer say when the phones might be fixed?'

'I was on my way out to speak to him when you came in, miss. Hopefully things will be up and running by the morning.'

Nora knows it isn't this poor man's fault. He looks barely old enough to have graduated high school, but he has managed to maintain his temperament, even as she lost hers. She takes a tentative step back from the desk, accepting defeat. Jess will be tucked up in her bed anyway, lost to dreams, so even if she could phone, it isn't like she'd be able to speak to her directly.

As she exits the sheriff's station, she looks up at

the fairy lights hanging between lampposts, which are now glowing orange, lighting up the sidewalk.

Heaven's Gate is little more than a straight road, with a few shops interspersed among motels and residences. More like a large UK village than a town. There are large banners hanging from lampposts and posters stuck to practically every surface advertising the upcoming Festival of Light further along the trail in Darby. Leanne did say all the local townsfolk participate and that it's a precursor to Thanksgiving.

There are only two restaurants along the strip: an American diner and a family-run Italian, but the shutters are drawn on the building on the latter, with no sign of life, suggesting it may have closed down. Nora finds Charlie, Bruce and Ken sitting in a booth in the diner, their packs nowhere in sight. The table is covered with plates of burgers, chicken wings, and fries.

Bruce waves the cuddly dinosaur in her direction, while shuffling along the cushioned seat to make room for her. 'I ordered you a chocolate shake,' he says, sliding a large metal cup towards her.

'Thanks,' she says as she climbs in next to him, placing the plastic straw between her lips and taking a long drink. The cold sweetness of the beverage is like a welcome slap to the face.

'And we ordered enough to feed an army,' he continues. 'Help yourself. I think my eyes were bigger than my belly when I saw the menu.'

The feast smells so good, but her appetite has yet to return since Frank mentioned Jess being in some kind of accident. She can't stop thinking about what kind of incident could have befallen her daughter. The fact that she's been off school and has had to wait for clearance from the doctor before returning means it must have been more than grazed limbs. A fracture of some kind? Worse?

Ken lifts the basket of onion rings and offers them in her direction. She takes one and drops it onto the plastic plate before her.

'You want to watch those,' Charlie warns. 'Got a bit of a kick to them. They must add tabasco to the batter. They're delicious before you realise they'll blow your tongue off.'

'We were talking while you were away,' Bruce says, and wipes the grease from his lips with a paper napkin. 'It's getting late, and we'll never make it to another hostel before midnight. Given the slippery conditions on the way down here, and our shared need for a shower and good night's sleep, we thought it would be an idea to get rooms at the motel. That okay with you?'

Hopefully things will be up and running by the morning.

'Spend the night in Heaven's Gate?' she clarifies.

'Sure. Leanne took us to the better of the two motels, and they had space so we reserved two twin rooms – if you don't mind kipping in with me?'

It might be days before they're next in a town and she's able to phone home. And if the deputy was right, then it could be a matter of hours until the phone line is restored and she'll be able to phone Frank again. If she's lucky, she might even get to speak to Jess while she's eating her breakfast.

She can't keep the smile from breaking across her face. 'Sounds like a plan.'

Charlie slaps his hands together in celebration. 'See, I knew she'd be okay with it! Are you going to tell her about tonight's planned entertainment as well?'

Bruce frowns and in her periphery Nora notices him quickly shake his head.

'What?' she says, her face curling in on itself in confusion. 'What entertainment have you arranged?'

She can't understand why Charlie looks so excited, but Ken and Bruce look as though they want the ground to swallow them up. And then the penny drops.

'Oh, God, tell me you three haven't found a topless bar or strip show to go to.'

Bruce looks genuinely hurt by the accusation, while Charlie has a light bulb moment.

'Wait, there's a titty bar?' he says. 'Oh, let's do that instead. My idea is lame in comparison.'

Judging by Bruce's and Ken's reactions, maybe Nora did do them a disservice.

'What was your idea, Charlie?'

He slurps from his milkshake, and grins like the Cheshire Cat. 'I'm not sure you'd be up for it. I shouldn't have said anything.'

He tosses a fry into his mouth, before signalling for the waitress and asking if they can have the leftovers bagged up to take away.

Nora senses the ploy of reverse psychology, but can't resist. 'Tell me what the three of you were planning.'

Charlie's smile widens. 'I met this kid outside the camping store. He was there asking someone to go into the general store and buy him a packet of cigarettes. He could only have been fourteen, topless astride a BMX. Reminded me of myself at that age, but I told him they were bad for his health and I didn't want to be the cause of him dying young. And then he said the strangest thing: nobody lives beyond thirty in Heaven's Gate.'

Nora waits for him to elaborate, but he shovels the final mouthful of burger from his plate into his mouth.

'And?'

He chews and swallows, sucking ketchup from his fingers. 'Think about it: how many people over the age of thirty have you come across here since we arrived?'

Nora thinks back to the spotty teenager behind the counter at the general store, and the sheriff's deputy who was also younger than her. She looks over her shoulder at the waitress in roller-skates and the man in chef's whites talking to her through the hatch into the kitchen. Both look to be in their early twenties if she had to guess, but given the time of day, it's not strange to see younger people working.

'It's funny now that I think about it,' Ken says, a finger pressed to his chin, 'I thought the girl who checked us in to the motel was on the young side too. Figured her parents must own the business and had left her in temporary charge.'

Charlie raises his eyebrows in an 'I told you so' manner.

Nora shakes her head. 'Some punk kid makes an audacious claim about the town's life expectancy and you lot are ready to condemn it as some kind of Twilight Zone?'

'Hey, I'm not saying he's right,' Charlie says, 'but when I challenged him on it, he reckoned he could prove it. Said for twenty bucks he would give us a guided tour of this virtual ghost town.'

'Is he going to knock on every door and ask residents to show their birth certificates?' Nora scoffs.

Charlie doesn't rise to the bait. 'Apparently some visiting witch doctor put a curse on the town twenty-five years ago. He told me he could take me to the exact spot where it happened.'

Nora howls with laughter, her mind finally distracted from thoughts of Jess's possible condition. 'Ah, I've heard it all now,' she says, wiping tears from her eyes.

Bruce and Ken are laughing now too, and even Charlie can see the funny side. 'He said the town used to be full of miners until the mine shut down after the curse. Then the lumber factory disappeared into some kind of sink hole that opened up in the ground, and gradually anyone over the age of thirty starting dying off, after one fatal illness or another. Tumours, cancers, heart attacks, you name it. But he said the trigger for the town's downfall was when the old mental hospital was burned to the ground. Get this, patients and nursing staff were still trapped *inside*.'

The laughter at the table ceases in an instant.

'The fire raged for several days and there was so little left afterwards, they reckoned it was impossible to tell how many had died.' He pauses, revelling in their disgust. 'Rumour was some of the patients might have escaped to the woods, hunting for meat and fish. Kid said he'd take us to the remains of the building.'

The waitress brings two paper bags of food back to the table, and Charlie follows her back to the counter to settle the bill.

'You're not seriously entertaining going on this ghost walk, are you?' Nora whispers to Ken and Bruce.

Neither answers, before they both shrug. 'Where's the harm?' Ken says. 'It's not like the motel rooms have television.'

She can't believe anyone would want to go and gawp at the scene of something so horrifically tragic. Silence descends.

'Well, I'm not going,' Nora says eventually, folding her arms with a huff.

'That's fine,' Charlie says, returning to the table and slurping the rest of his milkshake. 'Why don't you carry your pack back to the motel and get some sleep?'

At this, Bruce pushes the key across the table. 'Listen, I can come back with you if you don't want to be on your own.'

She takes the key, and slides out of the booth. 'I will be perfectly fine knowing I have three Ghostbusters out there keeping the streets safe.' She laughs. 'Besides, it'll give me the chance to record today's events in my journal. You boys have a good time, and I'll see you in the morning.'

She picks up the bags of food, and her pack, and double-checks the directions to the motel with Bruce. Then she watches as they head in the opposite direction in search of the kid with the BMX.

The motel is down a side road, and consists of a dozen conjoined rooms on one level, with parking spaces angled in front of each bedroom door. At the far end of the tenement is a similarly sized plot with the word 'Reception' in bright green neon in the window. Nora walks past it and stops at her and Bruce's room, room seven, unlocking the door and dropping her pack inside. The thin walls shake as she closes the door and locks it.

The room is fairly basic: two beds, a desk-cum-dressing table, a large mirror on the wall, and a toilet and walk-in shower at the far side of the room. The two beds are separated by a half-metre space, one against the outside wall, and the other up against the bathroom wall. Cigarette burns litter every surface, even though there are signs everywhere declaring it a 'No Smoking' room. Ken was right: no sign of a television set.

Nora places the bags of food on the bed by the window, claiming the other for herself, before heading into the bathroom and switching on the shower tap. After a minute, the water runs warm, and as steam starts to fill the room she begins to remove her layers of damp and smelly clothing. The thought of a hot shower has her pulse racing, but her blood runs cold when she sees a figure in a mask staring back at her through the window.

22

JESS

April 2023, Darby, Maine, USA

I remember Bruce telling me about the four of them stopping over in the town of Darby in the days before Mum ran off, but I hadn't realised how far it would be from Rockston. Given both are mountain towns within the Appalachians, by road they are a good hour apart.

Bruce told me how he prepared for the AT by gradually increasing his stamina with longer and longer walks, until he was walking miles and miles every weekend. He said, despite such efforts, he still wasn't prepared for what they encountered.

'It's not the same as walking along flat paving slabs and tarmac,' he would tell me back when I lived with him. 'The AT is unforgiving. One minute you're struggling to keep your footing on a muddy embankment, and the next you're physically free-climbing a virtual vertical summit. And then when it rains, it's hell on earth.'

His comments and stories certainly put me off the idea of ever attempting something so challenging. For Bruce, it was eye-opening, and after his return he began to take on other strenuous challenges. Last year he completed his fifth London marathon, all in the name of charity. I've seen how much the exertion takes it out of him, and yet I have no memory of Mum doing any kind of training before she left. I'm sure she must have prepared, but I've never been able to marry the mum I knew with the stories Bruce would tell of his time here. She just wasn't built to survive a place like this, so it really shouldn't have been such a surprise to anyone that she never returned.

I know, like her, I'm not cut out for this. I'm struggling to be without constant access to social media, but more so email and messaging apps. Writing for the newspaper, I would rarely be offline for more than an hour at a time, even during the night. I'm not a social butterfly like some of those influencers, and I very rarely share personal information online, but I like to know what other people are up to, so I can have an informed opinion.

The town of Darby is much smaller than Rockston, though the layout isn't dissimilar. Where Rockston is picture perfect – the kind of place destined for the front of postcards – Darby is more restrained. Half the shop fronts I drive past are boarded up, or covered with posters advertising other shops and events. Where Rockston looks as though it's thriving with its green grass and vibrant flower beds, Darby looks more like a town forgotten. There's nobody out on the streets even though it's nearly 3 p.m., just the kind of time when you'd be seeing people collecting children from school.

I complete a circuit of the town, but there's only a couple of businesses that appear to still be open or even in operation. I find a building a little further down the road which claims to be the offices of the local newspaper and radio station. I make this my first port of call.

Like Rockston, there are diagonal parking spaces outside each shop front, and when I first pull in, I'm not sure the premises are open, but then I see a woman milling about inside. It's hardly the cutting-edge face of media, but similarly is perfectly reflective of the town it's surviving in.

The glass door is locked, but the woman inside opens it when I bang my knuckle against it. She's wearing enormous glasses, the kind Deidre Barlow donned in *Coronation Street* – I know this because Bruce used to watch it regularly as he had a secret crush on Mike Baldwin. She pulls the hem of her knee-length cardigan across her chest as if I mean her harm and as if the polyester material will somehow offer her protection.

In my purse, I locate an old and worn copy of one of my business cards, back from when I sold my first freelance story. Back then, I dreamed of one day making it as the next Lois Lane, before swiftly real-ising why her character only operates in fiction. She takes the card, reads my name and title, and then smiles at me with confusion, before offering to hand it back.

'Oh, you can keep that,' I say warmly, thinking about the three boxes of unused cards in Bruce's spare room. 'I was hoping you might be able to help me. You know, one *professional* journalist to another.'

Greta – or so her name badge suggests – seems

quite taken by the compliment, and doesn't ask for any further credentials or identification, before welcoming me inside and offering tea and coffee. I thank her and request a tea, making use of the alone time to scan the printouts on the only desk with any papers on it, presumably hers. There's a poster advertising a school fête, a dog show in another town, and a farmers' market from the weekend before.

God knows where they find enough content to produce any kind of local newspaper.

I explain who I am and why I've come across to Maine. I don't mention that I'm Nora Grogan's daughter, and wait for her to make mention of the discovery of the remains, but she either isn't clued up, or doesn't want to give anything away – I expect it's the former. I tell her I'm trying to piece together Nora's final movements as part of an anniversary special.

'I have reason to believe she may have passed through Darby in the days before she vanished,' I tell her, 'and was hoping you might have access to copies of your periodicals from that time I could look at for background.'

'And you say this was 1993?' Greta mutters, heading over to one of the vacant desks, which has a large, box-sized monitor in the corner.

I follow her over, expecting her to turn towards one of the large metal filing cabinets lining the wall beyond the desk, but instead she reaches down and fiddles with the switch of the enormous desktop tower standing beside the desk. It whirs to life, making the sound like that of a speedboat motor.

'All of the pre-2000 papers were scanned and up-loaded to the archive, so you should find what you're looking for here.'

I take a sip of the tea while I wait for the screen to load. It's currently black with a single white flashing underscore. It reminds me of the first computer Dad brought home, back when the router used to sound like small plane taking off.

Greta pulls out a chair and pushes it towards me as a pixelated window opens on the screen.

'Just type the date into the box and it will present you with the output from that period.'

She moves away with no other words, leaving me to sit and stare at the outdated software. I'm expecting it to fail, but when I type in September 1993, it loads up four files. I open each in turn, which are all covering the run-up to, and the week after the sixty-third annual Festival of Light. For the town of Darby, it would appear to be the biggest event in the calendar year, though I can't say I'm familiar with the festival or its background, aside from Bruce's mention of a bad trip.

Greta is busying herself in a back office, and it's only when I see her through a small porthole into the soundproofed room that I realise she's more than just the local journalist, but also the resident DJ. I don't imagine Radio Darby plays many modern artists, judging by Greta's age and lack of fashion sense. But maybe I'm being unkind. Maybe she's the queen of grime.

The final chords of an Everly Brothers song play out as she exits the booth, before Roy Orbison's 'Pretty Woman' kicks in.

I print copies of the four newspapers, and a giant press beside the booth kicks to life, running the pages for me. I offer to pay for the printing, but Greta assures me that it isn't necessary, and enquires whether she and the *Darby Times* will get a mention in my article. I assure her they will, and take her email address to send her a link (if, and) when such an article goes to press.

I collect the pages, and return to the car, ready to read all about the origins of the Festival of Light, but can't shake the feeling that I'm being watched. I look around me, but the dusty sidewalk appears empty in both directions. Greta waves from behind the sheet glass, and I wave back as I climb back into the car, conscious that it's only a few hours until I'm due to meet a potential source at O'Reilly's.

23

NORA

September 1993, Appalachian Trail, New Hampshire, USA

Nora grabs a towel from the rail beside the toilet and
pulls it around herself as she ducks behind the wall,
back into the belly of the room. The curtain rail above
the window in the bathroom is broken, but it's so dark
outside that she didn't even realise the window was
there. Her heart is racing and the room continues to
warm as mist from the shower causes a cloud to form.

The figure outside the window was dressed in
dark trousers and was topless, but her eyes went immediately to the large white mask covering his face.

She's certain it was an animal's skull of some kind – possibly a bear? It immediately brought up memories of the room of skulls, but there's no way the owner of that cabin would have tracked them to Heaven's Gate. Is there? Even if he was angry about the broken window and stolen meat, he couldn't know this is where they'd end up so many days later.

Securing the towel around herself, she takes a deep breath, stands, and peeps her head around the wall. The figure is no longer outside the window. She breathes a sigh of relief, and turns off the shower, moving closer to the cold glass, and peering out, searching for where he could have disappeared to.

There is a mound of grass leading from the back of the hotel up to a wire fence, and beyond that a darkened forest. The way he was standing there, she could feel his gaze burning into her soul. God only knows how long he was watching while she slowly stripped off, oblivious to his presence.

But what if he's still out there, hidden from view?

There's no way he could have scaled that fence in the time she hid behind the wall, so where else could he have gone? It's too dark to see beyond the edge of her room, so it's possible he's still there watching.

A shiver runs the length of her spine, as if someone has just walked over her grave, and she darts back behind the bedroom wall, trying to gather her thoughts.

If he's not outside the window now, could he have come closer? Could he have misinterpreted her nudity as an invitation and be making his way around the motel?

She hurries to the door and checks the key is still secure in the lock, before daring to glance out of the curtains at the main strip. She can't see anyone out there, but the street light outside the room is broken, making it difficult to see much anyway. She draws the curtain, grabs a spare towel, and does her best to secure it in place over the window.

She knows she should go and speak to the motel manager and report what she saw, but she doesn't yet feel confident about stepping outside, in case that's what the figure is waiting for.

Frank repeatedly told her he didn't like the idea of her ever being left alone by the others. He'd made her promise that she would keep at least one of the group with her at all times. She'd offered so many reassurances that (a) she wasn't in any kind of danger, and (b) that she would make sure to keep Ken or Bruce with her at all times.

She knows his panic stems from watching movies like *Psycho*, in which a woman travelling alone is brutally murdered in a backwater motel. But that kind of thing only happens in movies and television shows.

Every time her eyes close, she pictures the mask. She only glimpsed it for the briefest of moments before she ducked out of sight, but it's all she can see now. The white bone seemed to almost glow against the dark backdrop. The skull of a bear, she's almost certain.

She starts at a gentle tapping against the door.

Her eyes dart around the room, looking for anything she can arm herself with, but there's nothing save for a lamp on a shelf, but as she attempts to pick it up, she sees it has been screwed down.

The tapping starts up again, louder this time. More urgent.

Nora grabs at the sweater she'd been so pleased to peel off, and pulls it back over her head, discarding the towel. She thinks about the contents of her pack, and in a flash, she removes her tent package, unfolds it, and grabs hold of one of the extendable poles. It won't do a lot of damage, but she only needs to be able to distract her attacker long enough to get to safety.

This time the thud on the door echoes around the room.

'I-I'm armed,' she shouts at the door. 'Go and I won't call the sheriff.'

'Nora, it's Bruce,' comes the hurried reply.

She dives to the front window, and peers around the curtain, relief flooding her body when she sees Bruce's lanky frame staring back at her. Dropping the tent pole, she moves to the door, unlocks it, and throws her arms around his shoulders.

'Is everything okay? Who did you think I was?'

She doesn't answer at first, clinging on to him, as her heart continues to gallop against her ribcage.

Bruce closes the door and manoeuvres her to the edge of one of the beds, where he sits her down. 'What's going on? You look like you've seen a ghost.'

'I-I think maybe I did,' she says, her eyes falling on the towel over the bathroom window. 'There was someone out there when I was trying to shower.'

Bruce leaps to his feet and hurries to the back of the room. He pulls down the towel and scans the perimeter. 'Out here?'

She nods. 'They're gone now. I think. When you started knocking at the door... let's just say my imagination got the better of me.'

'He was watching you shower?'

She chuckles as the adrenaline continues to dissipate. 'I was just about to get in, but my saggy boobs probably gave him the fright of his life.'

Bruce returns to her side, crouching down at her knees. 'What did he look like? Can you describe him? I'll get the others and we'll go and find him.'

'There's really no need. He's gone now, and there's no—' She breaks off as a thought crosses her mind. 'What are you doing back here anyway? I thought the three of you were going for a guided tour of the old mental asylum?'

'We couldn't find the kid, so it was a bust.'

'The three of you all came back?'

He nods.

She knocks him over as she stands, folding her arms as she glares at him. 'Oh, I get it. I suppose the three of you thought it would be hilarious to try and freak me out, right? Which of you was wearing the mask? Huh? I bet it was Charlie, wasn't it? Wait till I get my hands on him.'

'Whoa, whoa, you think one of us was spying on you?'

'Don't act all innocent. I've figured it out. What was the plan? Scare me until I beg one of you to sleep with me? Was that it?'

'No. No way. I don't know what you're talking about. We went to the camping store, but couldn't find the kid. We walked from one end of town to the other, but there was no sign, so we came back.'

He sounds convincing, and she wants to believe him, but ultimately she doesn't know him well enough to sense whether he's lying.

'And what's this about a mask? What kind of mask was he wearing?'

Nora can imagine how Charlie could have carefully secreted one of the masks from the death room, waiting to use it to try to scare her. She'd like to think that Bruce and Ken wouldn't be so easy to convince to help him.

She stops pacing the room. 'So you're telling me none of you donned an animal skull and watched me from out the back?'

He presses a hand against his chest. 'I swear on my life.'

'And Charlie was with the two of you the whole time you were out?'

'The whole time.'

'There was no point when he snuck off and you lost sight of him, even for a few minutes?'

He hesitates. 'We stopped at the store on the way back so that Ken and Charlie could buy some beers. But I was outside the store the whole time, and neither snuck out, until they both emerged with their drinks.'

She narrows her eyes, now picturing Ken keeping a look out while Charlie snuck out some rear entrance of the store to play his prank.

'I swear whoever was outside the window wasn't one of us,' Bruce continues to protest. 'I wouldn't do something like that, and I wouldn't allow the others either. I swear to you, Nora.'

She exhales sharply, knowing she has no way to prove the figure was Charlie, and nods in acknowledgement. She will have to keep an eye on Charlie and Ken.

'Did this guy in the mask do anything else?' Bruce continues. 'Was he... you know, exposing himself?'

In truth, she didn't notice and her stomach turns at the possibility. 'I don't think so.'

'We should probably report it to someone. I saw a sheriff's station in town. I'm happy to go with you if you want—'

'I don't think that's necessary,' Nora cuts him off. 'Listen, I really want a shower. Would you do me a favour and just stay in the room while I'm in there? I'd feel safer.'

He raises a thumb. 'Absolutely. Take all the time you need. I'm probably going to read and fall asleep.

I'll wash in the morning. I told the others we'd meet them at the diner at seven if that's okay with you?'

Nora doesn't answer, moving back to the bathroom. She secures the towel over the glass, and this time strips off behind the shower curtain. As she showers, she tries not to think about what she saw, but her mind continues to race. She can't determine what's worse: whether the figure was Charlie playing a practical joke, or some stranger from the woods, watching.

24

JESS

April 2023, Darby, Maine, USA

I've been on the road for fifteen minutes, my eyes rarely leaving the rear-view mirror, when I realise that downing the tea before I left the *Darby Times* offices was not such a hot idea. The satnav says I've still got forty-eight minutes until I'm back at the motel and there's no obvious sign of a rest stop along the route. I certainly don't remember passing one on the way out. There's no sign of anyone following me, which is a relief, and I have to put it down to my overactive imagination getting the better of me.

A sign on the side of the road indicates a beauty spot approaching, which I vaguely remember passing on the way. I slow as I near the gap in the security barrier separating the road from the cliff edge, before indicating and pulling into the dirt track car park. There are no marked parking bays, but two cars are parked beside one another, and I pull in beside them in a cloud of dust. Ahead of me, there are benches looking out over the rest of Maine, with two telescopes for those wanting a closer view. There is one family on a picnic bench slightly further back from the edge.

I climb out of the car, and despite my high hopes, there's no sign of a public toilet. It's literally a car park with benches and a breath-taking view. I approach the barrier, and can see Bangor International in the distance. Planes arrive and depart every couple of minutes. It seems so detached from the life I've already observed up here in the mountains; like a different world altogether. I briefly remember my conversation with Isaac – the 'them and us' culture he spoke of. I thought he was exaggerating, but now I'm starting to believe it. It's the Eloi and Morlocks all over again.

The family at the picnic table pay me no attention, and don't seem to notice when I creep out of the car park and make my way across the deserted road to the wall of trees closest to the side of the mountain. All I need is to find a shallow spot where I can squat down, and drop my jeans without fear of a stinging nettle or wild bug attacking me.

Squeezing between two trees, I'm surprised to find there's something of a pathway leading further into the darkness. It's rocky and uneven, and every now and again a tuft of weeds pokes through the well-trodden path, but at least there's no danger of tripping on tree roots and vines. It's much cooler under the leafy canopies high above my head, and I have to rub my arms which are peppered with goose bumps.

The pathway seems to split ahead, and I follow the bend to the right, figuring I should now be far enough from the road that I shouldn't be seen. I cut between more trees, until I find a small clearing. I quickly unfasten my belt, and drop my trousers, before resting my hands on two stumps, and squatting.

'I won't tell if you don't,' I whisper to a nearby tree.

The relief I feel when I'm finished is tantamount to one of the greatest feelings I've felt in a long time. There's nowhere to wash my hands or a mirror to check my appearance, but there's some hand gel and a vanity mirror back at the car, so I'll make do with that.

I head back out to the path, but stop when I hear a pained whimpering nearby. I think I'm imagining it at first, but then I hear it again, and I can't resist the compulsion to check it out. I continue to follow the path around to a wider clearing where I see an animal on its side several feet ahead. The fur is dark brown in colour, and I immediately know it's a cow. It's whimpering as I approach, but then I see it isn't alone.

I stop, wary of the creature gnawing at its side. A small bear cub, maybe. The poor cow is still alive as the creature tucks in, and the cruelty angers me, but I know better than to come between a bear and its food, and slowly step backwards, not seeing the dry twig until it snaps beneath my heel. The cub freezes, and its head slowly rises. I don't move, hoping it won't see me as a threat, but then it stands and my terror increases.

But there's something off about the situation. I can't quite understand why the creature seems to be wearing a khaki-coloured T-shirt and camouflage trousers, until a bony arm lifts the furry carcass from his head, and lowers the white skull mask from his face. I then recognise that this is a man in his early thirties. And he's staring back at me. He is stick thin, his shoulders as bony as his elbows, and his bald head shines as it catches shards of sunlight. He has more fingers than teeth, and blood drips from his chin from where he's been dining.

I feel sick, but I can't move. It's as if my feet have

somehow become frozen in the ground. He continues to move towards me, with barely ten feet between us now, and still my fight or flight response fails to engage.

He wipes his nose with the back of his left hand.

'Well, I asked the gods for something to eat and they've granted me mains *and* afters today,' he drawls, snickering in the process, before spitting on the ground.

If I've any chance of escaping I need to run. *Now*.

I don't stop to look back over my shoulder to check if he's following me, because I can't give up the slim advantage I've gained. I don't stop, even when my lungs burn and my muscles choke on lactic acid. I don't even stop to check the road is clear before darting across it and diving into my car. There's no sign of him when I look back, but I don't wait to see whether he's going to come searching for me. I accelerate out of the car park in a cloud of dust and terror, and floor the pedal until my heartrate returns to an even pace.

I know I should report what I saw, but I don't want to be anywhere near that man ever again.

I made a huge mistake in coming over here on my own, but now I need to make the best of a bad situation. I need to find out the truth about Mum. I reach into my pocket and pull out the scrunched piece of paper from the man in the tearoom. Despite Ashley's earlier reservations, I really don't have a choice: I'm going to have to meet this guy at O'Reilly's this evening and see what he can tell me about what really happened.

25

NORA

September 1993, Appalachian Trail, New Hampshire, USA

Sleep, when it comes, is in fits and starts. Nora spends half the night pushing back the thin blanket, double-checking that the door to the room is still locked, and that the towel in the bathroom is still secured over the pane of glass. Bruce sleeps through, oblivious to the crazed woman moving back and forth across the threadbare carpet. A whole night on an actual bed and she's failed to make the most of it. When sunlight starts creeping through the beige curtains, she's actually grateful for an excuse not to sleep any more.

She washes and moisturises at the basin before throwing on fresh clothes from her pack. She eventually wakes a gently snoring Bruce to tell him she's going to the phone box to try to call Frank and Jess. He mumbles something about taking a shower, but rolls onto his side without opening his eyes. He looks so peaceful that she leaves him where he is.

She opens the door a crack, half-expecting to be confronted by a topless man in a bear mask, but the sidewalk is empty. Opening the door wider, she takes a tentative step forward, again scanning the immediate horizon, but there isn't a soul in sight. Yet she can't shake the feeling of being watched. Keeping hold of the door handle, she scans the perimeter again, looking at the empty drag of road for anything out of place, before double-checking the windows of the rooms closest to her, but no sets of eyes stare back.

Should she go back inside and ask Bruce to escort her to the phone box? Would he think her mad?

She closes her eyes and takes a deep breath. The air is noticeably mustier than what she's become accustomed to on the AT. Down here, the toxic pong of exhaust fumes is never too far away. It's another reason to get out of the town and back where the air is clear and the views spectacular.

What she saw last night could just as easily have

been a figment of her overactive imagination. Given the stress of the trip, her inability to check in with her daughter, and the overall fatigue of hiking miles in the wilderness, who's to say what tricks her brain could be playing? The ghost-like figure in the mask could easily have been triggered by what they witnessed in the death room, connected to the story Charlie was telling them about Heaven's Gate having been cursed by some visiting witch doctor. She doesn't believe in witchcraft and ghost stories, and is embarrassed that she allowed such fiction to get the better of her.

In the cold light of day, a trick of the mind feels a lot more plausible than the alternative. Nora opens her eyes and actually laughs at the ridiculousness of it.

Taking another deep breath, she thrusts out her chest and releases the door handle; she's not going to allow her paranoia to get the better of her. Her priority is to speak to Jess and find out more about the accident Frank mentioned before they were cut off. She marches back to the main road, and turns towards the phone box. She silently curses when she sees a slight woman with ice-white hair already inside. She must be in her eighties, and has two large bags of groceries on the floor, and is gabbling away. At least it means the phone is working, Nora reminds herself as she crosses the road and sits on the wooden bench outside the sheriff's station.

Heaven's Gate is finally waking up, and as the minutes creep by, the footfall slowly increases with people going about their daily lives. A dozen cars pass in the street before her, workers heading to jobs in other towns, she assumes. She has no idea what the nearest city is, but she certainly isn't missing the hustle and bustle of Brighton. If she was at home, she'd probably be bogged down with worrying over the latest crisis on the news, or about what to cook for dinner. There's certainly a lot to be said for switching off all that noise and embracing a more nature-focused life.

The woman in the flowery dress returns the handset to the receiver and battles to get the door to the booth open, struggling to slide the paper bags out with her foot. Nora hurries over and helps her by lifting out the bags. The woman is full of thanks and tries to engage Nora in conversation, explaining she was phoning for a taxi, but Nora apologises and says she must make an urgent call of her own.

She fishes in her pocket, and grips two quarters between her fingers, before lifting the black phone and dialling the memorised number.

It rings.

And rings.

And rings.

She returns the handset, before picking it up and dialling again. It rings and rings, but still no answer.

Where the hell are they?

It's a Saturday lunchtime in the UK, so it's possible Frank could have taken Jess out somewhere, but he never normally takes her out at the weekend, more interested in sleeping late and catching up with reading than doing anything extracurricular. Why, of all times, would he have to choose to go out now when she's trying to phone?

Frustrated, she exits the phone box and heads back along the strip to the diner, deciding she will eat now, and then try to phone later, before they leave.

Ken, Charlie, and a freshly showered Bruce join her as she's finishing her plate of eggs and toast. They all look so much more refreshed than she's feeling.

'Did you manage to speak to Jess?' Bruce asks.

She shakes her head and finishes her mug of black coffee. 'No answer, so I'm going to try again in a minute.'

'We're agreed that we head back to the trail after breakfast?' Charlie checks, and the others shrug and nod.

Nora can't wait to see the back of Heaven's Gate. For all the discomfort, blisters, and effort trail hiking takes, Heaven's Gate has been the most unsafe she's felt since they arrived. She's keen to put as much distance between it and herself as possible.

Leaving money for her breakfast on the side of the table, she tells Bruce she'll meet him back in their room and returns to the phone box. The white-haired lady in the flowery dress must have been collected, as there's no sign of her.

She dials the number again, and this time it connects. She feeds coins in to the slot. 'Frank? It's me.'

'Nora? Is that you?'

'Yes, yes. Oh, thank God. Can you hear me okay?'

'Of course, of course, how are you?'

She feeds almost all of the coins into the slot, determined to make the most of the opportunity. 'I'm fine. I'm good. Tired, but well. How are you?'

'We're surviving. What time is it over there?'

She glances at her watch. 'Nearly 8 a.m. I've just had a plate of eggs and coffee. We're in a small town – well, it's more like a village than a town – called Heaven's Gate. It's a bit creepy, but we're going to be heading back to the AT in a bit. Is Jess there? Can I speak to her?'

'Oh, um… no, she's not here.'

'Where is she? Last night you said something about an accident?'

'Oh, yeah, she's fine, she's fine, but my parents have taken her to the beach for the day.'

Nora's heart drops. 'What about this accident?'

'It's nothing serious. She got knocked over at school and twisted her ankle. I had to collect her, and take her for an X-ray, but the doctor said it wasn't broken. He told her to rest the ankle for a couple of days, so I've had Mum and my sister over looking after her. When I got home last night, she was running about, as if nothing had happened.'

Nora knows how resilient Jess can be, and is relieved to hear she's on the mend.

'I don't know what it's like where you are, but we're having a mini heatwave over here, so when Mum suggested a day at the beach, Jess couldn't wait. They should be back around six if you can phone back then?'

Nora looks at her watch again, wondering whether she can convince the others to hang around for another five hours, but as her eyes wander back up, the breath is sucked from her lungs when across the street she sees a figure in a mask staring back at her.

Her hand shoots out as if it's somehow going to be able to provide protection, but when she blinks, the figure is gone. She can hear Frank calling her name, but instinctively drops the handset and exits the booth, rubbing her eyes and blinking, staring back at where she saw him, but there's nobody there.

When she comes to her senses, she returns to the booth, panting, and lifts the receiver. Frank is repeating her name over and over.

'I'm here. Sorry, I thought I saw... I must be cracking up. Um, I don't know when I'm going to be able to phone again. Listen, can you tell Jess I called? And that I love her so, so much. I'm missing you both tremendously. Tell her I'll phone again in a couple of days when we get to the next town.'

The pips sound, and before she can tell Frank she loves him, the line disconnects. As she exits the booth, again, she checks the perimeter for the figure she's certain she saw, but it's as if they vanished into thin air.

26

JESS

April 2023, Rockston, Maine, USA

What I don't realise until I arrive is that O'Reilly's is a biker bar – at least that's the conclusion I draw when I pull up on the dirt road and count more than a dozen motorbikes parked up on the gravel and mud, both outside and beside the building. A large neon sign hangs above the main entrance where a man and a woman dressed in dark leather jackets converse over a cigarette.

Squeezing between them, I head through the wooden saloon doors, and am immediately struck by how dim it is. I see now that the windows are covered with paper, and so the only light is provided by the two large halogen lights hanging by chains from the ceiling. You'd never know the sun is still shining outside. I guess in here it can be any time because it always looks the same. A ton of cardboard beer mats line the ceiling, somehow making the place feel smaller than it actually is.

There are empty beer barrels standing on their sides acting as tables with cocktail stools beside each. Three of the makeshift tables are occupied, but otherwise the place is empty. As I move closer to the bar, I hear the sound of balls colliding and realise there must be a pool table around the side that I can't see. A video arcade game stands unused adjacent to the bar, and there's an antique cigarette dispenser hanging from the wall with a big 'Not in service' sign pasted to it.

'You sure you're in the right place?' From behind the bar, a woman with long black hair calls to me.

She is wearing a thin, sleeveless green vest, and her hair looks in dire need of a wash, cut, and blow dry. She's thinner than me, but I get the feeling she can hold her own when called upon. She doesn't look intimidated by the largely male pack of drinkers.

'This is O'Reilly's, right?' I say with more confidence than I'm feeling. 'I heard this was the place to be.'

She shrugs at my comment and continues to wipe glasses and place them on a shelf. 'What you ride?'

'I don't have a bike.'

'And yet you came to a biker bar on a Friday night?'

'I didn't notice a sign saying non-bikers weren't welcome.'

She smiles at this and drops the towel. 'I admire your confidence. What you drinking?'

'I'll have a diet soda. Thanks.'

She reaches for a glass and places it beneath the soda fountain and begins to fill. 'What really brings you here? Given we're in the middle of nowhere, this ain't the kind of place you come to by accident.'

'I'm looking for someone actually.'

'Gay or straight?'

I'm thrown by the question. 'Not like that. I'm supposed to be meeting someone.'

'Blind date?'

'Not exactly.'

She places the glass on a coaster and I pay her. There are small glass bowls of peanuts on the bar, but I resist the urge to grab a handful, collect my drink and move to the barrel table closest to the door so I can see everyone who comes and goes, and can also make a quick escape if things turn sour.

It's not yet 7.15, but I chose to get here early so I can try to spot the guy in the porkpie hat before he sees me. I couldn't even say if he was fat or thin, or how tall he was, because the only time I saw him he was stooped over. Anyway, he was gone so quickly that the detail didn't register. For all I know, the guy in the porkpie hat isn't even the one who wants to meet me.

When I pull out my phone, I'm relieved to see I have a bar of signal. A message pings through from Ashley checking that I haven't come to meet him, but I choose not to reply as I know she worries too much. But then I think about how Mum went missing, and my earlier encounter with the man in the mask, and quickly write to say where I am. She's probably asleep, but at least she'll be able to tell the police should I not make it back to Rockston.

The woman behind the bar keeps glancing over at me, as she pours drinks for other customers, and I do my best not to return the looks.

The saloon doors open and a guy walks in, but he's in a leather jacket, and isn't wearing a porkpie hat. He asks for change before leaving again. Another five minutes pass before the next man enters, but he's the one who was smoking outside, and again there's no sign of a hat of any kind.

At half past seven, and with my drink almost gone, I decide I've been stood up and am about to leave when the woman calls out to me. 'Your name wouldn't happen to be Jess, would it?'

I nod and carry my glass over.

'Phone call for you,' she says. 'Think it must be your date.'

She nods towards the side of the bar where I spot a box phone. I move across and scoop up the handset.

'Hello?'

'Are you Jess Grogan?'

'I am, yes. Who is this?'

'A friend.'

'Are you the guy who left me the note?'

'No, but he works for me.'

I have a horrible sinking feeling, and my eyes dart around the rest of the room, but nobody is paying me any undue attention. Even the bartender is busy chatting to one of the customers.

'You said you knew about my mum. What do you want?'

'You're in danger.'

A cold shiver runs across my chest. 'Who are you and what do you want from me?'

'I told you: I'm a friend. I only want to get you away from the people who want you dead.'

The breath catches in my throat. 'What did you say?'

'There are people out there who will do whatever it takes to protect the truth about your mom. You want to live, you need to do what I tell you.'

My eyes dart across the strangers in the bar, searching for anyone paying undue attention to me. Is one of them a killer? Do they all want me dead?

'But I haven't done anything wrong,' I whisper into the mouthpiece.

'You're looking for her, and asking questions. Sometimes that's enough.'

Despite my fear, my mind snaps me back to reality. 'If I'm in danger, I'll go to the police, and they'll protect me.'

'I wouldn't bank on it. Listen carefully, we don't have long. You need to come and meet me now.'

I've seen too many movies about vulnerable women making the wrong choices in exactly these kinds of situations to go along with anything this stranger has to say.

'No, you come here and meet me.'

'It isn't safe. I'm taking a huge risk in even contacting you.'

'Tell me what you know about my mum.'

'She died in Rockston.'

It's like a punch to the stomach. 'Who killed her?'

'I don't have time to go into specifics. Meet me tonight and I promise I'll tell you everything I know.'

'I'm not going anywhere else until you tell me exactly who you are, and what you know.'

There's a burst of crackle as he sighs. 'Trouble waits for you back in Rockston. I will send someone to collect you, and then we can talk.'

My voice cracks under the strain of emotion. 'No. You tell me now.'

Another sigh. 'Fine. Your mom was killed by someone in Rockston and then the whole town conspired to cover it up. Your coming here was a mistake. They'll kill you too just to keep their secret safe.'

I think about Mrs Daniels adamantly telling me she'd never seen Mum, the shopkeepers reporting me to the sheriff, and the missing guest register from 1993.

Could he be right?

'Will you come and meet me? I can grant you safe passage off the mountain.'

'My passport is in my motel room. I need to go and collect it first.'

'Very well. How long will it take you?'

I look at my watch. 'Depends where you want to meet.'

'I'll text you an address, if you give me your number.'

She obliges. 'Wait, what do I call you?'

There's a pause on the line. 'Mr DeWalt.'

The phone disconnects, and the text message comes through but it's just coordinates, which isn't particularly helpful. I forward the message to Ashley, telling her this is where I'm headed next, before hurrying out to the car and hightailing it back to Rockston. There's part of me tempted to go looking for Jarod's grandmother to ask about the guest register, but if DeWalt is right and there is a conspiracy in this small mountain town, then she'll only deny all knowledge of it anyway.

As soon as I approach my room, I can see something isn't right. I might have left in a hurry, but I know I definitely closed and checked the door. So why is it ajar now?

27

NORA

September 1993, Appalachian Trail, New Hampshire, USA

Nora keeps one eye straight ahead, and the other over her shoulder, still unable to shift the feeling that she's being watched, even though there isn't a soul in sight in either direction. They're back on the short trail Leanne had taken them along to get down to Heaven's Gate twenty-four hours earlier.

Had it not been for all of Leanne's stories about Moon-Eyed People and figures with ten-foot-long wings, maybe she wouldn't have started seeing things. She looks down at the metal bracelet hanging from her left arm. She held her arm in a basin of ice-cold water for more than half an hour last night, and still the damned thing wouldn't come off. At least the antihistamine lotion Leanne gave her seems to be keeping the itchy rash at bay. How on earth that blonde girl managed to get the bracelet onto her wrist in the first place remains a mystery. She has a good mind to hunt for the girl when they eventually make it to Darby, and insist she remove it.

It's all in your head, she reminds herself, but that's easier to think than believe. No matter how much she tries not to picture the topless figure in the mask, he keeps returning to her thoughts.

When Nora revealed that she'd been unable to speak to Jess, Bruce kindly suggested they stick around in Heaven's Gate for another day, an idea that neither Ken nor Charlie were happy to agree to. Ken had managed to talk to both of his sons after breakfast, and despite a restful night's sleep, he couldn't handle another night in the world's least interesting town. 'When the highlight of a town is to watch the washing-machines spinning at the launderette,' he said, 'it's time to search for pastures new.'

And even for Nora, staying would mean having to deal with her visions of the figure in the mask. Though the fact that she thought she saw him just now in the middle of the road has her convinced that the incident in her bathroom was her mind playing tricks on her. She just needs to put him out of her head, and focus on something else.

She pictures Jess at home, and can imagine her making the most of her injury, demanding servant-like service from Frank's parents and sister. It wouldn't surprise her if Jess had asked for a bell so she could ring if she required anything. Nora laughs at this thought, but her head quickly snaps back around when she realises she's travelled several metres without checking the coast is clear.

Clouds of dust circle them as they make the most of the flat sections of track, and build momentum for the inevitable rises that will lead them back up to the AT. You'd never know this area had been coated in ice-cold snow only days before. The sun is so hot in the sky that it feels more like summer than autumn. How can things have changed so drastically in such a short period? It's so hot that Nora has retired her jacket to her pack and rolled up her sleeves.

The pathway ahead is narrowing, and she recalls this section of the small trail from yesterday. Leanne had warned that it was known locally as Dead Man's Passage on account of the number of hikers who'd fallen from the edge. It didn't seem as narrow yesterday, but now that they're ascending, Nora is conscious of the vast nothingness to her right. She's not going to be able to concentrate on what's behind her, so turns and places her front against the rough rock face, and takes sideways steps. Her pace slows as a result and Bruce's orange pack is soon shrinking into the distance, but she'd rather be safe than misplace a foot and fall.

She looks to her left to check they're not being followed, before reminding herself that she's being paranoid, and turns her head back to the right. The pathway below is so narrow that she's amazed the other three have made it along so quickly. Bruce's pack is nowhere in sight, but then the pathway is curling around the rock face, so it's impossible for her to see anything more than a couple of metres in front and behind.

She glances down and instantly regrets it as her boot catches on a loose stone, sending it hurtling over the side. She watches it as it bounces on outcrops of rock, splintering into a thousand pieces until it disappears from view into the ravine below. She gulps audibly, and reminds herself to watch her footing. Keeping her face to the rock face no longer seems such a good idea, and she slowly turns on the spot, rocks scraping as her pack comes into contact with them. Just as she feels the weight of the pack pulling her backwards, she manages to grab at a random sprig of branch poking out through a crack in the rock.

She can hear Bruce and the others calling back to her, suddenly aware that she isn't with them.

'I'm coming,' she shouts back, her legs feeling more like jelly, but only too aware that she can't stay here for the rest of the day.

Taking several long breaths to settle her nerves, she slides her right foot to the right, slowly bringing her left heel to join it, and then slides again, like a slow toe-to-heel ballroom dance. Every step forward, she reaches out for any kind of rough stone or plant she can use to keep herself glued to the rock face. Time ticks by slowly, and just as she thinks she's never going to make it off Dead Man's Passage, she catches sight of Bruce and Ken on a far wider platform a few metres ahead.

'Watch yourself,' Bruce calls out, 'it's pretty slippery at that bit. At least you were smart enough to use scissor steps. We thought we were going to lose Ken at one point.'

'I was fine,' Ken replies with an air of nonchalance, but the blood has yet to return to his face.

Nora's feet make it to the wider platform, and

Bruce practically catches her as she stumbles forwards, her legs yet to find their strength again.

'Are you okay?' he asks, and she offers a brisk nod, taking a secondary glance back over her shoulder.

'This would probably be a good spot for a rest,' he suggests, checking with the other two who nod in response.

Ken unfastens his pack, and is starting to slide it off when it catches on a sharp spike of branch, and in a fraction of a second, he's stumbling forwards, grabbing on to Charlie who isn't expecting the approach. And then Nora watches on helplessly as the two of them go over the edge of the platform. Bruce clutches out, but the momentum is with them, and he too disappears over the side, leaving Nora staring openmouthed into nothing.

28

JESS

April 2023, Rockston, Maine, USA

I creep steadily closer to the door as it gently flaps in the cool breeze. The smell of pine in the air is no longer as welcoming as when I arrived. I think of De-Walt's warning about the people in this town wanting me dead. If there is someone in my room, I don't want to go in unarmed. So I hurry back to the Smart car, open the boot and rummage around inside until my hand touches something cold and metallic. I unclip and pull out the tyre iron, holding it up to the darkening sky.

If now is my turn to go, I'm going out as I came into this world: kicking and screaming.

I thrust the metal rod through the air a couple of times to get a feel for the weight of it. It won't help if the person in my room has a gun, but it might make them think twice. I never should have left my passport in there, but I naively thought it would be safer inside than on my person.

With my back to the wall, I slowly sidestep until I am just outside the door. Taking two deep, silent breaths, I swing round and push it open with my foot, the tyre iron held high above my head. I scream when I see two eyes staring back at me through the darkness.

The figure is sitting on my bed, and quickly stands, raising his arms, and moving towards me. I should be running back to the car, or off to reception, but my feet are frozen, and I can't move.

DeWalt's words fill my mind: I only want to get you away from the people who want you dead.

'Stay back,' I manage to gasp, swinging the tyre iron in front of me.

He stops advancing, but I can't make out his face, as my eyes blur with tears.

'Jess, it's me... it's Bruce.'

I stop swinging in an instant as instinct recognises

that voice. The figure stretches out an arm, and a moment later the room fills with dim light from the bulb overhead. The tyre iron clangs as it drops to the floor. I don't think I've ever been so equally surprised and relieved, yet my feet remain planted, as if my mind doesn't trust my eyes.

He steps before me, but my fight or flight response dissipates the moment he places his arms around me and I breathe in his deep, familiar scent: moisturising cream and Old Spice. It feels good being held, and my body melts into his warmth.

'Thank God I found you,' he says, pressing his lips to the top of my head.

'W-what are you doing here, Bruce?' I muster.

He leads me over to the bed, and sits me down on it, before locating a bottle of water, and offering it to me.

'Sorry it isn't something stronger,' he mutters, as I take a swig, and try to compose my racing heart.

I think my heightened paranoia genuinely had me believing that the figure waiting in my unlocked room was in fact here to do me harm as DeWalt had suggested. I don't want to admit how embarrassed I am, and besides, I'm more interested to know what Bruce is doing here, and how he found me.

'Ashley called me,' he volunteers, as if reading my

mind. 'It was early – Paolo didn't appreciate the wakeup call – but she said she'd just spoken to you and that you'd flown here in search of your mum's remains. Bless her, she was hyperventilating so much that I feared she'd go into premature labour, so I promised I'd come over and try to find you.'

Guilt splashes at the edge of my conscious mind, but I never asked him to drop everything and come to my rescue.

'I caught a flight from Heathrow this morning at ten, and after a three-hour stopover in Newark, arrived in Maine just after six local time.' He stifles a yawn. 'I've no idea what the time is now, because my body clock is telling me I should be asleep, particularly after the early start.'

I give his hand a squeeze. 'How did you know where to find me?'

'I arrived to a slew of messages from Ashley, recounting your exchanges. The last one said you were going to meet some stranger at a bar or something. I feared I was already too late.'

Something isn't right here, but my adrenaline-addled brain can't quite figure out what it is.

'But how did you get to Rockston, and how did you get into my room?'

'Ashley said you were coming here and as it's the

only motel in the town, I spoke with the lovely lady at reception, and told her... forgive me: I told her I was your dad, and needed to speak to you urgently. I guess I can tell a convincing fib when I need to.'

I shouldn't be focusing my attention on questioning Bruce's motives for being here. Given DeWalt's warning, I need all the friends I can find.

'We're not safe here,' I tell him, following another sip of water. 'I went to the biker bar, and spoke with the source over the phone. He said Mum was killed here, and that the town covered it up. He said I'm in danger.'

I don't elaborate on the exact threat to my life, as I don't want to panic Bruce.

His brow furrows. 'Who is this source? Ashley said something about him leaving you a note?'

I show him the note I collected from the floor of the tearoom, and he studies it.

'And what exactly did he say on the phone?'

I try to recall the exact words, but I didn't commit them to memory. 'Just that he's a friend, that he knows someone in the town killed Mum, and that the rest helped cover it up, and that me being here asking questions is putting my own life at risk. He sent coordinates, and wants me to meet him tonight.'

Bruce's eyes widen. 'No way! Are you kidding me?

For all you know this mystery voice on the phone could be the killer himself, luring you into the open so he can tie up loose ends.'

I can't say the thought hadn't crossed my mind on the drive back to Rockston.

'He said he was taking a huge risk in contacting me, and... I don't know, I guess I want to believe him. In my experience, people often want to protect their identities when reporting serious crime. That's the whole reason the contact form on my website doesn't demand a name or email address.'

He looks far from convinced. 'If he has information pertaining to what happened to Nora, why hasn't he reported it to the police?'

I sigh. 'Maybe he has, and they ignored him. I don't know.'

'And why reach out to you now? How did he know you were in the town asking questions? How does he know that your life is in danger? There are too many unanswered questions.'

I want to agree with him, but we're disturbed by a knock at the open door. I don't know if I'm relieved or worried to see Sheriff Randy Whitaker tipping his hat in my direction.

'Miss Grogan, I hope I'm not disturbing you?'

My eyes are drawn to the gun in the belt holster,

and I feel protective of Bruce, so rather than inviting Whitaker in and allowing him to kill us behind a closed door, I quickly stand and cross to the door, stepping out into the open.

'What can I do for you so late, Sheriff?' I ask once we're outside.

I meant for Bruce to stay in the room, but feel his body warmth directly behind me.

'I wanted to give you an update. I've sent the DNA swab I took from you earlier today to the lab for them to compare against what was recovered, but they're unlikely to have results for twenty-four to forty-eight hours. By all means, you're welcome to stay, but there's nothing you can do here to influence matters, so if you want to leave me your contact details, I can be in touch when we know more.'

He eyes Bruce with interest. 'I'm sorry, we've not been introduced. I'm Sheriff Randy Whitaker, and you are?'

'This is Bruce,' I speak up. 'He's... um, he's...'

My mind blanks. I don't know how to describe Bruce in this instance. He's not technically family, and yet isn't that how I think of him deep down?

Bruce offers his hand to the sheriff. 'I'm Bruce Simmonds, an old friend of the family.'

The sheriff closes one eye and tilts his head. 'Wait,

that name rings a bell. Don't tell me.' He pauses, presumably turning the name over in his mind. His eyes widen as he makes the connection. 'Wait, you're not the same Bruce Simmonds who first reported Nora Grogan missing thirty years ago?'

Bruce's cheeks redden. 'I am indeed, though this is the first time I've stepped foot in your quaint town.'

The sheriff's face widens into a smile. 'I'm sorry, it's the strangest thing: I was reading a statement you made about Mrs Grogan's disappearance only this morning. So weird that you're now standing before me here.'

An odd silence overcomes us as they continue to stare at one another in an unnecessary game of one-upmanship.

'That's why I'm here,' Bruce eventually offers, resting his hands on my shoulders. 'I came to bring Jess home and to keep her safe.'

The sheriff fishes into his pocket, and offers me a business card. 'My email address is on here. Drop me a message whenever you're ready, and I'll let you know when we have the results of the DNA test.'

I pocket the card, and watch as he bids us good evening and moves away. I wait until he's out of sight before exhaling.

'Are you okay?' Bruce asks, maybe sensing the tension in my shoulders.

I don't answer, instead, heading into the room and gathering up my limited possessions and shoving them into the holdall. I collect my passport from the drawer beside the bed, and push it into my pocket.

'We probably won't make it back to the airport before dawn,' Bruce says, 'so it makes sense to rest up here—'

'I'm not staying another second in this town,' I say firmly. 'I'm not so convinced the sheriff didn't come to my room with malice in mind.'

'Okay, well, hopefully we can find another motel between here and the airport—'

I raise my hand to cut him off. 'Let me be clear, Bruce: I'm not giving up and going home without knowing exactly what happened to Mum. Whether those are her remains or not, I've spent my whole life waiting to hear the truth, and now that I'm here, I can't just turn my back on her.'

His face softens into an empathetic frown. 'Can I play devil's advocate for a minute? What if you don't find the answers you're seeking? How long are you going to stay here until accepting that you – *we* – may never know what really happened to her?'

'As long as it takes,' I say defiantly, but the truth is I

don't know where to start searching for answers. It's clear the townsfolk of Rockston have no intention of helping me, and I'm not sure I can trust DeWalt. Right now, I'm too exhausted to get my thoughts clear in my mind.

'Let's go find a room somewhere, and we can make a decision in the morning.'

29

NORA

September 1993, Appalachian Trail, New Hampshire, USA

Nora wants to scream, but no noise escapes as the sound of their bodies falling winds her like a punch to the gut. She pinches herself, wanting to wake from the nightmare, but she's still on the side of a mountain, desperately clinging to the rock face to keep herself from following her team mates over the edge.

One moment they were then, and then gone. Never to be seen again.

An eerie silence settles, and her mind races with how she's going to be able to find someone to tell them what's happened. She daren't go back along Dead Man's Passage, but she has no clue how much further she's got to go before re-joining the AT proper.

And then finally she hears a pained groan coming from somewhere just below the ledge. It's followed by a cacophony of swearing and griping, and it is music to her ears. Dropping to her knees, she carefully removes her pack, and rests it on the platform, flattening her body against the dusty, rocky floor, and ever so carefully edging forwards. As her eyes move over the lip of the platform, she's relieved to see her three friends in a crumpled heap on another ledge maybe ten feet below her.

'Oh, thank God you're still alive,' she shouts down to them.

Bruce's entire face is covered in white sand, as he blinks back up at her, trying to avoid the blazing sun above her head.

Charlie pulls off his baseball cap, and uses it to swat at Ken. 'What the hell, man? If you wanna commit suicide that's your business, but why the hell did you have to drag me into it too?'

The relief pulses through Nora's body, but she can see the ground has broken away where Ken stumbled, almost as if it had been deliberately manipulated.

'Are you okay?' Nora calls, wiping her eyes with the back of her hand.

She can see Bruce has sustained a nasty cut to his forehead, and Ken's glasses appear to be missing a lens.

'Looks like you're going to have to try and climb back up,' she tells them.

Charlie runs his hands along the jagged rock face and shakes his head. 'I don't think any of us are climbing this without some kind of rope. You might have to go and call for search and rescue.'

She remains where she is but tilts her head to stare back at the narrow path she just came along, and desperately prays for an alternative idea. From here she can see there are no similar ledges beneath Dead Man's Passage. A slip from that will mean certain death.

Nora freezes as she hears the near sound of voices. She tells the other three to be quiet so she can listen, and a moment later she sees a young man in his twenties, his bleached-blond straggly hair hanging down over his face. His friend is also in shorts and a T-shirt, with equally long hair, but dark brown.

'My friends went over the edge,' she says quickly, clinging to the ground for dear life, as one of them leans over the edge with no apparent concern for his own safety.

'Whoa, bodacious. How you doin', guys?' he shouts down.

'We need rope to climb up,' Charlie replies.

They exchange glances, mouthing words that Nora can't hear or interpret. 'Um, Jeez, sorry, but we're really in a hurry. We'll send for help when we make it to the next checkpoint.'

They move to go around Nora, who remains flat on the ledge, too terrified to attempt to stand in case more of the ground gives way. They seem to know exactly where to tread.

'You can't just leave us,' Nora pleads, angry that they're even considering leaving.

'Listen, you could try stripping off and tying your clothes together to make a kind of rope,' the blond one is saying, but his friend is already dragging him away.

There's nowhere obvious to tie a rope even if she did manage to create one. 'Please, we're all alone out here, and we're not experienced hikers.'

He pulls the blond one back. 'Okay, that ledge will eventually lead them back to the AT, all they gotta do is follow it. If you join us now, we can lead you to where it comes out. But that's the best we can do as we gotta keep moving.'

She can't say why, but she has a bad feeling about these two already, and is wary of going off alone with anyone she doesn't know. She looks back over the edge, and can see the narrow ledge does appear to continue around the side of the mountain, but it's in a downward trajectory, whereas her path is heading up. Her only alternative is to try to climb down to the others, but one misplaced foot and she'll continue past them until she hits the dry riverbed.

They're already moving on, so she has no time to make a decision. Catching sight of the bracelet on her wrist, she prays there is some truth in the protective powers it's supposed to grant, and scrambles back to her feet, passing on the information to the others.

'Hey, wait up,' she calls after them, walking as quickly as she can manage, but clinging on to bits of branch and roots sticking out of the side of the wall. 'Thank God you came by when you did,' she says, remembering what Leanne had said about the wonder of Trail Magic. 'I'm Nora, by the way.'

The blond one grins back. 'Cool. I'm Weasel, and this is my friend Snake.'

She instantly hears Andy's ominous words in her

head: *Have you warned her to steer clear of Snake and Weasel yet?*

The breath catches in her throat and she coughs and splutters, daring to glimpse back over the edge, wanting to tell the others to turn back so she can join them below, but they're already several feet lower. She desperately tries to recall what Joanna said about them. Something about them begging for food and stinking of weed, but that she too picked up a bad vibe. Scanning the floor, she looks for anything she can retain as a weapon in case she needs to, but there's nothing but rocky debris. They're taking the narrow path at some pace, though it isn't clear what they're hurrying to or from. She allows the one called Weasel to get a few feet ahead to give herself space should she need to think quickly.

Eventually the narrow path widens, and Nora finds herself in the shade of tall trees, but they don't stop to rest as she'd have liked, so she's forced to take a drink from the canister hanging from her neck while still moving. She can't be certain they'll be good to their word, and is keen to find out more about them, should she need to report them later.

It turns out the names Snake and Weasel were adopted during their time on the AT. A trail name – essentially a nickname either personally chosen or suggested by another hiker – is something some thru-hikers use as a means of ingratiating themselves further in trail tradition, or so Weasel advises Nora as they continue.

'Like, you know, you could meet a dozen Kyles while hiking the AT,' he tells her as they heave themselves over a fallen tree trunk, 'and then when you arrive at, like, a hostel or something, you might be like, hey, has anybody seen Kyle, and they be like, "Do you mean Kyle with the tattoo, or Kyle who is really hot, or some other Kyle?" It gets confusing, like, you know? So, the idea is that by adopting a special trail nickname, you're easier to remember.'

'Plus it helps break the ice,' Snake shouts out from further ahead.

'So how did you choose those particular names?'

Nora had already grasped the fact that neither of them were given the names at birth, but she's curious to know why these particular animals were chosen.

'So you see how Snake's hair is so dark yet seems to shimmer in the sunlight? It kind of looks like a snake's skin, don't it?'

Nora considers the straggly hair hanging down over Snake's cheeks as he grins back at her inanely. It reminds her of the leather handbag her mother would never be without, but keeps the comparison to

herself. The pair of them look as though they've mod-
elled their 'look' on *Bill and Ted*. With long, baggy
shorts, Van Halen T-shirts and no apparent fear of
traipsing through the wilderness, she envies how relaxed they seem.

'And Weasel?' she asks, turning back to look
at him.

He looks over to his friend and bursts out
laughing.

'Do you know much about weasels?' Snake asks,
as they begin walking again.

Nora shakes her head. 'Can't say I've ever seen
one.'

'Well, they're, like, super long, right? They look a
bit like a cat, but they can stand on two legs, though
their legs and arms are quite short.'

Weasel lifts his arms into the air as if on cue. Nora
considers him, but wouldn't have said his arms or legs
look abnormally small.

'Ah, dude, you should quit messing with her,'
Weasel says, laughing again. He fixes Nora with a sincere stare. 'My folks run a small farm back in Sonoma
County, and breed all sorts of furry critters including
weasels. We were trying to think of a trail name for
me, and it just kind of stuck.'

Her shoulders relax when they finally hear Bruce

berating Ken and Charlie for allowing Nora to go off with two strangers. When she sets eyes upon Bruce, she can tell the sweat shimmering on his cheeks is from worry as much as it is exertion. He attempts to hug her, but it's awkward, and Nora is quick to thank Snake and Weasel and bid them well on their journey.

'Actually,' Weasel tells them, 'we were just talking and we thought we'd hang with you guys for the next stretch.'

Nora can't understand their sudden change of heart, but can't object as Charlie and Ken formally introduce themselves. She hangs back with Bruce while the others go on ahead.

'Do you remember what Joanna said about these two?' she says quietly, through gritted teeth.

'Not specifically. Did something happen when you were alone with them?'

'No, nothing like that. I just... I don't trust them. I can't put my finger on why.'

'Listen, I'm sure there's nothing to worry about, and I promise I'll look after you. Let's just get to camp and I'm sure they'll have moved on a day or two. Okay?'

She keeps her head down, willing time to pass quickly, but it drags, and when Ken finally announces they've reached their camping spot, she's relieved to be able to eat and rest. Snake and Weasel remove their packs before heading into the nearby trees in search of firewood.

Bruce puffs out his cheeks, and shakes his head as he closes his eyes. 'I don't know if it's something I ate, but my gut's been in a spin the last couple of miles.'

She helps him unfasten his pack, and lays it down on the sandy floor, before reaching inside and extracting his water bottle.

'Maybe a bit of heat stroke?' she suggests. 'It has been warm.'

He takes a sip of the water, before his eyes widen and he lurches towards the trees before throwing up. The sound of his retching echoes off the large boulders surrounding the camping spot. The smell is enough to make Nora's own stomach turn. She moves the water bottle closer to him, before beating a hasty retreat.

'Whoa, someone's got a case of the D and V,' Weasel declares as the two of them return moments later, carrying a bundle of thick branches. 'You all should stay well clear of that. Unless he's been undercooking his own meat, then what you've got there is a case of norovirus. It's practically a wonder of the AT in its own right. And if the rest of us don't steer well clear of him, we're gonna have a case of Spewmageddon on our hands.'

Nora eyes Bruce carefully as he continues to retch into a bush. 'You're saying he has a sickness bug?'

'Damn straight! And this is just the start of it. Before you know it, he's gonna be shitting all over the place too.'

Charlie lifts his pack and moves to the opposite side of the camp, before starting to unpack his tent. Ken follows suit as the fire begins to crackle.

Bruce eventually stops vomiting and moves himself just outside of the circle, a stone's throw from the treeline so he can get there in a hurry. The mood in camp is noticeably quiet. Weasel asks whether Charlie and Ken party, and Nora looks away when he produces a joint and sparks it. She declines when it's offered to her, and chooses to go and stretch her legs; the smell of it is as off-putting as what Bruce deposited in the bushes.

She doesn't wander far, the image of the figure in the bear mask still burned in her memory, but as she's returning to the camp, she freezes when she hears Snake and Weasel talking quietly away from Charlie and Ken, who are giggling like drunk students.

'We can't hang around here forever,' one of them

whispers. 'There's no way I'm dealing with the D and V again so soon.'

'We don't have a choice right now, dude. The cops will be looking for two dudes hiking alone. Sticking with these guys means they won't look at us. Okay? Just avoid the sick one, and then when the coast is clear we can move on.'

'And what happens if they figure out what's going on?'

Nora dares to poke her head above the bush she's cowering behind, and sees Snake pull a shiny handgun from his pack.

'We do what we have to.'

30

JESS

April 2023, outskirts of Rockston, Maine, USA

I know there's so much Bruce hasn't told me about what happened over here all those years ago, and he thinks he's protecting me, when in fact, the truth could set me free. When he first invited me to move in with him and Paolo, I thought he was doing it out of guilt for not keeping Mum safe, but as the years have progressed and he's continued to show me kindness beyond necessity, I can't help but wonder if there's more to it than that.

We're sitting in a small diner drinking strong

coffee and splitting a plate of doughnuts when he tells me he will pay for my ticket back to the UK. We're a stone's throw from the motel we found late last night, which is not nearly as far from Rockston as I was led to believe. Half the booths in the joint are filled with a mixture of hikers and those in more formal work attire.

'I understand why you would want to stay and search for answers,' he says, wiping his greasy chin with a paper napkin, 'but don't you think if there were clues as to what happened, the police here would have checked them out?'

It's a fair question, and one I asked myself between intermittent bouts of sleep during the night. Back when I was interning at the newspaper, my mentor there told me there was no story that couldn't be written; you just have to be prepared to keep searching for answers. When I first decided I wanted to become a journalist, it was driven by wanting to discover what happened to Mum, and that desire has never left me, despite all the rejections and knockbacks. I have been ignoring the voice in the back of my head for too long, and now it is screaming at me to stay and fight. If I return to the UK without answers, my mind will never rest. But how do I explain that to someone who seems convinced I'm going to follow in Mum's footsteps?

I take a long sip of the coffee, savouring the kick of the caffeine. 'Somebody somewhere knows exactly what happened to her, and I feel my whole life has been building to this moment; everything that's gone before was to give me the necessary experience I need to solve this thing. I feel it in every sinew in my body.'

'And what if that *somebody* doesn't want you to uncover the truth? Are you really prepared to put your life at stake?'

What life?

In fairness, Bruce doesn't know how difficult things have been since the divorce, because I haven't told him. He's invested so much time and love in me that I don't want to disappoint him. If he knew about my rent arrears, I've no doubt he'd offer to settle them and invite me to move in with him and Paolo, but at thirty-five, I'm too old to be a third wheel, and to rely on his generosity. It's time I stood on my own two feet and showed the world I'm ready to fight.

'I want to retrace Mum's final footsteps in the days leading up to her disappearance,' I say instead. 'Maybe if I can tread the same ground as her, I'll be able to put myself in her head and find out what caused her to run off into the woods to begin with.'

'You want to join the AT?'

I shrug. 'If that's what it takes.'

'But you're in no state to start a weeks-long hike. No disrespect, but when was the last time you walked for more than an hour straight?'

He knows me better than I gave him credit for. 'It doesn't matter. I'm in good enough shape, and I'll rest when I need.'

'And you don't have the necessary equipment. God, I section-hiked the trail thirty years ago and even I wasn't fully prepared for what to expect.'

'I'm sure there are stores nearby where I can get supplies.'

'Well, I'm in no condition to start hiking again.'

'I don't want you to stay anyway, Bruce. You can fly home and tell Ashley that you found me and that I'm fine, and I promise I will keep you updated with my progress every day.'

It's one thing to put my own life at risk, but I can't allow Bruce to suffer the same fate.

He takes a slurp of his coffee, shaking his head. 'I'm going nowhere without you. So, like it or lump it, you're stuck with me.'

'So be it. You can be Watson to my Holmes. Now, I think we start by finding this DeWalt character to see what he knows.'

'Absolutely not!'

I flinch at his outburst as the eyes of those in the booths nearest to us turn in our direction.

'He's our only source that Mum is definitely dead, and we'd be crazy to ignore him.'

'You have no idea who this guy is or what motivation he has for contacting you. He could be a kook who's trying to involve himself in the story, or he could be a crazed killer. The fact is you know nothing about him, and that for me is a major red flag.'

I had similar reservations when I spoke to him on the phone, but maybe it's because it's now daylight, or because Bruce is with me, but I feel less scared about meeting DeWalt.

'So what do you suggest?' I counter.

Bruce wipes his mouth for a second time, and pushes the plate away from him, contemplating the question. 'Okay, I have an idea. We could go to Heaven's Gate. It's a small town not far from here, and was where I first started to have concerns about your mum's mental health.'

'What sort of concerns?'

His eyebrows not together. 'It's hard to remember exactly what triggered it. She was seeing things that weren't necessarily there, I suppose. You said you want to retrace her steps? Then that's where I suggest we begin, Holmes.'

* * *

The town of Heaven's Gate is little more than a long road with a few storefronts scattered either side of it. Bruce tells me it's more built-up than he remembers, and points out the motel where they spent one night thirty years ago. He says it doesn't look any different to how he remembers, although the name of the motel has changed.

'Your mum was certain she saw a peeping tom watching her while she showered, but we didn't find anyone matching the description she gave. I think she suspected it might have been Charlie playing a prank, despite my protestations.'

'You never speak much about him and Ken. Are you still friends?'

He shakes his head as he pulls us into a bay in the supermarket car park. 'I think Ken moved back to Swansea to care for his parents a few years after the hike. We weren't really friends before it, and after... I think it was easier to avoid one another than process what happened.'

'And Charlie?'

He looks away. 'I haven't spoken to him for thirty years.'

'Why not?'

He turns back to face me. 'A clash of personalities, I guess. We were from different places, and once I returned home, I had no need to speak to him again. And I guess the same must have gone for him.'

What is he not telling me? I feel there's more to his words than he's prepared to admit, but when I press him on it, he tells me it's because he's tired, and I'm reading too much into it. We head down one side of the road, and back up the other, with Bruce telling me how Charlie had met some kid on a bike who'd told them stories about a hospital burning down.

'Ghost stories for the curious tourists,' Bruce adds, as we arrive at a café offering free Wi-Fi.

I'm melting in the heat of the April sunshine, and there only appears to be two other people inside, so I offer to buy him a drink. We both order Frappuccinos, and wait at the counter. Thank God for the air conditioning.

'You've never mentioned these ghost stories to me before,' I say.

'That's because that's all they are. We were brought to this place by a hiker we met at one of the hostels. She spoke to us about all kinds of local myths – people in the woods, and that kind of thing – but your mum seemed to be the only one who bought into any of it.'

'What do you mean she bought into it?'

Thick lines pepper his temple. 'I don't know. As an example, she bought this bracelet from some local girl who claimed it offered protection from evil spirits. At first I thought your mum was just playing along with it – trying to prank Charlie back – but now that I'm thinking about it again, she really did become convinced that it offered some kind of power. You probably don't remember, but was she always interested in mystical things?'

It's my turn to shrug. The few memories I have of Mum are of a woman whose smile could brighten a room.

'Anyway, I think maybe it was a mix of exhaustion from hiking and her feeling guilty about leaving you behind that was messing with her mind. I sensed something was wrong, and I tried to encourage her to take a rest, but it only seemed to make her more determined to complete the hike. She was incredibly stubborn,' he adds with a smile. 'I guess that explains where you get it from.'

'Do you think that's why she ran away from camp?'

'That's the only way I can explain it,' he says, taking a sip from his drink when it's placed in front of him. 'We were nearing the end of the hike, and had every reason to get back to you, but there just seemed to be something playing on her mind.'

I can't say why, but I still feel like there's more he's not saying, but Bruce is a closed book when I ask him questions about what happened in the days before she bolted. His answers are always the same – almost word for word – as if they're a lie he's spent years rehearsing. But why would he lie? He had nothing to gain from Mum not returning, and if anything became a makeshift parent. I guess he's trying to protect me, but I'm not a child any more. One way or another, I need to crack the wall he's putting up.

I collect my cup from the counter and savour the cool liquid through the straw, bracing myself for the heat as we step out and slowly make our way back to the car. It's nearly midday and it definitely feels like July in the UK, and I realise that if I am going to stay for longer, I really should purchase some more clothes.

I'm about to suggest as much to Bruce, when I spot a figure at the far side of the car park. He is standing close to one of two enormous dumpsters, but he's staring straight at us.

'We should probably get going,' I suggest to Bruce, as the figure stops what he's doing and starts striding across the car park towards us. There's something about his speed that's unsettling.

Bruce hasn't noticed and is reading something on his phone.

'Bruce, can you unlock the car, please?' I say, louder this time.

He glances up, confusion on his face, and fiddles about in his pocket, searching for the keys.

The figure is wearing a navy-blue jumpsuit, open at the middle, revealing an enormous tattoo of a lion's head on his hairless chest. His head also looks clean-shaven, and he appears to be eating a bruised banana that I sense he recovered from the dumpster. I can't stop picturing the figure I saw eating from the wounded cow on my way back from Darby, and suddenly Bruce's mention of ghost stories doesn't seem so fictitious.

The beep of the car unlocking breaks the silence, and I jump in, inadvertently leaving my drink on the roof of the car. I quickly lock the door as the figure's shadow falls across my window. When I look out of the window, he's staring in at me, sipping from my drink.

'Your mom go missing from here?' he calls out. 'I might know what happened to her.'

31

NORA

September 1993, Appalachian Trail, New Hampshire, USA

We do what we have to do.

Snake's words play over in Nora's head as if she's only just heard them, even though it's been almost three days since she saw him remove the shiny weapon from his waistband. Three days of her trying to get just two moments alone with Bruce to tell him about what she saw without sounding like a crazed madwoman. But it's been impossible with him spending the last forty-eight hours in self-imposed segregation from the rest of the group. And then with

Ken coming down with the same excruciating stomach bug, they've barely managed to trek ten miles.

Writing about it in her journal has been the only way to get it clear in her mind, but she doesn't want the others to read the detailed accounts she's written about them.

Charlie is no use, trying to relive his youth, spending every waking minute with his two new best friends. She's sure Snake and Weasel are just humouring him, and whenever she's tried to subtly suggest they move on with their own hike, both told her they're only happy to lend a hand, after all, they'll need help with navigating to less crowded spots so they don't spread the virus.

Back home, Nora would have treated a bad case of gastroenteritis with plenty of fluids and rest. She would have consigned Bruce to bed, only to come out in a bathroom emergency. But when you're being sponsored thousands of pounds to complete a hike through a remote wilderness, and you've agreed to a fairly strict timeline, resting is not an option.

Since starting the hike, a good day means the group completing eighteen miles over fairly even terrain. But since the dam on Bruce's bowels was breached, they've barely managed six miles a day, which means they're now behind schedule. They've not yet passed the point of no return, and with some extended day hikes, reaching Mount Katahdin by the end of next week is feasible, but not at the current rate.

And no sooner does Bruce start to show signs of being on the mend, she finds herself darting for the bushes, hoping to stay downwind of the others. This is the sixth time she's had to squat and gurgle and she's certain there can't be anything solid left inside.

'Has anyone seen Nora?' she hears Bruce shouting.

'I'm back here,' she groans in response, as her gut contracts.

She hears footsteps wading through tall grass nearby, indicating one of the group is approaching.

'No,' she gurns, poking out an arm and willing whoever it is not to come any closer.

It's bad enough the rest of the group knowing what she's doing without one of them witnessing the grim reality. Yet still the footsteps continue.

'Guys, seriously,' she yells as her gut cramps again.

She is ducking behind a boulder, but the footsteps are still coming from behind.

She clenches and grabs for a handful of green leaves, praying they're not poisonous and vowing never to take toilet paper for granted again. She just manages to get her underwear and trousers up before a pair of figures stumble out from behind the low-hanging branches.

She opens her mouth to protest, but it hangs limp as she sees the startled faces of Brynjar and Inga staring back at her. Brynjar studies her in silence as if trying to place her face, and then the bell clearly rings as his features soften and indecision becomes a warm smile.

'You're the British lady,' he says, nudging Inga with his arm.

The smell of what's hidden by the long grass wafts across in the air. Nora wills the wind not to send it towards the two newcomers. Do they realise what she's been doing?

'Um, yes, that's right,' she replies, sidestepping from the evidence and hoping they mirror her move. 'I'm surprised to see the two of you again. I thought you'd be long gone. You overtook us weeks ago.'

'We stopped over at one of the towns,' Brynjar says coyly, as if he's hiding some top government secret that only the two of them know.

She continues to sidestep, relieved to put distance between herself and the smell.

'Shall we tell her?' Brynjar says, beaming at Inga, who nods eagerly in response. 'We got married!'

They both raise their left hands into the air as if proof was required.

'Oh, congratulations to you both! That's wonderful news.'

They look into each other's eyes. 'Thank you. We've been engaged forever, and were going to get married when we got home anyway, but then Inga asked why we're waiting, and I couldn't think of a reason, so we found a town with a court house and filled in the paperwork. It was easy and now we are one.'

Nora averts her eyes as they share a long and passionate kiss.

'Oh, here you are,' Bruce says coming around the corner with Charlie, but then is somewhat surprised to see Brynjar and Inga staring back at him. 'The Norwegians.'

They wave.

Snake, Weasel and Ken are next to appear, and Nora really doesn't want to watch the 'just married' re-enactment again.

'We should get going,' she says peeling away, careful to keep distance between herself and the others. 'Congratulations to the two of you again, and good luck with the rest of your hike.'

'Oh, wait, we didn't tell you the craziest part yet,' Brynjar says, squeezing Inga's hand tightly. 'A day or two after we were married, we were arrested and held in a local jail because they thought we'd held up the bank in another town.'

Nora blinks several times.

'It was crazy,' Brynjar continues. 'The morning after we'd married, we were coming back from breakfast at a café when a sheriff came and arrested us and confiscated our packs. Said he'd been looking for two masked hikers who had robbed a bank and that they'd had a tip-off about us. He wouldn't let us speak and put us in back of two different cars. My mind was like is this a bad dream? It was only when we showed them the marriage certificate and they spoke to the registrar that we were allowed to go. The security guard at the bank said the robbers looked like hikers, and so the sheriff is speaking to everyone that passes through to find the culprits.'

Nora's eyes immediately fall on Snake and Weasel who now appear to be trying to hide behind Ken and the nearest tree. She looks away, keen not to let on that she now knows the real reason they've been so keen to stick around. There's part of her that wants to point the finger, but she can't be sure Snake won't pull out his gun and shoot them all. If it's fully loaded, he has six shots, plenty to take care of the problem. She doesn't want to endanger the newlyweds as well, but is more determined than ever to share her concerns with Bruce as soon as she can.

'Don't let us keep you,' Nora says. 'Probably safer for you to get ahead of us as well, as we've got a sickness bug.'

Brynjar immediately lifts the scarf from around his neck and presses it against his mouth and nose. Inga does the same. Nora and the others step aside, allowing them to pass, before re-joining the path themselves.

Snake and Weasel must already be wondering whether any of the group have linked them to the robbery, and so she waits until they're further ahead with Charlie, before hurrying over to Bruce and whispering for him to hang back.

'Is everything okay?' he asks, keeping a safe distance between them, hoping to avoid a repeat of the illness.

Nora glances towards Charlie and the others, but the path has diverged to the right and she can no longer see them.

'Snake and Weasel are... that is to say, I *believe* they're the bank robbers. I overheard them talking the other day and they were saying something about keeping a low profile and how nobody would bother them if they believed they were part of a larger group.'

Bruce frowns. 'What is your problem with them? First you moaned about them smoking a bit of weed, then I heard from Ken that you reckoned they were the ones who brought the bug into camp—'

'It didn't hit until after their arrival,' she interrupts, 'and how come neither of them have been sick?'

'Doesn't mean they gave it to me. Charlie's not been ill yet either, and he's probably spent more time with them than the rest of us!'

'Well, how do you explain Snake's gun?'

Bruce's eyes widen. 'How do you know he has a gun?'

'I saw him with it.'

'When?'

'The other night.'

He raises his eyebrows. 'And you're only just telling me now?'

'I've been trying to tell you since I saw it, but it's been impossible to get you alone.' She sighs. 'Andy and Joanna warned us that they were trouble, and I think they were right. We need to ditch them as soon as possible, but without letting on that we know what they've done.'

'They're many things, but I don't think they're killers.'

'You didn't hear Snake's threat the other night.'

A twig snaps loudly and they start, turning to see Snake, Weasel, Ken and Charlie staring back at them.

'Now, you really shouldn't be so smart,' Snake says quietly, slowly shaking his head. 'We were going to leave you people and be on our way after tonight, but now you've gone and connected the dots. You really don't leave us any choice.'

He reaches behind his back and pulls out the handgun.

32

JESS

April 2023, Heaven's Gate, New Hampshire, USA

There's mashed banana smeared against the side of his cheek where he's been eating so quickly, and his stare is so intense that I'm forced to look away. And yet, there's a mania in those eyes that I'm sure I've seen before. I can hear Bruce yelling for the guy to get away from the car from the safety of the driver's side.

'I said I might know what happened to your mom,' the guy repeats, and it's this, and a nagging sense of familiarity, that makes me look back at him.

The truth you seek will bring nothing but trouble. Your

life out here is trapped in a bubble. If you see a gun, run, run, run.

My eyes widen as the words explode like fireworks in my head. It can't be, but as I continue to look at the face of the man slurping my Frappuccino, I realise it is the guy who confronted me in the diner yesterday morning, before I'd even made it to Rockston. The shock of blue hair is gone, as is the nose ring, but if it isn't him then he has a doppelganger. I don't believe in concepts like fate and destiny, but I do believe that everything happens for a reason. My inner journalist can't accept that it's merely coincidence that Chester has now reappeared in my life.

As I lower the window, the breath catches in my throat at the smell of rotten food wafting in off his jumpsuit. 'What do you know about my mum?' I say, gagging in the process.

He rests his forearms on the top of the car, and leans closer. 'She go missing from near here?'

I nod, conscious that this guy could be anyone, and I don't want to feed him too much information in case he's trying to hook me in a confidence scam of some kind.

'Then *they* probably took her,' he replies matter-of-factly.

'They?'

'The mountain people.'

The woman who rescued me yesterday said he was on day release from a mental health facility and had had his medication mixed up. He certainly seems less out of it today, but that doesn't necessarily mean he won't become violent if provoked.

'They take all sorts of people,' he continues, taking two steps back from the side of the car, and bouncing into a burst of star jumps.

The car shakes as Bruce clambers in, slamming and locking the doors. 'Let's get out of here.'

'They've been taking people from these towns for years,' Chester calls at us, between jumps.

Bruce starts the engine, but I press my hand against his as he attempts to put the car into reverse. 'No, wait a second.'

I lean my head out of the window. 'What did you just say?'

It's difficult to hear his response over the sound of the engine, so I do the unthinkable and get out. The Frappuccino is back on the roof where I left it, so I collect and carry it over to Chester.

'Please finish the drink,' I say, handing it to him.

He smiles and takes a long slurp through the straw. Bruce is hurrying to get out and to come over to us, but I resist his hands as they try to pull me away.

'Your name's Chester, right?' I say.

He looks at me quizzically. 'Are you from the hospital?'

I shake my head. 'No, no, we met yesterday. At the diner. Do you remember?'

He frowns. 'Yesterday? Sorry, I was a bit out of it yesterday. The doctors messed up my meds. Did I hurt you?'

I shake my head gently, my stance softening. 'Gave me a bit of a scare, but no, you didn't hurt me.'

He scrunches his nose. 'Yeah, I can go a bit cuckoo when I'm off my meds. All better now, though.'

Taking in the stained jumpsuit, I'm not sure I'd agree with that statement.

'This is my friend Bruce,' I continue. 'Bruce, this is Chester.'

Neither proffers a hand to shake.

'You two married?' Chester asks.

'No. Bruce is... Bruce was a friend of my mum's.'

He snickers at this. 'Good, because you're definitely hotter than him.'

'Chester, did you lose someone to them as well?'

'No, we know the rules, and if you follow the rules then they won't come for you.'

'What rules?'

'You know: *the rules.*'

I guess, because I can still picture yesterday's outburst, there's an element of condescension in my tone,
but it's better to be safe than sorry. 'We're not from
around here, Chester. We're from England, so we
don't know what the rules are.'

'Don't go in the woods after dark is the main one.
They don't take people in the daytime, because they
don't want you to see them. But if you do *have* to go in
the woods at night, then you have to remember three
things: if you see something, no you didn't; if you hear
something, no you didn't; if someone calls your name
– don't look, run.'

A shiver runs the length of my spine. It's the same
warning Isaac gave me when I first landed in Maine.
'Who taught you these rules, Chester?'

'My grandma, but everyone around here knows
them. Break the rules and you're fair game. But I'm
careful, and I have my own place in the woods now. I
had a friend cast a hex on it to keep me safe when I'm
not at the hospital. You want to see it?'

Instinct says yes before I have chance to even consider the question. Chester beams proudly, and heads
off back towards the dumpsters. I feel Bruce's cau-
tionary hand on my shoulder.

'Are you seriously considering going with this
guy?'

I tap his hand. 'I've been here a day and Chester is the second person to suggest someone within these mountains may have taken Mum. Everyone else has denied she was ever here. What do you suggest?'

'Are you guys coming?' Chester calls out, now some distance away.

Bruce relents with a groan, and we hurry across the car park where Chester is pointing at a rucksack beside the dumpster. The odour of rotting food is stronger here, and I have to breathe through my mouth in an effort to combat it.

'Can one of you carry that for me?'

'What's in it?' Bruce asks, eyeing it suspiciously.

'Groceries.'

With that, Chester hoists a second bag onto his shoulder and leads us to a hole cut in the fence that separates the car park from the forest beyond it. Chester ducks through the hole and I follow, taking the bag from Bruce so he can crawl through.

'This is a bad idea,' he mutters, but I'm more interested in what Chester has to say.

'Can you tell me more about the other people who've gone missing?' I ask, hurrying to catch up with him as he crosses through plants and bushes as if they're not even there. For someone who seemed so uncoordinated yesterday, he clearly knows where he's heading.

'I can do better than that: I can *show* you.'

This triggers an alarm in my head, and I try to ignore the image that we're going to suddenly arrive in some unofficial cemetery surrounded by bones and handmade tombstones.

The forest is unwieldly, and it really is a struggle to keep up with Chester as he ducks below low-hanging branches, and jumps to avoid tree roots poking out of the ground.

Is this what it was like for Mum when she was hiking the trail?

I'm out of breath when we finally make it to a clearing, and am astounded by the shack before us. It isn't much larger than a garage, and appears to be made from clay and wood as best as I can tell. The roof is a series of interlaced branches over a canopy of some kind. There are holes for windows, but no glass, though there are also shutters, presumably to keep out bad weather. There is a smaller wooden shack beside the property, with a run-off cut into the muddy floor, which I can only assume is the latrine. It reminds me of the kind of den Ashley and I would make at the far end of her parents' long and narrow garden when we were kids.

Chester pulls open the door to the shack, if door is the right word: it's made out of some kind of tarpaulin, stretched across a thin wooden frame, lightweight, but strong against the elements. Inside the cabin, it's roomier than I'm expecting. Immediately to the left is a stove linked to a small gas bottle; the kind I've seen attached to Ashley's patio heater. Beside that is a cooling box, and a shelf with two ceramic plates, two bowls, and two plastic drinking cups. Then there are two pans, one large, one small, and a tray of mixed cutlery.

To my right I see a small round table made out of a large tree stump, around which are two smaller stumps or stools. At the rear of the cabin there are two hammocks secured to hooks in the clay walls. The floor is warm and hard, but is essentially dry mud and clay. I can't deny the homely feel to it.

'Home sweet home,' Chester says, taking the holdall from Bruce, who is sweating worse than me, and looks grateful to have been relieved of his burden.

Chester invites us to sit on the stumps, whilst he proceeds to empty the bags. He removes a carton of sweetened almond milk, only a day past its date, or so he comments. Tinned custard, desiccated coconut, and baked beans. It really is quite the haul.

'Did you collect all of this from the dumpsters?' I

ask, and he nods as if I've asked a basic maths question.

'My grandma used to say one person's trash is another's treasure,' he chimes.

I wonder as to the legality of dumpster diving over here, but don't want to upset him. The final item he extracts is a box of cookies, which he proceeds to open and place on the stump-table between us.

'Help yourselves. Can I make you coffee?'

Despite the shade provided by the canopy roof, it's still sweltering inside the shack, and we both pass, also not entirely sure where he would find water to boil. I can't imagine he has many guests come to visit, and that might be why he's buzzing around the place, constantly checking if we're comfortable or need anything.

'You said you'd show us the people who went missing?' I press gently, and he snaps his fingers together with glee, disappearing behind a curtain at the rear of the shack, emerging a moment later with a large bundle of papers. He places them on the table in front of me, and hovers nearby, waiting for me to look through them.

The top sheet of yellowing paper is a newspaper cut-out, but I can't see the name of the journal. The headline reads:

THE MAN WHO WALKED INTO THE SMOKY MOUNTAINS BUT NEVER WALKED OUT

It talks of a hiker called Dan Trebine, thirty-eight, who was last seen on Monday, 3 July 1978, having left a message on his sister's answering machine, simply saying, 'Don't follow me.' Several key hours had passed before anyone realised he hadn't turned up for his night shift at the factory, and so Tennessee troopers were late starting their search. His car was found abandoned less than a mile from the Great Smoky Mountains National Park two days later. A stack of unpaid bills were recovered from his rented apartment in Maryville, but Trebine has not been heard from since. No witnesses have ever come forward to say they saw him on the Appalachian Trail.

It's a story I'm vaguely familiar with, having spent several months searching for other missing persons stories from the area. I seem to recall I dismissed this story's relevance as it was fifteen years before Mum's disappearance and several states away at the southern entrance of the AT. At the time, I was looking for clues as to who might have killed Mum, but maybe it was a mistake to dismiss it out of hand so quickly.

'They took him, I reckon,' Chester says confidently, reaching for one of the cookies. 'Anyone who goes into these woods and doesn't come out, you can almost guarantee that *they* took them.'

Bruce raises a sceptical eyebrow while I skim through the rest of the pages, scribbling down names and dates on a draft email on my phone to check later.

'What can you tell me about *them*?' I ask Chester, but he doesn't answer, instead staring out of the window, and nodding as if listening to someone talking.

'You have to go now,' he says, scooping up the clippings, and disappearing back behind the curtain. 'It will be dark soon and you need to get back to your car.'

It's not yet 1 p.m., I want to say, but Chester has become decidedly agitated, and I'm remembering the way he was waving his arms around frantically yesterday, so Bruce and I thank him for his time and head out of the shack.

The last thing we hear is Chester shouting, 'Don't go in the woods after dark!'

33

NORA

September 1993, Appalachian Trail, New Hampshire, USA

Bruce takes a tentative step in front of Nora, spreading his arms as if trying to put a protective force field around them. Nora's eyes don't leave the gun in Snake's hand, as the sun glints off the barrel.

Before any of them can react, Snake grabs Ken and kicks the legs from beneath him, forcing him to his knees, and placing the gun's barrel to his temple. 'If any of you have anything you want to say to Ken, I suggest you say it quickly.'

Ken's face drains of all colour, and his eyes stare

pleadingly back at the group, willing one of them to do something – anything – to get the gun away from his temple.

'Whoa, there's no need for any of this,' Charlie says, self-appointed mediator. 'We haven't seen or heard anything incriminating. If anyone asks, we never met you guys. And we don't even know your real names, so it's not like we can tell the police or sheriff anything anyway, is it? I don't care if you robbed a bank. And in the grand scheme of things, it's not a big deal. But if you shoot us, then you'll have committed a felony and you'll be hunted until you're caught. Do you really want to spend the rest of your lives behind bars?'

Nora's heart breaks as she sees a damp patch spread across the crotch of Ken's shorts.

'He's right,' Bruce chips in, his voice an octave higher than any of them are used to. 'The sheriff doesn't know that you two are guilty, nor where you are. I'm with Charlie on this one – we *all* are – just go and you'll have no trouble from us.'

He nods at Nora, encouraging her to echo his thoughts.

'Yes, no trouble from any of us,' she says, adding a weak smile.

Snake draws back the gun's hammer with a menacing thwack, and Ken's whimpers grow louder.

'P-please, I have a family. I have t-two sons,' he says, his eyes welling up with tears.

'Dude, I think they have a point,' Weasel says, slapping the back of his hand against Snake's shoulder. 'At best they're three days from getting back to Heaven's Gate if they're going to inform on us, and I'm not sure any of them want to cross Dead Man's Passage any time soon. So we have a few days' grace to get away before they can tell anyone they saw us. I don't want to spend the rest of my life on the run, dude. I got college next year, and my mom and dad will be pissed off if they have to watch another son being hauled off to prison.'

Snake lowers the weapon, and leans closer to him, so they can talk quieter. 'If we kill them and bury the bodies, nobody is going to come looking for them or us.'

'They will,' Nora quickly shouts, only catching the last part of their conversation. 'If we don't make it to Mount Katahdin by the end of next week, all the people back home are going to question what happened. It'll be an international incident so you won't be safe going anywhere. We're doing this for charity, don't forget. Our progress is being tracked nationwide on UK television, so if we don't check in at the next town, they'll know instantly that there's a problem, and you won't even make it to the next state before your pictures and trail names are plastered all over the media.'

She has no idea where the bluff has come from, and she wills Ken and Bruce not to undermine it.

Snake extends his arm and points the gun in her direction. She has no idea how good a shot he is, or whether he'd miss from that distance, but it isn't a chance she's prepared to take.

'Killing us only worsens things for you. Do us all a favour, and go while you still can. The longer you hang around here, the more likely it is that someone else will come across you.'

'So maybe we just kill you and don't hide the bodies. No grave digging means we can get going as soon as you're dead. And if we do kill you, nobody will know that *we* did it. There's nothing to connect us to you.'

'The Norwegians,' Bruce pipes up. 'They saw you with us, and when the police recover the bodies, they'll be able to narrow the time of death. Depending on how quickly they catch you, they might find gunshot residue on your hands and clothing, which is the equivalent of leaving a sign saying, "I did it".'

Snake looks back at his friend, and it's clear to Nora that he is also against this plan.

Snake has lowered his arm. Against her better judgement, Nora decides to chance her luck. Reaching down, she grabs a handful of small pebbles and hurls them at him, hoping to cause a distraction allowing one of their group – or even Weasel – to wrestle the gun from him.

But the surprise causes Snake's muscles to twitch and the gun fires, and Nora dives to the ground, wincing as something sharp strikes her side.

He drops it instantly, shocked that it has gone off, and Charlie quickly snatches it up, the tables finally turned. He points it at Snake and Weasel, though Nora has no doubt he wouldn't use it unless provoked. But then she thinks back to how easily he dispatched the snarling wolf, and doubt clouds her mind.

'What now?' Charlie asks the group.

Ken doesn't answer, still in shock, and yet to get off his knees.

Bruce is the first to speak. 'We should try to get to a phone and contact the police.'

'We're days from a phone,' Charlie counters. 'And we've already lost ground.' He narrows his eyes and looks at Snake and Weasel. 'You two get out of here. We have your gun. And if we see you again, I won't hesitate to use it.'

He shakes the weapon at the two of them, who hightail it away into the trees, leaving the four of them grateful to still be breathing.

'Is everyone okay?' Charlie asks, helping Ken to his feet.

Ken sighs. 'I need to change my trousers, but otherwise fine. Bruce?'

'I'm fine. Nora?'

She's about to say she's fine, but when she tries to stand feels something sharp digging into her side. Her hand instantly shoots to the cause of the pain.

'Nora?' Bruce says again, now twisting around to try to understand why she hasn't responded.

Nora pulls her hand away from her side, disbelieving the warm, sticky red dripping through her fingers. She holds the hand out to Bruce, unable to form the words with her lips. Her vision blurs into a hundred colours, as if someone is holding a kaleidoscope in front of her face.

He rushes over, crashing to his knees and catching her head before it falls back against a rock. 'Oh, Jesus, guys, I think she's been shot. Shit. I need a first aid kit.'

34

JESS

April 2023, Heaven's Gate, New Hampshire, USA

It takes far longer to find our way back to the car park, and maybe it's more luck than judgement in the end.

Is that why Mum never emerged? Did she lose her bearings too?

Bruce has made no secret of his thoughts about Chester and his wild-eyed theory. 'I spent many nights on the AT, and there were no people hiding in the trees waiting to abduct us. It's all just myth and nonsense.'

I don't actually disagree with him. The fears most

of us have are ideas that prey on our insecurities: kids being scared of the dark; monsters under the bed; black cats bringing bad luck. I can't imagine what life has led someone like Chester to abandon the world and hide out in a shack off the beaten track, but I've no doubt he's struggled with his mental health for some time.

That said, there were so many newspaper clippings and notes in his collection, and *something* must have happened to those people. But for those still missing, where are they? Did they lose their lives at the hands of guilty people? It's easier to swallow than the idea that they're still alive and living off grid. I know Mum would have done everything in her power to get back to me. And I'm more determined than ever to find the guilty culprit.

I look back at Bruce, who's puffing and wheezing as he crawls back through the gap in the fence. The smell of rot emanating from the dumpsters is even worse in the midday heat, and we hurry back to the car, but while Bruce opens his door to get in, I remain where I am.

He looks up at me. 'What are you waiting for?'

'The café we were in earlier had free Wi-Fi, right?'

He nods. 'And?'

'*And* I want to dig into some of those names Chester gave me. Come on, you can buy me lunch.'

I don't wait for Bruce to argue, marching purposefully back towards the air-conditioned café, and grabbing the table with two sofas in the window. I don't even look at the menu, instead connecting to their network, and searching for the first name, Jeanette Barnes. It doesn't take long to find what I am looking for:

FORMER OLYMPIC SWIMMER DROWNS IN VIRGINIA LAKE

According to the article, winning silver at the Montreal Olympics in 1976 was Jeanette Barnes's proudest achievement, and had it not been for a major rotator cuff injury, she might have gone on to win gold in Moscow in 1980. Not willing to give up on her athletic dreams, she ploughed her energies into marathon running instead, and her AT hike in 1985 was in preparation for the NYC marathon that same year. On a hot spring afternoon, she and fellow hiker Judith Ramsay decided to cool off in the lake, but as Barnes swam farther from shore, she suddenly vanished beneath the lake's surface and never rose. Despite a desperate rescue attempt from Ramsay,

Jeanette could not be found. Weeks later, the body was dredged, and with no other obvious injury, cause of death was pronounced as drowning.

Bruce drops into the armchair opposite me. 'Find something interesting? You have that excited look in your eyes like when you were a teenager and you first discovered boys.'

'An unexplained drowning in Virginia.'

'Okay. Not a missing person, though.'

He's right, so I search for the next name. 'Here we go, what about twenty-five-year-old Padraig Murphy?'

'What about him?'

'Well, apparently, he told his mother he'd had a calling from God, telling him he needed to hike the AT. He quit the seminary, emptied his savings account, and armed only with basic hiking equipment and a copy of the New Testament, he joined the trail at the northern entrance in Maine. He spoke to numerous hikers about his mission over the following days. But then he simply disappeared within a week of starting. His pack was discovered one hundred miles from the foot of Mount Katahdin, but there was no obvious sign of why he'd left it behind, nor where he'd gone.'

Bruce doesn't respond, instead choosing to stare at the menu standing on the table.

'Didn't you say Mum was hearing voices or seeing things?'

He doesn't answer, eyes glued to the menu.

'Bruce? You said Mum was acting strangely, talking about mysticism, and the like.'

He finally meets my stare. 'Yes, I told you I was worried about her mental state.'

'Well, according to this, Padraig's mother later discovered he'd been recently diagnosed schizophrenic, and that this could have accounted for the calling he'd heard. But get this: his remains have never been recovered. Sound familiar?'

'Of course it does, but it doesn't mean it's connected to what happened to Nora. Yes, I see the similarities, but what that story doesn't give you is an outcome. If the former priest's body was never found, then what happened to him? Is he living in some ramshackle house like Chester? Is that what you think happened to your mum?'

I know he doesn't mean to be so brutal, but I bite my lip anyway.

'I'm sorry.' He eventually sighs. 'Listen, let's order some lunch, and then we can chat some more. I'm having a BLT. You want the same?'

I nod, as I'm more interested in my phone than looking at the menu. Bruce leaves the table and goes to order at the counter, whilst I search the next name on my list.

SEASONED HIKER SUCCUMBS TO HYPOTHERMIA ON MCAFEE KNOB

Park rangers searching for an overdue hiker made a gruesome discovery on Wednesday, January 18, 1995 at a shelter along the Appalachian Trail. Concerned friends had reported seasoned hiker Justin Torrance, 46, missing when he'd failed to rendezvous with them on Saturday night.

The local sheriff was unable to rule out foul play owing to vicious scratches discovered on the victim's back and the fact he was found without clothing or his pack. CSIs have suggested he may have succumbed to an animal attack and then crawled to the shelter, but unable to start a fire, he was powerless to resist the seasonably cold temperatures. To date his belongings have yet to be recovered.

A wild animal attack would definitely be a palatable explanation for why Mum never exited the AT, but that doesn't explain why her remains have never been recovered, unless it was so far off the main trail that nobody has yet stumbled across them. And yet I know from what Bruce has told me that the official search for Mum lasted several weeks, and involved a huge team of police and rescuers scouring the trail for clues.

Bruce once told me a story about them coming under attack from a pack of wolves early on in their hike, but them overcoming it when Charlie found a rifle in a nearby cabin. He never did tell me what happened to that rifle.

UNSOLVED MURDERS ON BLOOD MOUNTAIN

The bodies of singer Bernadette Poisson, 65, and her partner Collette Benoit, 59, were found in the shadow of Blood Mountain a little after sunrise on Saturday, September 4, 1999. On holiday from their native Paris, the pair had decided to scale the mountain over a long weekend stay on the Appalachian Trail, before they were due to head to New York City where Poisson was set to appear on Broadway. The discovery was made by hikers who'd risen early to watch the sunrise, and they immediately contacted authorities; however, the pair were pronounced dead at the scene. They'd suffered fatal knife wounds to the throat and sternum. Apparatus found abandoned at the scene suggested this may be ritualistic, though no weapon has been recovered. No witnesses have come forward to say they heard or saw what happened.

I hear Chester's words in my head: *They've been taking people from these towns for years...* for their blood sacrifices?

I shudder at the thought. Just because I don't believe in mysticism and magic doesn't mean others don't, even if they are deluded in those beliefs. How many millions have continued to believe in Christianity for centuries based purely on word-of-mouth accounts? Rightly or wrongly, faith is faith.

Could Mum have stumbled off the trail and wound up at the hands of the same people who murdered Bernadette and Collette? I search up the next of Chester's names.

UNMARKED GRAVE REVEALS DEADLY SECRET

On Friday, April 11, 2008, a group of hikers stumbled upon a young man, murdered and lying in a shallow grave near the Cow Camp

Gap, which is part of the George Washington National Forest. Minus head, hands and feet, and with no identification documents, the cadaver was processed by a team from the FBI, but its identity remains a mystery. The DNA recovered has been shared with missing persons databases globally, but no match has been made. The surgical removal of body parts led investigators to conclude that the death was not the result of a wild animal attack.

If this is the only news that Chester has been reading for all these years, I can begin to understand why he's so willing to accept the dangers of 'the mountain people' as he called them. There's no updated story to suggest the body of this man has ever been identified in the last fifteen years. I can only assume Mum's DNA wasn't collected at the time of her disappearance, otherwise Sheriff Whitaker wouldn't have needed to collect a sample of mine.

'Shouldn't be long,' Bruce says, returning to the table. 'Wait, are you okay? You look like you've seen a ghost.'

It's because I've just searched for the final name on my list, and it's like the rug has been pulled from beneath me.

BEWARE THE BLOOD-RED EYES

The final words of the victim of a vicious wild animal attack are enough to make the hairs stand up on the back of your neck. Alicia Chivers, 45, from Vermont was found strung up to a fence a short distance from the famed Appalachian Trail, warning of 'blood-red eyes'. The victim of a prank gone wrong, or something more sinister? Paramedics who treated her at the scene described slashes consistent with claws, but such was the blood loss, she was pronounced dead at the scene. The Manchester sheriff is now appealing for any witnesses who can help trace Ms Chivers' final movements.

I show Bruce the story, and catch him up on the others.

'What if Chester's right and someone in the woods did take her?'

Bruce buries his face in his hands, and for a moment I think he's going to chastise me for getting ahead of myself, but when he does finally lower his hands, I can see the worried lines at his temples. 'There's something I've never told you – never told *anyone* – and it's about your mum: she was shot not far from here.'

My mouth drops open. 'Shot by who?'

He's perched uncomfortably on the end of the armchair. 'A pair of crooks we happened upon called Snake and Weasel.'

I don't know how to react. My mind is racing with so many questions, and the only thing I can think is that I always suspected Bruce was keeping something from me, but I never expected it to be this.

He offers out a hand in a calming gesture. 'Before you overreact, the gunshot didn't kill her, but I now wonder whether what happened after may have played a part in her running off.'

35

JESS

April 2023, Heaven's Gate, New Hampshire, USA

'You have to bear in mind,' Bruce says, 'seeing that much blood, I was panicking. The three of us didn't know what to do. None of us were medically trained. Ken had some first aid experience, but she was losing so much blood and we were in the middle of nowhere. Bandages and gauze were doing little to stem the flow, and I thought she was going to die there in my arms.'

I can see his eyes watering, but I don't want to interrupt him while he's finally opening up.

'From nowhere, this Stetson-wearing guy with

hair as white as snow appeared, saying his name was Billy-Ray Nelson, and that he could remove the bullet and save Nora, but we had to trust him. He said he lived off grid and didn't have a phone, and we were several days from the nearest town, so we had little choice but to agree to go with him.

'He took us off the trail, down through the trees, in much the same way as Chester did earlier. It was clear he knew where he was going. Charlie and Ken said it was a bad idea, with Charlie fearing the hillbillies he'd seen in *Deliverance*. I carried your mum as I felt responsible for her, and tried to ignore all the painted signs warning us to turn back and return to the trail. He eventually led us to a cabin made from scavenged fence panels and large rocks; more like a den than a house. A couple of old oil drums were propping up one of the fence panels, and at the front a large waterproof sheet covered half the property, tied to the ground using taut guy ropes. Outside the front of the cabin was a rotting wooden bookcase, bearing the weight of the skulls of small animals: chipmunks, skunks, and deer. Branches, shaved of their bark, propped up the other fence panel, but the whole cabin looked like it would collapse under the pressure of a heavy sneeze.'

Bruce pauses as a waitress carries over our sandwiches, but neither of us has any interest in eating them right now.

'He had this dog, the size of a small bear, with enormous teeth and a loud bark, but it quietened the moment he told it to. He made Charlie and Ken wait outside, even though it had started to rain, but I was relieved they were nearby in case anything bad happened inside. I think I was less fearful for myself than I was for your mum. She seemed to be passing in and out of consciousness, and when I put her down on his makeshift table, she was so pale. He told me he had to extract the bullet or she'd die, and then proceeded to use a hunting knife to cut it out. It was like something out of a nightmare, and even now it feels more like a dream than reality.'

I can see how much he is struggling to recount this story, and it's hard to keep control of my frustration that this is the first time I'm hearing it. But if I criticise now, I may never learn the truth.

'He had this jar containing a goo substance as black as tar. He claimed it was a kind of homemade sanitiser, but that it was made purely with natural ingredients, which is why it smelled like an old gym sock.' He offers a thin smile at me. 'It made my eyes water it was so bad. He cleaned his knife and the wound with the stuff, and I was too scared to stop him. In the back of my mind, I kept thinking that I was deluding myself to believe this guy was actually going to save her life, but hope was all I had. I'm certain she would have died had we tried to get her back to Heaven's Gate.'

He lifts up his sandwich, considers it a moment, and then returns it to his plate.

'He managed to get the bullet out, but she'd lost so much blood, and we were miles from the nearest hospital, and nobody knew what blood group she was anyway. I was sure she was going to die on that old table. Billy-Ray reckoned an able-bodied person on foot could probably get to the highway in a day and a half, and maybe hitch a ride to the nearest ER, but carrying an injured person, it would be double that. He said she needed to rest and recover, but that the blood loss could still kill her.'

He fixes me with a desperate stare. 'You have to understand: I had no other choice. I'm sure in my position you would have made the same call.'

'What did you do, Bruce?' I whisper as the words stick in my throat, dreading his answer.

He reaches for a paper napkin and wipes the corners of his eyes. 'Billy-Ray told me there was one chance to save her. I thought he was trying to convince me to part with money, and I swear in that instance I would have paid any price to save your mum. But he didn't want money. Instead, he asked me if I was religious. Such an odd question! I said I wasn't, and he told me that what he had to offer required faith.

'He then proceeded to tell me about the history of the Appalachian Mountains. He spoke of ancient gods bestowing gifts to the communities residing here. He said it's why the trees and plants continue to thrive after so many centuries. I know what you're thinking – that it's all mumbo jumbo nonsense – and I thought the same thing. But then he spoke about medicines being handed down, made from the same crops and minerals provided by these gods, and he said he had something specific he could give her. Said it was packed with iron and promoted healthy blood cell production. I pushed him for what was in it – worried that he was going to poison her – but he wouldn't say. Told me it was a secret he couldn't share.'

I don't like where this is heading, and the more pained Bruce looks, the more I'm fearful of what he did. I'm suddenly reminded of Isaac's warning at the airport: *all manner of strange goings-on in those parts, you mark my words.*

'She'd lost so much blood, and he wouldn't let me

speak to Charlie or Ken. I had to make a decision. She would have died if I hadn't tried something.'

My frustration can simmer no more. 'What did you do, Bruce?'

Tears stream from his cheeks, as he searches my face for empathy. 'Oh, Jesus, I told him to give her the medicine.'

36

JESS

April 2023, Heaven's Gate, New Hampshire, USA

I snatch up the keys from the table without another word, my vision blurring as I hurry towards the door to the café. I can just about hear Bruce calling my name as I race into the overwhelming humidity, but the rush of blood to my ears drowns out all other background sounds.

He lied to me. He's been lying to me for thirty years!

I trusted Bruce, even though I've always felt the version of events he painted wasn't quite the whole picture, and I am done listening to his lies. A car horn bares somewhere to my right as I stumble across the dusty road, and back into the supermarket car park. The rental is where we left it, and the engine fires up with a roar. Flooring the accelerator, I skid out of the car park just as Bruce is trying to cross the street, and he's lucky I manage to swerve out of his way.

I never should have come, and now I desperately want out of these mountains. Wiping my eyes with my wrists, I have no idea where I'm going until I see the 'You're now leaving Heaven's Gate' sign on the road up ahead.

There's never been any mention of Mum being shot. Not from Bruce. Not from Charlie. Not from Ken. I have read countless articles from that time about her disappearance and on subsequent anniversaries, but nowhere have I read that she was shot. And my instinct tells me that isn't the only truth Bruce has been keeping from me.

I see it now. All the years of supporting me weren't born out of any duty, but out of guilt. And can I even believe his claim that two random thieves – Weasel and Snake, or so he claims – were responsible? For all I know, it could have been Charlie or Ken, or even Bruce himself. All I can see now is that she died at their hands and they've spent the last thirty years covering it up. And *that's* the real reason for Bruce suddenly showing up in Rockston.

I wipe my eyes again, my anger boiling over as my brain slots the final puzzle pieces into place.

He must have panicked when I showed him the article originally, and figured he was finally rumbled. And then when Ashley told him I'd flown across, he knew I'd stumble upon his lies and he came across to try to mitigate the damage. Feeding me lines about two random people I've never heard of – couldn't he have created more convincing names for them? – so I won't figure out the truth.

How could I have been so gullible for so long?

I pull the car over to the side of the road when I can no longer see the outline of Heaven's Gate in the rear-view mirror, and I bury my face in my hands. Hot tears sting my eyes as I think about my poor mum left in an unmarked grave somewhere out here for thirty years. I need to bring her home, and I will do everything in my power to make those responsible for her death face justice.

But right now, I need help, and I don't trust Bruce. I don't want to believe that he lured me out of Rockston to silence my questions once and for all, but I'm not going to make the same mistakes that Mum did. There is one person who has offered help with no demand for anything in return. Unlocking my phone, I find the text message DeWalt sent, and punch the co-ordinates into the satnav.

* * *

Almost an hour of driving through twisty, winding roads, and I finally arrive at another town, but this one has none of the glamour of Rockston. The main strip of shops are all shuttered, bar one, which appears to be a liquor store, based on the posters plastered on the shop windows. It's like a ghost town, and even as I follow the satnav's instructions and arrive at a residential area, there's no sign of anyone on the street, nor any cars parked on driveways. The lack of people is unsettling, and I'm now beginning to question my choice to come here.

On the phone at O'Reilly's, DeWalt told me it wasn't safe for either of us in Rockston, and that I had to come and meet him here, but I'm not sure it was so smart to come here alone; not that Bruce left me much choice. He was the one who was so persuasive in convincing me not to seek out DeWalt, but maybe that was part of his efforts to cover his tracks.

'Your destination is on the left,' the robotic voice tells me, and I pull over at the corner of a building that looks as though it was once a bank. The brick-work is smeared in different coloured paints; one piece of street art overwritten by another, and by an-other again.

This doesn't seem right, and there's no knowing whether DeWalt is still around. He sent me these co-ordinates last night, but what if he was only here for a short window before moving on? The text message was sent from a private number, so I have no way of replying or phoning him. Every braincell is telling me just to get the hell out of here, but adrenaline keeps me from starting the engine. Exiting the car, I push the end of the key between the index and ring fingers of my right hand, and ball my fist around it, should anyone try to jump out at me.

It's much cooler here, the sky a blanket of light grey cloud, and I actually shiver as I close the car door, and move closer to the abandoned bank build-ing. It is deathly quiet, and the air smells of damp soil and decay.

What happened here?

It's like I've wandered into an alternative universe where mankind has been eviscerated. It's so quiet, and if I had any sense I would get back into the car and abandon this idea, and yet that's what piques my journalistic interest most. What could make an entire town of people disappear and abandon their homes?

I freeze at the sound of a tin clattering somewhere behind me. Turning, I tighten my grip on the keys, but the street behind me is empty. It could easily have been a gust of wind pushing a piece of litter, and yet I suddenly sense I am not the only person to find myself in this strange place. I'm certain the sound came from within the bank building, and as I examine the shutter over the front door, I see that it has been yanked clear of its runners, and is just resting over the door. Lifting the shutter, I'm able to squeeze beneath it, and through the broken glass of the door. Fragments of glass crack beneath my feet as I try to quietly make my way through the darkness.

Switching on the torch on my phone, I shine the beam through the gloom. More graffiti stares back at me from the walls, and yellowing pamphlets advertising loans and credit cards cover the worn carpet. I strain to hear any sound over that of my racing heartbeat, but there's nothing. Moving further into what was once the banking hall, I can see someone has had a good attempt at yanking the ATM from the wall, presumably in search of cash.

I start at a stifled cough, and whip the torch's beam into a gloomy corner. There, beneath large sheets of cardboard, I see a hand reaching to block out the light. I take a tentative step closer, and see now that the man was sleeping before I wandered in. I can't be certain that he isn't armed, nor that he will do me harm, so I take a couple of slow backward steps towards the main doors, but stop the moment he says my name.

He's too far away for the torchlight to properly penetrate the dark corner he's holed up in.

'How do you know my name?' I whisper, and I'm not sure he's heard my question at first.

'I didn't think you were going to show,' he croaks back. 'When you didn't arrive last night, I figured they must have got to you and that I was too late.'

I recognise his voice, and yet it sounds different to what I remember of the phone conversation.

'DeWalt?'

I see him struggle to his feet, and take another two steps backwards, the key between my fingers primed.

'Do you mind if we go outside?' he croaks. 'There's no electricity in here, and we need light.'

My whole body wants to turn and break into a sprint as adrenaline floods my brain, but I picture Bruce's face in the café, and my resolve hardens. If I'm ever to learn the truth about Mum, I'm going to need to take chances.

'W-what do you want from me?' I stammer.

I can see his shadow moving closer to me, but my feet remain fixed.

'I want to help you learn the truth about what happened to your mom, but more importantly, *why*.'

I remain where I am, allowing him to move closer. He's frail, and hunched over, and instinct tells me I'm probably more of a threat to him than he to me, but when he is no more than a foot away from me and I see his face, the breath catches in my throat.

'Isaac?'

37

JESS

April 2023, outskirts of Boar Creek, New Hampshire, USA

He looks even more dishevelled than when I met him at the airport, but I would recognise those warm, tired eyes anywhere. I knew there was something familiar about his voice, but I hadn't placed it at first.

'I don't understand. What are *you* doing here?'

He shields his eyes. 'Would you mind lowering the light?'

I point the phone in the direction of the broken shutter, and hold it up to allow us both to pass back through and into the dusty, but lighter street. It takes several moments for my eyes to adjust, but when they do, I see he is still wearing the same navy coat worn thin at the elbows and shoulders. The grey, wispy beard somehow seems more unkempt than yesterday.

'I tried to warn you not to come here,' he says quietly, every word a struggle.

'I told you: I'm here to find out what happened to my mum. You're the man I spoke to on the phone last night, aren't you? You're DeWalt?'

He nods unsteadily, but looks as though he'll blow away in a sudden gust, and so I take his arm in mine, and lead him to the car, helping him get into the passenger seat, before joining him inside.

'I could have told you who I was at the airport, but I hoped you would heed my warning. When you didn't, I knew I had to intervene, or they'd come for you next.'

'Who's they? I don't understand what is happening here, nor why you're trying to help me.'

He takes a moment to steady his breathing before pulling out a crumpled photograph from the inside pocket of his jacket. He passes it to me. The photograph is of two men in their early twenties. The one on the left must be Isaac, but it isn't clear who the white, ginger-haired man is. They're both dressed in ice hockey shirts, and grinning in that way best friends do in one another's company.

'Jonny and I were inseparable since kindergarten. Attended the same schools, and were due to go to college together, until the summer I convinced him to hike the AT with me.' A solemn frown settles across his features. 'The plan was to hike to the top of Katahdin, so we'd feel like kings on top of the world, but we never made it after he was taken in by them folks in Rockston.'

I turn the image over in my hands, seeing the year 1982 scrawled in the top right corner of the underside.

'What do you mean he was taken in by them?'

Isaac runs a hand over the grey whiskers on his chin. 'When we met yesterday, I warned you there was things go on up in these mountains that folks just don't realise.'

'What kinds of things, Isaac? I'm sorry, but I'm not sure what you're getting at.'

'You've been to Rockston, though, right?'

I nod.

'And what did you think of it?'

My eyebrows knot together. 'It was a pretty town, I suppose; a bit old-fashioned maybe.'

'Looks like the sort of place they make model villages out of, don't it?'

I nod again. 'And?'

'How many churches you see in that town?'

I try to recall, but can't say I noticed any, but then I didn't spend that much time there.

'We only stopped there for a couple of days to rest, but Jonny met this girl and the two of them got talking, and before I knew it, he was telling me he was staying. It was like some switch in his head was flicked. He went from being my best friend and a smart as hell guy, to turning his back on college and his future overnight. I got no other way of describing it. It was like they'd brainwashed him or something. I tried talking to him about it, but he pushed me away. Started dressing different too, and cut himself off from all his friends and family. I was worried about him, but I was already too late.'

'I don't understand what you're telling me, Isaac. Are you saying they were holding him against his will?'

'Once they got their claws into him, it was like his body and mind was taken over by some stranger. I no longer recognised my friend.'

I can hear the sadness in Isaac's voice, but I can't see what any of this has to do with my mum.

'That whole place – every person in Rockston –

they're all part of a cult, and that Sheriff Randy Whitaker is their leader.'

I don't know what to say. My gut instinct is to laugh out loud at the ridiculousness of the statement. When I think of cults, I picture hippies in gowns, with flowers in their hands, offering praise to some ethereal being. Rockston just didn't strike me as that; certainly no communes that I saw. And yet, there is no trace of humour in Isaac's tone or body language. Whether he's right or not, he certainly believes the words he's uttered.

'We tried to get Jonny out,' he continues sombrely. 'Me and Jonny's sister Meryl. We went to Rockston and begged him to come back with us; to see a doctor. But he refused; claimed we were the ones who needed psychiatric help. So, I did what any good friend would, and I took him against his will. I knew that I'd never convince him to come away willingly, not with them all listening in and keeping tabs on us, so I had to get him away from the town to try and talk sense into him.

'I forced him into my car, and brought him here, but back then this place was a thriving mining town. I tried to get him to remember what he'd been like before, showing him old home movies we'd made growing up, but he was having none of it. I booked him in to see a therapist, to get specialist help, but he wouldn't have any of it. Kept saying there was nothing wrong with him and that I was the one who'd lost my mind.'

I give him space to talk. If there's one thing I've learned as a journalist it's that people like to fill silences and reveal far more when they're left to speak freely. But my mind can't stop drifting back to my time in Rockston. The picture-perfect picket fences; the cleanliness; the feeling that life is just so perfect there.

Too perfect.

But thinking about it through this new lens, I can suddenly understand why nobody seemed willing to help when I asked about Mum.

'I refused to drive him back there, kept him locked in my house, praying that he'd snap out of it, but he didn't. And then when I was running out of ideas, he took the decision out of my hands.' He looks away, maybe unwilling to let me see his tears. 'He took his own life in the basement of my house, using a noose fashioned out of torn bedsheets. The Jonny I knew would never have chosen that path; but he did it because they were in his head.'

Several minutes pass, and when it's clear he has nothing further to add, I ask, 'What does all of this have to do with my mum?'

He dabs at his eyes with a handkerchief. 'Before he died, Jonny told me the people of Rockston believe that there are beings in the mountains protecting them. It sounded like mumbo jumbo to me, but he really believed in it too. Referred to the power as some weird name I couldn't even begin to pronounce. Said that in order to keep the beings happy, blood sacrifices had to be made; that they selected their victims by giving them a bracelet, and would then kill them at a festival. It is my belief that your mother was one of their victims, that they killed her as a sacrifice to their gods.'

It sounds so preposterous, and yet I know from history that such cults do exist and that their leaders are able to manipulate their followers into all kinds of menacing acts. It's impossible not to think of David Koresh in Waco as well as Charles Manson and his 'family' in recent history.

'You must have gone to the police, what did they say?'

'I spoke to the Feds, but because Jonny had a history of mental health issues, they didn't take my claims seriously. I've no doubt they would have sent someone to Rockston, but you've seen the place; they hide it well. They cover their tracks too. Two months after Jonny died here, a major storm hit the area. The mine collapsed, killing thousands of men, and the town was abandoned, and with many saying it had been cursed. It was the strangest thing. I don't believe in curses and Voodoo, but it was like someone placed a veil over this town and it died. The money I once had was invested in property here, and I lost everything. But I refuse to leave. I can't allow them to win, and that is why I had to get you out of there, before you became their next victim.'

For someone who says he doesn't believe in mythology, he's not convincing, but I'm not buying the story.

'How did you know I'd be at the airport?'

The question is out of my mouth before I've even thought about it, but I think that's what's been troubling me since I found him inside the abandoned bank.

He sighs heavily, as if he's carrying an enormous burden. 'I have a contact – a friend of sorts – who still lives in Rockston. He feeds me information from time to time, and he was the one who left the note for you to meet me at O'Reilly's. He told me they wanted to lure Nora's daughter to the States and to offer her – *you* – as a sacrifice on the anniversary of her death. They lured you here to kill you, Jess.'

'And what if I don't believe you? Can you prove any of what you've told me today?'

'You can search for my friend Jonny. His full name was Jonathan Kamminsky, and he died on 4 November 1985. Look him up.' I pull out my phone to do just that and see I've missed a dozen calls from Bruce, along with a long text message.

'Trouble?' Isaac asks when he must see my face drop.

'Nothing I can't handle,' I respond, pocketing my phone. 'How do I prove that the sheriff had my mum killed?'

Isaac considers the question a moment. 'I don't think you ever will. They've covered their tracks for this long, and I doubt they'll slip up now. Your mom was one of a long line of people they've abducted and either manipulated into joining their group, or killed for their own ends. I'm sorry to be so blunt, but unless you want to wind up as their next victim, you need to steer clear.'

At least Isaac has given me reason to believe that Bruce may not have killed her, and according to his message, he reckons he can prove she didn't die in his company. I'm so confused about all of this right now. I've known Bruce for most of my life, and I always believed he had my best interests at heart. I want to believe that again. But I won't have him lying to me any more. He either needs to tell me the whole truth or I will sever all ties with him.

'Let me reach out to my contact,' Isaac says as he opens the door and clambers out. 'Maybe there's something he can dig out that will at least prove she was there at some point. I'll let you know if or when I hear anything. But please don't go back there unless you hear from me. Enough innocent blood has been spilled.'

38

___

JESS

April 2023, outskirts of Boar Creek, New Hampshire, USA

I should probably feel guilty as I park on the road outside the café and see Bruce staring forlornly back at me through the window, but I don't. Stealing his keys and abandoning him in Heaven's Gate was both rash and petulant, but the betrayal I felt was valid. Once my dad passed, I wasn't sure where I'd end up, with my sixteenth birthday just passed, and the local authority uncertain what to do with me, but Bruce was like a guardian angel offering me rent-free accommodation. He said it was because he and his wife had separated and he needed the company, but I always felt that was his way of making me feel less like a freeloader.

His generosity allowed me to complete my GCSEs and it was his influence that saw me make the first tentative steps towards journalism. I liked puzzles and writing, and he encouraged me to follow my dreams. It was clear he didn't like to talk about what happened over here, almost as if he was scared to remember, but that didn't stop me asking questions as often as I could, although I was also conscious that he could kick me out at any time.

He became the surrogate parent I needed at a time when I was most vulnerable. Maybe that is why he felt he couldn't tell me about Mum getting shot up here. The way he described the event, I don't think he was at fault, so I just don't understand why he didn't tell me until now.

I kill the engine, but remain in my seat, trying to compose myself. His message said he can prove that she survived the gunshot wound, and based on what Isaac DeWalt has also shared, I've reason to believe him. I will give him a chance to share his proof, and then I'll decide whether to share the rest of what Isaac told me, though I'm not sure I believe it. The concept of human sacrifice goes back to biblical times, but in this day and age, with technology as advanced as it is, and with such ready access to information through the internet, surely people don't still believe in the practice.

That said, it would explain the creepy sensation I had when wandering around the town, asking questions, and showing Mum's picture. Would I want to remember the face of someone I killed?

Bruce waves, and I know it's my cue to face the music. Exiting the car, I take a deep breath before entering the café, and the wall of cool air brings welcome relief. An empty takeaway cup stands on the table in front of Bruce.

'Are you hungry?' he asks, standing, and reaching into his back pocket for his wallet. 'I gave your BLT to a homeless guy I met downtown, as I wasn't sure you'd seen my messages or were even coming back.' He catches himself and offers an apologetic smile. 'You're right to be upset, but I wish you'd let me finish explaining before you took off.'

I haven't eaten since breakfast, but I have no appetite right now, so I sit in silence, and give him the space he's craving.

'You definitely share your mum's headstrong determination,' he says, chuckling lightly in an effort to ease the tension. 'I don't think I've encountered anyone with such resilience, apart from you, of course. And for what it's worth, I'm sorry I've never told you any of this before.'

He sits forward, pressing his hands together in a prayer-like stance, resting his lips momentarily on the tips of his fingers. 'Charlie convinced Ken and me that the authorities didn't need to know about our encounter with Snake and Weasel, and we naively went along with it. I think he was concerned that the police might have looked deeper into his connection with them.'

'His connection?' I interrupt.

He seems thrown by the intrusion, as if he's been rehearsing this part and wasn't expecting to have to improvise. 'Um, yeah, well, they hung out with us for a few nights, and he was smoking pot amongst other things with them, and what we didn't know until your mum vanished is that he was out on licence, and he was convinced they'd look to put him back inside if they suspected he'd been dealing again. He was also paranoid that they'd wrongly think we had something to do with the robberies Snake and Weasel had committed. It was probably all the drugs making him so paranoid. I couldn't see the logic in mentioning what had happened, as I genuinely didn't think it had anything to do with your mum leaving.'

'*Didn't* think? Does that mean you've changed your mind now?'

'Maybe.'

He reaches behind him, and I see now he has the pages I printed at the newspaper office when I was in Darby yesterday.

Gosh, was that really only yesterday? So much has happened since then.

He lays the pages out on the table, and it looks as though he's been reading them as he's circled certain passages. 'Your mum's recovery from the gunshot was nothing short of miraculous. All my panic and worry was unnecessary. After a couple of days, she was strong enough to be moved and I managed to get her to a hospital so the wound could be checked to ensure it didn't become infected, but they were amazed by her recovery. Despite the amount of blood she lost, whatever Billy-Ray gave to her seemed to boost her immunity and even the skin repaired itself in what must have been record time. If I hadn't seen it for myself, I wouldn't have believed it possible. He saved her life.'

'What exactly did he give her?'

'He wouldn't tell me what was in it. Claimed it was something handed down by their elders centuries before.'

I can hear Isaac's voice telling me about Rockston being a cult, but as far as I know Mum and Bruce hadn't made it into Maine at this point. Maybe the cult-like nature spreads further than just Rockston.

'It stank; I can tell you that much about it. It was just as well your mum was barely conscious at the time, as it must have tasted pretty awful too.'

'And you just allowed him to give her this potion without questioning what was in it, or trying it yourself?'

I don't mean to snap at him, but his actions were so reckless.

He holds his palms out in a passive gesture. 'He wouldn't let me. In hindsight, I could have made a hundred alternative choices, but in that moment – with how stressful the situation was – I felt powerless. But,' he turns one of the printed sheets to face me, 'as you can see: it worked.'

I don't recognise anyone in the black and white grainy image at first, but then I see her eyes, and my heart flutters. I don't know how I missed it originally, but there is Mum: one of five apparent revellers above a caption describing the Darby Festival of Light in September 1993. I'd say she looks more distressed than jovial; something close to panic in her eyes, but then it isn't a great printout.

'This was days after she was shot,' Bruce says tri-
umphantly, 'and she doesn't look as though she's suffering, does she?'

I only have his word that the shooting occurred
before this picture was taken, but I have no other
reason to question what I'm seeing.

'I know I could have explained all of this to you
years ago, but there was never a good time. The longer
a lie lasts, the more it becomes truth. I think I'd even
got to the point where I thought maybe I'd just dreamt
the shooting. But then being back here... I don't know,
suddenly the memory is stronger. The sights, sounds
and smells of places can do that.' He pauses and fixes
me with a sincere frown. 'I am sorry I didn't tell you
sooner. I never meant to upset you, but it's time you
know the truth. The *whole* truth.'

I'm suddenly conscious that we're not the only
people in the café, though at the moment nobody appears to be paying us much attention. I shuffle in
closer, not wishing anyone to overhear our conversation.

'I found DeWalt,' I whisper. 'He told me things
about Rockston and the surrounding areas. I'm not
sure how safe we are here.'

He shakes his head dismissively. 'I don't think your
mum died in Rockston, despite what this DeWalt

character will have you believe. While you were away, I started replaying those events in my mind. In Darby, something changed in your mum. I was worried about her mental state before, but she was worse when we left Darby. And now that I'm back here and remembering more things, I think it's possible she was killed by Snake and Weasel.'

The statement throws me. 'What's made you so certain?'

He points at the printed pages again. 'Because there was a bank robbery in Darby a couple of days after the festival. That means they were in the area when your mum tore off into the trees. They'd already shot her once, but what if she stumbled into them again, and this time they finished the job? She could identify them as responsible for the robberies and attempted murder. It isn't an angle the police ever followed, because we never told them about our run-in with the two of them, but now it makes perfect sense to me.'

Whilst this sudden leap sounds like a stretch, I find the theory more palatable than Isaac's suggestion that Mum died at the hands of a power-hungry sheriff with a Messiah-complex.

'I think we need to contact the police or the FBI and relay this story,' Bruce says, while I'm still processing. 'I can tell them about our encounter with them, about them shooting your mum, about the robberies; the lot. And if they arrest and question them, maybe they'll reveal the truth.'

I want to tell Bruce his theory is probably the result of listening to too many true crime podcasts, but maybe there is some truth in it.

'We can't blame it on people called Snake and Weasel,' I say, tempering his enthusiasm. 'What were their real names? Do you remember?'

He stares blankly at me, and I can almost see the inner workings of his mind, as his eyes dance. 'Um, I don't think they ever actually said. I remember one of them was from Sonoma County in California.'

I roll my eyes, search the names Snake and Weasel on my phone, expecting to see the usual sponsored links to social media pages, but one news story stands out above them all.

SEARCH CONTINUES FOR MISSING CALIFORNIA HIKER

The story is decades old, and I freeze when I read and learn Kyle Daws (a.k.a. Weasel) was last seen while hiking the Appalachian Trail in Maine in 1993 – the same year Mum disappeared. I've never been a

believer in coincidences, and my mind races with con-
nections between the two disappearances. I instantly
rule out the possibility that Mum turned her back on
Dad and me to get together with someone who
adopted the name Weasel over Kyle, but could Bruce
be right, and something happened to the two of them?
Gary Horowitz (a.k.a. Snake) is quoted in the same
article, describing how his friend vanished from camp
one night after an argument, and hasn't been heard
from since.

I try to relay as much of the story to Bruce as I can,
but my phone is ringing in my hand, and although it's
a private number, I answer, and my worst fears are
confirmed when I hear Isaac's voice.

'I spoke to my friend, and he says he has proof
your mom was definitely in Rockston at some point.'

39

NORA

September 1993, Appalachian Trail, Maine, USA

Nora wakes to the unfamiliar sound of bleeping and whirring. Her head feels as though it is trapped in a vacuum, as muffled conversations happen just out of reach. Her eyelids crackle as she prises them apart, and it feels as though they've been glued shut for weeks. She doesn't know what she's expecting to see, but the white sheet covering the length of her body isn't it. In fact, the whole room is bathed in white: the walls, the blind covering one wall, the door at the far side of the room.

Is this heaven?

She tries to sit up, leaning on her elbows, but her arms ache and her shoulders creak as they engage. She lifts herself fractionally, blinking several times in an effort to clear the dried gunk, and eventually rubs them with her left hand, surprised to find something grey and plastic pinched to one of her fingers. The plastic is attached to a thin grey cable that she follows back to a white box on a stand beside the bed, which she now realises she's lying in. There is a silver frame or rail, cool to the touch, trapping her inside the bed.

How did I get to a hospital?

She racks her brain, trying to recall the last thing she remembers, but all she can see is the endless paths through trees. She pushes the thin sheet back, and is surprised to see tight strapping around her waist and abdomen, and as she runs her fingers over the bandages, she winces as she remembers the gunshot. She also sees the bracelet hanging from her wrist, and thinks it did little to protect her from getting shot.

On cue, the door to the room opens and a man with grey skin and dyed black hair enters, keeping his eyes fixed on the paper connected to the clipboard in his hand.

'Hello, good morning, and how are we feeling today?'

Nora tries to speak, but can't get the words past the frog in her throat. She coughs and tries again. 'Where am I?'

'You are in the Critical Care Unit of Darby Hospital, and I am the physician overseeing you today. I'm Dr Terry Copeland. And you are...' he studies the notes on the clipboard, 'Mr Jacob Feeney.' He peers at her around the side of the clipboard. 'I'm just kidding. You are Mrs Nora Grogan from the UK, right?'

She nods, wincing as she tries to shuffle into a more comfortable position in the bed. 'What happened to me?'

He looks back at the clipboard. 'Well, let me see. Seems you were presented with a gunshot wound on Tuesday, and have been in recovery ever since.'

'Did you remove the bullet?'

'Nope, says it had already been taken out. Looks like you were assessed, opened up to check for any internal damage, then sewn back up. They've had you on a saline solution to keep your fluids up, but you're allowed solids now, so someone should bring some food by in a little bit.'

He places the clipboard on the end of the bed and moves across to her. He shines a pen torch in her eyes, and checks her throat and mouth before collecting the clipboard and heading for the door.

'Do you know if any of my friends are here, or who brought me in?'

He stares blankly back at her. 'I'll send one of the nursing team in, and they should know more.'

'How long will I need to stay in here?'

'Well now, for a wound like yours, we'd usually keep you for a day or so more before letting you return home, but it is the darnedest thing: you are healing right up as if you've been kissed by the Lord our God Himself. The way your wound is healing up is nothing short of miraculous. So, really, unless anything changes, we can probably let you go home tomorrow. Now, I need to carry on with my rounds, but if you have any difficulties, just buzz for the nurses and they'll attend to your needs.'

He ducks out of the door before she can ask him anything else, but a moment later, Bruce strides in, all smiles, and offers her a grape from the brown paper bag he's carrying. 'You're awake!'

'The doctor said we're in Darby, but I have no recollection of how we got here.'

'Your life was saved by a cowboy of sorts. Long story short: he removed the bullet and stitched you up, but you'd lost so much blood that it was touch and go as to whether you'd recover.' He leans in closer, lowering his voice. 'Nelson said he had some magical medicine that would aid your recovery, and... I told him to do whatever was in your best interests.'

'What kind of medicine?'

Bruce shrugs. 'He refused to tell me what was in it, though I have to hand it to him, whatever it was, it did the trick. Once you started to recover a couple of days later, he helped me carry you to a town where I managed to get us a ride here to Darby. I thought it best to get you properly examined, and this is the biggest hospital in this area.'

'W-what about the trail? What about the sponsorship?'

He rests a warm hand on her head. 'You don't need to worry about any of that. Ken and Charlie are still hiking, and should be with us by tomorrow. Nobody back home is going to worry an inch about us driving part of the course given the fact you were shot. Anyway, how are you feeling?'

She drops back onto her pillow. 'Like I've been shot. It's going to be tough going for me to get back on the AT.'

He snickers. 'You're kidding, right? Nobody expects you to finish the trail. I'll hook up with Ken and

Charlie and complete the course, and then we'll come and collect you, before—'

'No! I said I would walk the course for my god-daughter and that's exactly what I intend to do!'

Bruce frowns again. 'Listen, I know that your recovery is miraculous, but there's no point in putting your life in any more danger. Rest up. Ken has Rex the cuddly lion, and is getting plenty of photographs of him. Let us finish it from here.'

She shakes her head. 'Please. I want to do it for Ashley. And for Jess. I don't want to have caused her so much upset and then not complete the trail. I know I'll be a bit slower than before, but I'm going to do it one way or another, and I'd rather not be on my own.'

He glances at his watch. 'Well, the doctor did say you're free to go for a little walk if you fancy stretching your legs. If you're serious about heading out with us, it might be an idea for you to get you up and moving about before we're ready to continue in a couple of days.'

'Where's my pack?'

'In my motel room. Do you need something from it?'

'I have a photograph of Jess. Could you get it for me?'

He stands. 'Absolutely. Sorry, I should have

thought about that. Anything else you need? Your diary?'

She shakes her head, and then changes her mind. 'Oh, actually, can you find my least dirty and smelly clothes?'

'I have taken the liberty of washing all our clothes at the launderette, so is there any specific outfit you'd like me to fetch?'

'What's the weather like outside?'

'I'd describe it as Brighton in late October. Not cold and wet, but not warm and sunny either. Why don't I choose you something weather-appropriate?'

She nods, and he disappears through the door. She counts to sixty, and then pushes herself up and off the bed. An alarm sounds from behind her, and a nurse appears at the door, looking in uncertainly.

'The doctor said I could go for a walk.'

The nurse nods, ducks past her, and switches off the bleeping machine, before returning to hold open the door. 'I'd suggest you use the elevator if you want to get down to the cafeteria. It's only one floor, but you probably shouldn't be using the staircase.'

She leads Nora to the bank of lifts, and calls one, making sure she's inside before carrying on her duties. When the doors open, Nora feels as though she has woken in Narnia. All around the corridor, there are decorations of lanterns hanging, shiny bolts of lightning, and candles. A poster hanging from one of the walls advertises the town's Festival of Light, and as she moves slowly along the corridor, she is amazed by the lengths the townspeople seem to be going to for the event. There are tables and stalls just outside the hospital building advertising raffles and games, but there is one particular table that draws her eye.

A woman in a green wig and dark purple cloak is shuffling cards, and looks up when she feels Nora staring at the handmade poster advertising tarot. 'Would you like your fortune told?'

'I don't have any money,' Nora says, patting her hospital gown.

'Well, that doesn't matter.' The woman smiles, nodding at Nora's arm. 'I can see by the bracelet on your arm that you're a fellow believer.'

Nora's hand shoots to the silver charm bracelet. 'You know what this is?'

'Of course. I'd recognise the Bracelet of Utlvyidedi anywhere.'

'Oo-thla-ee-day-dee?' Nora tries to sound it out. 'What can you tell me about it?'

'Only that it brings good fortune to whomever wears it. Would you like me to see what good fortune it will be bringing your way?'

Nora chuckles. It's been years since she had a tarot reading. Her mum used to drag her along to them once a month when she was younger, but Nora had seen how obsessed she'd become with fortunes and fate, and has been cynical of such practices since.

'Thank you, but I don't really believe in that kind of thing.' An image of Jess forms in her mind, and she feels compelled to know that she's okay. 'Perhaps you could do a reading for my daughter instead?'

'What's her name?'

'Jess.'

The woman hands her the deck of cards. 'I need you to shuffle the pack three times while thinking only of Jess – I need the cards to get used to your energy about the relationship the two of you have – and then hand them back to me.'

Nora does as instructed, and hands them back, subconsciously twirling the bracelet, while she watches as the woman rests her palm on the top card and silently recites unintelligible words. When she is finished, she looks at Nora.

'The Major Arcana cards represent the life lessons, karmic influences, and the big archetypal themes that are influencing your life and your soul's journey to enlightenment,' she says as she cuts the pack into three piles, face down on the table.

'Which pack do you feel most connected to when you think about Jess?'

Nora stares at the three piles and points at the middle.

The woman picks up that pile and places it on top of the other two, before fanning the cards out across the green tablecloth. 'I want you to pick out three cards. The first will tell you where she is right now; the second will tell you where she's headed; and the third will tell you where you fit in with that. Okay?'

Nora does as instructed, but when the tarot reader turns over the final card, the blood drains from her face.

She looks from the card to Nora and then back again. 'There must be some mistake... No, this can't be right.'

Nora's pulse quickens. 'What mistake? What is it?'

The woman drops the card to the table and points at the bracelet. 'It's not possible.'

Nora tilts her head and stares at the image on the card: a knight on horseback, but where his head should be is just a skull.

The woman's face twists in pained surprise. 'Someone wearing the Bracelet of Utlvyidedi can't be a bringer of death.' She fixes Nora with a horrified expression. 'Who are you? What do you want from me?'

Nora doesn't even question the possibility that this dramatic response is just for show; nobody could be that good an actor. 'Please, I don't understand. What does this mean? Is my daughter okay?'

But the woman doesn't answer. She pulls off her wig and cloak and throws them at the table, before running off, shouting back over her shoulder. 'Y-you stay away from me. Do you hear me? You stay away!'

40

JESS

April 2023, outskirts of Rockston, Maine, USA

I continue trying to find out as much information about Snake and missing Weasel while Bruce drives us back towards Rockston, but the news stories I find seem to be duplications of each other. In my previous research into Mum's disappearance, I had stumbled across the name Kyle Daws, but hadn't seen any connection between the events, as they were on different parts of the trail when they went missing.

From what I've now read, Snake and Weasel were heading away from Maine when their argument flared up, and it isn't stated exactly what their argument was about. But if they were headed away from Rockston, it seems unlikely that Weasel would have ended up there as one of the blood sacrifices that Isaac DeWalt spoke of. I also can't fathom why the name Kyle Daws didn't feature in Chester's list of names.

Gary Horowitz – the man formerly known as Snake – set up his own investments company in the late nineties and was imprisoned on charges of fraud in 2016. He has seven years of his twenty-year sentence still to run. According to one article, his private equity firm was little more than a complex pyramid scheme, and the monies he stole were never recovered. I desperately want to understand what he remembers of his time on the trail, and whether he suspected a cult of abducting his friend, but have no way of phoning and speaking to him now. I will look to follow up with his lawyer as soon as I've collected my rental from the Rockston motel car park.

Coming here no longer feels like a mistake. There are layers of conspiracy – I'm certain of that now – and I just need to keep unpicking until I find the truth.

I can't escape the niggling voice in the back of my head suggesting that Snake could have killed Weasel and hidden his remains on the trail after their argument. It seems more likely than him being abducted and sacrificed, but I'm not ruling out any possibilities.

Bruce is noticeably quiet, his jaw set as he focuses on the endless highway ahead of us. He has made it clear he thinks returning to Rockston is a bad idea, but I need to collect my rental either way, so we have little choice. We have no evidence of wrongdoing to take to the police and FBI, and if Isaac can be trusted, then hopefully his friend will give us something tangible. It's a risk I have to take.

The 'Welcome to Rockston' sign looms ahead, and I shiver involuntarily as we pass it.

Isaac said he would meet us there, but we're the only car on the road as far as I can see. Tall trees now darken the route, casting a dark shadow over our progress, and inside the car there's a noticeable drop in temperature. Neither of us speak as we reach the first buildings of the town centre, and Bruce follows the signs to the motel.

Bunting hangs from every lamppost, as if there's a celebration planned. We pass a group on the street, dressed in brown fur coats and Davy Crockett-style coonskin hats. I'm not au fait with all the public holidays in the US, so I can't think what event or festival would lead to such revelry. An online search reveals he lived far away in Tennessee and Texas, and celebrations for his birthday don't occur until August, so maybe the outfits are symbolic of something, but I can't be sure.

'Looks like we've got a welcoming committee,' Bruce says, nodding towards the patrol car just inside the entrance to the car park. 'Do you want me to keep driving?'

I crane my neck for a better look, but it isn't obvious whether the car has anything to do with me, so I direct him to continue in regardless. It won't be long until the sun sets, so the timing is suspicious. Bruce parks up in the bay outside the room at the end of the row. The rental is where I left it, and it takes me a moment to fish through my bag for the keys.

'I'll go and settle the bill,' Bruce tells me, unclipping his seatbelt. 'Whatever happens now, there's no way we're hanging around this place for longer than necessary. Agreed?'

I nod, but there's still no further word from Isaac and I have no means of contacting him. Any one of the growing number of people could be Isaac's insider, but there's no way to know which. Maybe this key piece of evidence is the missing motel guestbook with Mum's name in it, but I hope it's something more conclusive. Right now, I have nothing to prove Mum ever came to this town, apart from Isaac's verbal statement. It's not enough for the police to launch an investigation into some of the shadier dealings Isaac has suggested go on here.

I remain in the car, while Bruce climbs out and jogs to the reception building, disappearing through the doors as the neon light flashes. I will use what is left of Ashley's money to settle up with Bruce once this trip is over. But right now I can't concentrate on any of that. The minutes tick by slowly.

I close my eyes, trying to picture Mum emerging from the trail and finding herself in this picturesque town. Did she realise how much danger she was in? I will never know what was going through her mind when she bolted from the group, nor what the true cause was. Did it have something to do with that weird medicine she was given after the gunshot? Or was her mental health suffering as a result of her exertions on the trail itself?

I start at a tapping against my window. Sheriff Randy Whitaker stares back through the glass, asking me to get out. There's no sign of Bruce, and panic explodes out of me.

'Go away,' I shout at him.

'Miss Grogan, I've been looking for you. I have news about the remains. I have the DNA test results.'

Where is Bruce?

'I'd rather not have to shout it through the window,' the sheriff continues.

Is this what they did with Mum: separate her from the group and then whisk her away?

I know I don't want to get out of the car, but I also need to see the test results. I need to see the truth with my own eyes. But if I was at home reading about this, I'd be willing me *not* to get out of the car.

I see the sheriff turn, as if distracted, and as he does, I see Bruce standing there, now engaging him in conversation. It gives me the courage I need, and I open the door, and move next to Bruce.

'It would be better if we spoke somewhere less public,' he tells us, but I'm not going anywhere, and cross my arms in a show of defiance.

'The results are in my office,' he continues, pointing over his shoulder in the general direction of the town centre. 'We could walk there, the three of us. I would say you could drive, but the town is getting ready for a bit of a celebration tonight and most of the roads are cordoned off.'

'I presume you've read the results,' I say, my heart beating so fast it feels as though it might erupt out of my chest.

'I have, yes.'

'And is it her?'

He fixes me with a sincere look, and I find myself reaching for Bruce's hand, and squeezing it hard.

'The remains discovered in the cave are not a familial match to you. In other words, there is more than a 99 per cent chance they are *not* your mother's remains.'

It's like I've been punched in the gut, and the wind knocked from me. I came here looking for answers about why my mum never returned home, but it was naïve to assume it would be neatly tied up with a bow.

'I can give you a photocopy of the letter confirming the results, if you come with me to my office. I'm sorry to be the bearer of bad news. This was why I would have preferred to notify you somewhere more appropriate.'

'Can you tell us who the remains belong to?' Bruce whispers, his voice straining with emotion. 'Is it one of the other missing people?'

'The Medical Examiner should be finished with her findings by this time tomorrow, and then we'll know more.'

This doesn't sit right with me. Why would someone send me a link to the story about the remains if they weren't hers? To trick me in some way? Or maybe to try to get a rise from me? I feel lost at sea all of a sudden. Isaac was so adamant that she'd come here and that they'd killed her, but now I don't know what to think; maybe she didn't come to Rockston at all.

I want to run away from this nightmare, and wake up back at home to the sound of Mum and Dad arguing over who used up the last of the milk and didn't buy a replacement. I just want the chance to hold her one last time; to breathe in her scent and feel that unadulterated love.

'I'm sorry,' Sheriff Whitaker says again. 'Take all the time that you need. I need to go and get ready to open the celebration, but if you want to speak more, or collect the letter tonight, please come and find me, and I'll be happy to assist.'

'These results,' I suddenly blurt out. 'You're sure they're accurate?'

He holds my stare. 'Positive.'

'And there's no way they could have been... I don't know, altered in some way?'

'Altered?'

'To cover up the fact they are actually her remains?'

The confusion pushes his eyebrows together. 'I'm sure this news hasn't been easy for you to hear, but I can assure you there's no cover-up or conspiracy here.'

Take some time, and we can talk again in the morning.'

Suddenly I picture Chester and his words fill my mind: *They've been taking people from these towns for years.*

I fish for my phone and unlock the screen, staring at the long list of names I wrote down. 'Do the following names mean anything to you, Sheriff Whitaker? Dan Trebine? Jeanette Barnes? Padraig Murphy? Justin Torrance? Bernadette Poisson and her partner Collette Benoit? Alicia Chivers?'

His brow knots. 'Sure, a couple of those sound familiar. What about them?'

'They all died or went missing in these mountains, and I'd like to know if you care to comment on the alarming number of deaths that stalk the trail?'

'I would be happy to talk to you about those cases when the office reopens in the morning. In the meantime, I need to go and open the ceremony.' He turns to leave.

'So you're denying any involvement in their deaths?'

He turns back to face me. 'I can understand the emotional strain you're under right now, so I'm not going to dignify that question with a response.'

A car door opens nearby, and a figure emerges. 'Ha, I bet you're not!'

Isaac is hunched over, looking almost breathless from the exertion of opening the car door. I hadn't realised he was here, nor that he has been listening in to the conversation.

Sheriff Whitaker narrows his eyes. 'What are you doing here, Isaac?'

They know each other?

'I wanted to hear whether you would continue with your usual lines of bullshit, or finally come clean. Why don't you tell this young lady exactly what you did to Alicia Chivers and why she was found strung up to a fence, babbling about blood-red eyes?'

I suppose Isaac and the sheriff could have crossed paths when Isaac tried to break his friend out of the cult, but there's something more than a passing familiarity between the two men.

'This isn't the time or the place,' Whitaker fires back, breaking from his cool exterior for the first time.

'Sure it is,' Isaac shouts back. 'Don't worry, I've already told Jess about what goes on around here when the moon is full.'

'You shouldn't have come back here, Isaac. You're no longer welcome.'

No longer welcome?

'She deserves to know the truth, Randy.'

The sheriff shakes his head. 'And what do you know about truth, Isaac? Does she know the real reason you lured her here?' He looks straight at me. 'When you first arrived, asking about your mom, it felt like there was a puppeteer at work, but I couldn't figure out who or why. Now I understand. You should both get out of here.'

I shake my head firmly, pleased to see Isaac picking at another layer of the conspiracy. 'I want to hear what else he has to say.'

'You can't trust this man; he's been lying to you.'

'He's the one who told me you killed my mum, as well as these other people.'

'But did you ever stop to question why he told you that? You're a journalist, right? A good story is not about the what, who, or how, and everything to do with *why*.'

I turn back to look at Isaac, but his glare is fixed on the sheriff.

'Why don't you tell her why you really came back here, Isaac? It's the same reason we banished you all those years ago: you still want the Bracelet of Ut-lvyidedi.'

41

NORA

September 1993, Appalachian Trail, Maine, USA

Despite her best efforts, Nora hasn't been able to take her mind off the tarot card reader's reaction to that final card. She's never seen anyone look so terrified.

Someone wearing the Bracelet of Utlvyidedi can't be a bringer of death.

She spent the afternoon applying grease to the bracelet, trying to get it over her thumb joint, but all she achieved was red raw skin and a frustrated mind. Although she's been visited by nurses every hour, she didn't really engage with any of them, stuck inside her own head and desperate to get back to Jess. Ever since Frank mentioned Jess's accident, she's been having nightmares that always end with Jess in danger, and the tarot reading has heightened her paranoia. Her own mother's certainty in a spiritual, ethereal world is what has kept Nora cynical, but now she's starting to question her own beliefs.

Much to her relief, Bruce lives up to his word and arrives at midday with a bag of fresh clothes. The nurses change the bandage and are simply amazed by how much the scar in her side has already shrunk. Nora also sneaks a look, certain it looks more like a large insect bite than a gunshot wound. She knows it's impossible, and can't have anything to do with the bracelet, and yet she's more open to the possibility than she's ever been.

Bruce suggests they catch a taxi back to the motel, but Nora insists they walk to help build the strength in her legs. He reluctantly agrees but doesn't realise the real reason she wants to walk is to find and question that tarot card reader further. Clearly the woman knew something of the bracelet's history, and Nora is desperate to know how to get it off so she can get back to Jess.

The town of Darby is alive with excitement. Bunting and banners advertising the annual Festival of Light are hung between department stores and shops the length of the main street, but as they cross roads, she can see that the decoration and fun extends down each of the side streets as well. It reminds her of Brighton on Pride weekend. There are stalls and tables set up on sidewalks, inviting passers-by to sample delicacies from the local area. They stop to sample cheese, chipotle chillies, and frozen yoghurt.

They stop at a phone booth, and Nora attempts to phone home, desperate to speak to Jess, but there is no answer, and this adds to her growing concern. She desperately wishes she'd never agreed to buy anything from the elfin-like girl back at the hostel. It feels like she's been dogged with nothing but trouble since putting it on. But it's the fear of what's to come that is troubling her the most.

She keeps telling herself that she doesn't believe in magic and mythology, but cannot silence the voice in the back of her head, warning her that the bracelet will put Jess in danger somehow. She tries to talk to Bruce about it, but his response is to tell her she's exhausted and needs to rest. But she's not going to give up on completing the challenge; not when they're so close to the end.

Ken and Charlie arrive at the motel half an hour after them, looking exhausted and slimmer than Nora recalls. They both seem delighted that she is up and about again, but smell as though they haven't washed for days. They agree to shower and change before heading out into the festival. But Nora doesn't want to wait, and agrees to meet up with them later. Bruce is reluctant to let her go on alone, but she insists, telling him the town is too small for her to get into any trouble.

Nora's first stop is the payphone stand across the street from the motel. She has no idea what day it is, but in the back of her mind she's sure somebody said the Festival of Light was being held on a Saturday. Either way, it's nearly 1 p.m., which means it's coming up to six back home, and regardless of what day it is, Jess will be at home getting ready for bed. She dials the number and holds her coins, ready to drop them in as soon as it connects. There is so much she wants to tell Jess: how much she's missed her; how she'll never leave for this long again; how she'll do everything within her power to keep her safe.

She decides she won't tell them about being shot as they'll only worry. There's only a few days left until they'll be scaling Mount Katahdin in Baxter Park, and then she'll be free to return home and put this whole sorry episode behind her.

The phone rings and rings, but goes unanswered

yet again. She hangs up and tries again, carefully pressing each number this time to avoid misdialling, but again the line rings without connecting. All she wants is to speak to Jess, and in her frustration, she slams the handset against the phone.

Nora heads back through town, this time on the opposite side of Main Street, eyes peeled for the tarot card reader. She passes stall after stall, but there's no sign of the woman. Now, on the outskirts of the town, she's about to give up – figuring the tarot card reader is in hiding to avoid running into Nora again – when she does spot somebody she recognises. Sitting at a table covered in green baize, the same colour as the tarot card reader's table yesterday, is the girl who sold her the bracelet. She's still as pretty and waif-like as Nora remembers, with that angelic face. The table is covered in handmade bracelets, but no metallic ones that resemble her own.

What had the tarot card reader called it? The Bracelet of Oo-thla-ee-day-dee?

The table is also adorned with crystals, candles, incense, rings, and books on mysticism. If the woman in the green wig was to be anywhere it would be this stall, but it can't be a coincidence that the elfin-like blonde girl is sitting there instead. Are they in this together? Con artists trying to make her part with cash to have the stupid bracelet removed?

Nora doesn't hesitate, approaching the table, and standing in line behind a man in a kaftan who is asking her questions about one of the hardback books. He eventually heads off and the girl looks up at her, smiling innocently.

'Hello, how can I help you today?'

Nora narrows her eyes. 'You don't recognise me, do you?'

The girl studies Nora's face, and then shakes her head. 'I'm sorry, have we met before?'

Nora raises her wrist into the air, the bracelet dangling. 'How about now?'

The girl stares blankly back at her, not a trace of recognition.

'You sold me this bracelet over a week ago at a cabin in New Hampshire. I told you it was too small, and you grabbed it and manipulated it in some way, and now I can't get it off.'

The girl stares closer at the bracelet. 'You think *I* sold this to you?' She shakes her head. 'I only sell handmade bracelets if you'd like to buy one of these,' she adds, waving her hand over the selection on the table.

'I just want it removed,' Nora says between gritted teeth.

The girl frowns. 'I'm sorry, but I really have no idea what you're talking about.'

Nora thrusts her arm forwards, and yells, 'Take it off!'

A number of people at neighbouring stalls turn and watch them closely.

'I'm so sorry,' the girl repeats, 'but I don't know who you are or what you want.' She begins to cry, loud enough to attract a tall, barrel-chested man who asks what the trouble is.

Nora takes off down the street, but swings back around and positions herself on a bench, where she watches the back of the girl's head for several hours. Other customers stop by and purchase the mystical trinkets she's selling, and eventually, the girl stands, and asks one of the other stallholders to keep an eye on her table while she goes for a toilet break.

Nora hares across the road, and as soon as the girl has turned the corner, grabs her arm and drags her down the street, ducking into an alley between two shops. 'I know you know who I am, and I know you know that this is the Bracelet of Oo-thla-ee-day-dee.'

The girl laughs, but tells her to shush. 'Your pronunciation isn't quite right, but you need to keep your voice down. Do you realise what others would do if they knew you were in possession of that?'

The tension in Nora's shoulders eases a fraction. 'So, you admit you recognise it?'

'I told you in New Hampshire that it is the most valuable charm of them all; that it will provide the wearer with protection from evil spirits. Why would you want to take it off?'

'I don't want protection from evil spirits. I made a mistake in buying it from you, and now I want you to remove it for me.' She holds out her wrist in front of the girl's face. 'Please?'

The girl gently pushes down on Nora's wrist until it lowers. 'I'm sorry, but I can't do that. *They* wouldn't like it.'

Nora scoffs. 'I don't care, just take it off! I don't want to be protected from evil spirits, because I... I don't believe in them.' She says it more firmly than she's feeling, and hopes the girl doesn't pick up on any doubt. 'My daughter... I'm worried that... I'm worried that something bad is going to happen to her. Yesterday, someone did a tarot card reading and freaked out when she saw the bracelet.'

The girl considers this for a moment. 'Have you had any dreams since I put on the bracelet?'

Nora nods. 'Nightmares would be a better description.'

'Nightmares? Why? What happens?'

Nora pictures the latest one, and it's like a knife punctures her heart. 'I see my daughter terrified, as if she's running from a monster, and I feel so scared for her.'

'What happens at the end of the dreams? Do you protect her?'

Nora opens her mouth to answer, but thinks again. 'I'm not in the dreams. It's just her.'

The girl shakes her head. 'How can you not be in the dreams? They're *your* dreams. You have to be in them.'

'Well, I'm not. It's just Jess and whoever she's running from.'

The girl's cheeks flush. 'If you can't see yourself in the dreams, but you see Jess running from a monster, that means... it means *you're* the monster.'

'No. *No!* I would never do anything to hurt Jess.'

'If you remove the Bracelet of Utlvyidedi, the gods will destroy your friends and family. You will bring a plague on everyone you know.'

Nora half-laughs at the response, in an attempt to hide her growing fear. 'I don't believe in your mystical gods.'

'Doesn't mean they aren't real. If you'd seen half the things I have, you'd be left in no doubt. The Appalachians aren't like other parts of the world. Where we are now is really special. Why do you think so many people have flocked to Darby today to celebrate? People come from miles around to commemorate the light that they provide us with. In this place, miracles really do happen. And now that you've accepted the blood of the elders, you'll see for yourself.'

Nora subconsciously presses a hand to the strapping beneath her jumper. 'So, what? You're expecting me to believe that I have to wear this piece of crap for the rest of my life?'

'You make it sound like a curse. Whilst you wear it, no harm will come to you. You will live a long and prosperous life.'

'What about the tarot card reading? The woman in the green wig said I would be the bearer of death to my daughter. All I want is to keep her safe.'

'No harm will come to your daughter so long as you continue to wear the bracelet.'

Nora doesn't want to admit how much of a relief it is to hear those words, but doesn't want to fall into the same traps as her own mother had. She's certain it was belief in other worlds that eventually drove her to her death.

'When I return to Brighton and see my daughter... she'll be perfectly safe?'

The girl's smile drops in an instant. 'You can't leave here. You have been chosen, Nora. You have a different path now.'

Nora grips the bracelet hard, and pulls and yanks at it, desperate to get it off. 'Chosen? It's just a crappy piece of metal.' She pulls with all her might until the jarring pain in her thumb becomes too much. 'I demand you take it off this instant! I didn't agree to anything when you sold this thing to me, and you have to be off your rocker if you think I'm just going to turn my back on the life I've built on the say-so of a child!'

'You don't understand: the bracelet chooses who it wants, and it chose you. Don't you remember feeling drawn to it when you looked at it? I know it's a lot to take in, but you have to realise you have no choice in this.'

Nora wants to stalk away, laughing, but that little voice in the back of her head is getting louder and louder. She tries to remind herself that she doesn't believe in magic; that her mother was insane to believe in anything irrational, but clearly this girl believes everything she is saying, regardless of how ridiculous.

'I'm from a town called Rockston, not too far from

here. Go back to your motel and sleep and then come and find me. Once you hear what my father has to say, and how important *you* are, you'll understand what is now expected of you.'

It feels like a bad dream, but Nora can't wake up. She wants to scream and stamp her feet and demand that whoever is playing this trick on her just stop, but it's only the two of them in alleyway.

'You're actually insane, aren't you?' she declares, wanting to pull out her own hair. 'I gave you ten dollars for two shitty bracelets because I felt sorry for you, and now you've lost the plot.'

The girl's eyes remain fixed on Nora's. 'I told you it was the most valuable charm of all and the power it bestows. You never said you didn't want the burden of that power. You agreed to me bestowing it on you. You cannot leave the Appalachians. If you do, you *will* be the cause of your daughter's death.'

Nora grabs the girl's wrist and pulls her close. 'I don't want any of this. I just want to go home and be with my little girl. Now take this sodding thing off me.'

'Hey, hey, what's going on there?' a voice calls from the top of the alley, but Nora ignores it.

'You take this thing off me now, or I swear it won't be your gods you need to fear.'

A hand grabs hold of Nora's arm and pulls her away. 'Nora, stop this. What are you doing?'

She's surprised to see Ken is the one prising her away.

The girl's face changes in an instant. 'Oh, thank you, sir, thank you. This woman just attacked me, and I don't know why.' Her crocodile tears are back immediately.

'I'm sorry about my friend,' Ken says, keeping a tight grip on Nora. 'You go on.'

The girl keeps up her tears as she peels away, and Nora tries to reach for her, but Ken pushes her back with his shoulder and full body weight.

'Y-you can't let her go,' she says as her own eyes fill. 'She's the one who put this bracelet on me. Please, Ken, let me go.'

He grabs hold of her hand and drags her away in the opposite direction. 'I don't know what's wrong with you, but you can't be violent with a child. I saw you grab her in the street. What were you thinking?'

'She wants to hurt Jess. You don't understand.' Tears fall as she battles to free herself, but Ken is far stronger than she estimated.

At the end of the alley, Bruce and Charlie are waiting.

'That girl is here,' she says to Charlie. 'The one

who sold me the bracelet. She said that Jess is in danger. I need to get this bloody thing off me.'

Bruce and Ken exchange looks. Charlie stares off into space, high as a kite on God knows what, his hands trying to catch invisible stars.

'I think she must have sampled the special cookies as well,' Ken says, rolling his eyes. 'They really should warn people that they're laced with LSD.'

'I'm not stoned,' Nora shouts, but suddenly the world is spinning and she collapses into Bruce's arms with exhaustion.

He scoops her up, and asks Ken to lead Charlie as they return to the motel.

42

JESS

April 2023, Rockston, Maine, USA

Isaac is panting hard, but he shrugs off my attempt to help him.

'I am the rightful heir to Utlvyidedi,' he grizzles at Sheriff Whitaker. 'It was *you* who broke with tradition and appointed an outsider. You put everyone at risk with your misinterpretation of the prophecies.'

My mind is spinning: the Bracelet of Utlvyidedi; heirs, prophecies? I have no idea what they are talking about, but it's now clear to me that these men are more than just passing acquaintances.

A small crowd has now started to gather around this stand-off, but with most dressed in frontiersman costumes, it almost feels as though we've been transported back in time. Only the motel's flashing neon sign is keeping me rooted in the present.

'I did what was necessary,' Whitaker replies spitefully. 'The bearer of the bracelet must be worthy, and you showed you were anything but. The prophecy said it would pass to one with outsider's blood who would bring a new dawn of life to our people.'

'You had no right to take it from me. Everyone knew I was next in line; you shouldn't have interfered.'

I feel like I'm just a pawn in some game for which I don't know the rules. So, Isaac lied to me about wanting to help, but I'm still not clear on why he wanted me to return to Rockston with him. He said it was to share proof that Mum had been killed by those in this cult and that her murder had been covered up, but he hasn't shared any of this ulterior motive. And frankly, I don't care about their petty feud; all I want to know is who murdered Mum.

I step between them. 'Isaac, please give me what I came for. Help me prove what happened to my mum, and then I'll do what I can to help you figure out whatever this is.'

He ignores me. 'I came here because I was seeking

a different way of living,' he barks back at Whitaker. 'I heard the calling in those trees, and I gave up everything to be part of this world. And in return *you* betrayed me. You and that bitch daughter of yours. I know it was her who took the bracelet and gave it away, and I am certain you're the one who told her to do it.'

There are now at least a dozen people gathered around us in the motel car park, each eager to see what scene is unfolding. I need to get control of the situation, but I'm also curious to hear where this argument is going. If Isaac won't tell me exactly why I'm here, maybe he'll let something slip.

'You're not welcome here any more, Isaac. You should leave now, and allow us to continue with our celebrations—'

'I'm not going anywhere until you give me back what is rightfully mine.'

The sun has virtually disappeared on the horizon, and there is little light left in the sky overhead. A streetlight has flickered on, casting a golden spotlight on us.

'The gods tested me by sending my old friend Jonny to drag me away, but I dealt with his betrayal. I sacrificed him for them to prove I was worthy of the bracelet. I have always been ready to do whatever was necessary.'

The sheriff scans the crowd before replying. 'You knew the rules when you joined us. The Bracelet of Utlvyidedi chooses the next bearer, and we must all stand by that choice.'

'Bullshit! You were just jealous of me, and didn't want me to be in control. You knew you couldn't put the bracelet on yourself because people would see your true motivations. So you did the next best thing: you gave it to someone you could easily manipulate for your own ends.'

He pauses before turning to address the crowd. 'Don't you people see: this isn't the life you were promised; there is one person controlling all of you and you blindly follow because *he* tells you it's what *they* want. But he's lying to you. It's time to rise up and do what your ancestors always intended. *We* should be the ones driving change across this country; not those slimy two-faced politicians in Washington. Have you even seen what's going on in the real world? It's on the brink of collapse, but rather than helping, Randy Whitaker has you sheltering and living in fear.'

The crowd has doubled in size now, and I can't make out all of the faces in the shadows beyond the golden spotlight. Isaac wasn't lying about them being part of a cult, and my fight or flight response is telling me we should get out of here, but I can no longer see the rental through the crowd.

I clear my throat. 'Sheriff Whitaker,' I say, trying to keep the anxiety from my voice, 'I'd like to see the DNA result confirmation letter now, please. I don't care what you and your cult are doing. I just want the results and then we'll be on our way.'

'You remind me of her,' he says, and the statement floors me. 'When I first met your mom, she had that same stubborn resolve; convinced we meant her harm. And if you don't mind, we are a *community*, not a cult. Everyone here is free to leave should they desire to do so. Nobody is being held against their will. We are a peaceful community, striving to live off what the gods provide for us.'

'And at what cost?' I snap back. 'Did you kill Dan Trebine, Jeanette Barnes, Padraig Murphy, Justin Torrance, Bernadette Poisson, Collette Benoit, and Alicia Chivers?'

'No, of course I didn't. People die on the trail from time to time, as they do in the real world. In fact, more people are murdered every day in the real world than have died as a result of hiking through these mountains. Statistically, you're far safer on the trail than anywhere else in the world.'

'I'm not so sure the FBI will agree when I report your little commune to them, and especially when Mum's remains are finally recovered and it's proven she suffered at your hands as well!'

I'm expecting him to react, but he simply smiles back at me. 'You're so certain of that, are you? I guess that's your mom's stubbornness shining through again. Let me save you the time of embarrassing yourself.' He looks out into the darkness. 'Are Dan and Paddy here? Show yourselves; it's perfectly safe.'

'Dan's on the stage doing a sound check,' a voice calls out from the crowd, but then a barrel-chested man with a thick and dark bushy beard steps forward, pulling the coonskin hat from his head, and holding it tightly to his chest, his head bowed.

'Brother Padraig was training to be a priest when he joined us, weren't you, Paddy? But he chose a different way of life. And look at him now. You'd never know he turns sixty next year, would you?'

In fairness, I'd have said the man standing before us was in his late forties, but I only have their word that he is who he claims to be. I certainly didn't expect Whitaker to produce a stooge, but maybe Isaac is right about the level of control he exerts over his followers.

'You have nothing to fear from us, Miss Grogan, I can assure you of that. In fact, as a show of good faith, can everyone step back from the cars so that Miss Grogan and her friend can depart?'

The crowd separates, and I see the rental. I don't think twice before moving towards it.

'Before you hare off,' Whitaker says quietly, 'I'd think twice about what stories you listen to about this place. Have you ever stopped to question who notified you about the remains being discovered?'

I freeze and look at him; his eyes dart in Isaac's direction.

Surely not.

'You expect me to believe that this homeless man found my website and emailed me a link to the news story? Why would he?'

I stare at Isaac, waiting for him to argue the point, but he remains quiet, seething.

'Isaac?' I say, swallowing the distance between us. 'Tell him you didn't send me the article?'

He meets my gaze with a shrug. 'I had to get you here somehow.'

My mind can't process any of this, and Bruce looks as confused as I am.

'You sent me the article? But why?'

He shrugs for a second time. 'I needed leverage,

and I knew you turning up unannounced would have *him* panicking. A simple case of misdirection like the great magicians of the past. I needed a way back here, and you were the perfect distraction.'

'But why?'

'He's dying,' Whitaker interjects. 'Just look at him: hunched over because he's in too much pain to stand straight; sweating profusely as his heart races to pump enough clean blood to counter the disease ripping through his organs. I'm right, aren't I, Isaac?'

He wipes the sweat from his upper lip, but scowls in silence.

'You see, Isaac here isn't on some mission to save the country. As before, he wants the bracelet for his own selfish gains: he thinks it will bring him a cure, but it doesn't work like that. No piece of metal – no matter how powerful – can cure disease. The bracelet brings the bearer guidance on how to protect those that need it. That's what you never truly grasped about its power, Isaac. We live here illness-free *not* because of magic, but because of the minerals and vitamins in the food grown in the rich soil; the chemical-free water filtered by the rocks surrounding us; the clean air not polluted by factories and cleaned by the vegetation that shelters us. There is nothing here can save you now, Isaac.'

I pull on Isaac's arm to get his attention, and he almost topples over, knocking into my shoulder. 'Tell me he's lying, Isaac. Tell me you didn't use me.'

He is panting so heavily that I can't believe I didn't realise how seriously ill he was before.

'Desperate times,' he gasps, leaning back against the vehicle he arrived in. 'I met you at the airport because I needed to know whether you knew what had happened to your mom; whether she'd been in touch about what happened. But I could see you knew nothing, so I had someone fit a tracer to your car and tracked you here, but I was worried someone would recognise me if I approached you here, so I had an acquaintance leave you that note. But when you didn't turn up after our phone call, and the tracer said you were still here, I wondered whether you'd figured out who I was. And then you turned up this morning and I knew I had to act quickly.'

'You son of a bitch,' I shout, wanting to lash out, but conscious that he'd probably wilt under a breeze.

But then he does something I'm not expecting, and pulls me in front of him, placing an arm across my chest, and before I can react, I feel the press of something cold and sharp against my throat.

'I'm not leaving without that bracelet,' he shouts

out. 'The bearer better come forward and give it to me now, or this woman's blood will be on their hands.'

For someone so weak, his hold on me is firm, and I feel the blade break my skin. I'm searching for Bruce, hoping he has a plan to save me, when a hooded figure emerges from the crowd, and my mouth drops.

43

NORA

September 1993, Appalachian Trail, Maine, USA

Bruce is already dressed when Nora wakes, her right arm asleep from where she's been lying on it all night. She blinks the sleep away, trying to focus on him, where he stands by the door, the pack already on his back.

'You're ready to go already?' she asks, pushing back the sheet with urgency, trying to remember whether she laid out her clothes the night before. 'Why didn't you wake me?'

He lingers by the door, but sighs. 'I... I don't think

you should come with us, Nora. I was going to leave a note, but you've beaten me to it.'

She stops still and turns to look at him. 'You were going to go without me?'

'I think it's for the best. Given everything you've been through these last few weeks, not to mention the fact you got shot...' He closes his eyes. 'I just think it would be best for your health if you stayed here and rested. I've spoken to the motel manager and he's happy for you to stay until we return.'

She pulls off the nightdress she doesn't remember putting on, and quickly pulls on a T-shirt and jeans. Bruce looks away.

'I told you at the hospital that I'm going to complete this hike. As Ashley's godmother, it's my duty.'

'No, Nora,' he says firmly. 'I know you feel obliged to complete what you started, but I'm genuinely concerned for your health; both mental *and* physical.'

She stops pulling the sweater over her head. 'Why? Because of what happened last night?'

'Yes, that, but not just that. You and Charlie were both out of it after whatever you ingested, and that's not your fault, but given how guilty you feel about leaving Jess, I just think it manifested itself last night.'

'You don't understand. That girl was the one who sold me this impossible bracelet, and when I demanded she remove it, she feigned tears and injury. I didn't hurt her like Ken said. She—'

'I'm not talking about *that*,' he snarls, flinging his arms into the air in frustration. 'I mean, attacking a little girl while under the influence is bad enough, but what you were doing in this room when we returned... you're not well, Nora.'

She shakes her head. 'What are you talking about? I don't even remember coming back to this room.'

'You don't remember the conversation we had? At midnight?'

She tries to picture any such conversation between them, but she's certain this is the first time they've had any kind of talk here.

'I carried you back here after you collapsed in the street, around five o'clock. I helped you change into your nightdress and told you Ken and I were going to head back to the festival so you and Charlie could sleep. You said that was fine. But when we returned at midnight, there was shouting coming from inside this room. I thought you were being attacked. When I opened the door, you were standing on your bed pointing at the mirror and shouting into it.'

Nora slowly turns towards the full-length mirror on the wall beside her.

'When I called out to you, you glared back at me,

and I've never seen such... such fear. You threatened to stab me with a pair of nail scissors if I came closer, and I genuinely thought you were going to hurt yourself or me, or both of us. I told you that I meant no harm, and when I made it over to you and pried the scissors from your hand, you kept screaming, "They're going to kill us. They're going to kill us." I tried to talk to you but you were unresponsive, as if you couldn't hear me, so I figured you must have been having a nightmare – about Snake and Weasel, maybe – so I helped you back into bed and sat with you until you calmed down and your eyes closed.'

She has no recollection of any of this, but can't think of any reason Bruce would make up such an imaginative story. Could she really have been acting out a nightmare? No matter how hard she searches, she has no recollection of it. She can still remember the doctors taking her mum away, and her dad describing how she'd threatened him. Nora doesn't want to consider that she could be losing her mind in the same way.

'I know how upsetting this must be,' Bruce says, moving closer, 'but the next few days are going to be very demanding. We need to average fourteen miles a day, starting now, and I just think it's asking too much of you. The others agree with me.'

Nora notes that Ken and Charlie aren't brave enough to be delivering this message to her face. She also notes that the three of them have been talking about her behind her back, and she doesn't appreciate the taste of betrayal; even if Bruce's intentions are pure, she can't say the same for the other two.

She's come too far to give up now, but convincing Bruce of that is going to be yet another hurdle. She knows he cares, and that might just give her an opportunity.

'You're right,' she says eventually, sighing as if she's baring her soul now. 'I was having a nightmare about Snake and Weasel, and I won't feel safe staying in this motel room on my own.' She pauses, allowing the seed to root itself. 'I'd feel far more comfortable with the three of you there to protect me. My scar has healed so well that I don't think it will slow me down. Please, Bruce, don't abandon me when I need you the most.'

She hates to be this manipulative, but there is more truth in her feeling unsafe alone than she's prepared to admit to herself. She can see the unease gripping his taut jaw.

'Look, I'm dressed now and ready to go,' she adds positively. 'I promise I won't slow you down, and I think getting back on the AT is exactly the mental recovery I need. Space and a chance to quietly process all that's happened.'

* * *

As they hitch a lift back to the trail entrance, there is no further mention of the incident in the alley and the scene in the motel room, and they are soon hiking back through the dark and overbearing forest.

Nora was right when she said being back on the trail would allow her to reflect on all that had happened in the last few weeks. But all she can think about is the girl's muttering when she appended the bracelet to her arm, Bruce's talk of lifesaving potions, and the tarot card of death. She tries to rationalise that these are nothing but isolated incidents in an unfamiliar environment. They're under the pressure of raising money for a dying child, and sacrificing time with her own daughter.

Was her mum aware of her own failing mental health? Nora always believed her mother's obsession with mysticism and searching for answers was a cause of her being sectioned, but was it an effect instead? Did she know something was wrong and was desperately seeking answers? She can't mention her fears to any of the others, because they'll call a halt to the trek, and Nora can't bear the thought of that. She just has to get through the final few days, and then she can get back to Jess and Frank, and deal with her concerns.

The pack on her back feels heavier than it ever has, and the deeper they move into the forest, the more acutely aware of her surroundings she's becoming. It's as if she can hear the birds chattering to one another, sharing details about the progress the hikers are making. She can feel the protection the trees want to offer, and the moment she thinks that she's thirsty and in need of refreshment, a stream miraculously appears. Is this what Leanne meant by Trail Magic?

'I think we should take a five-minute breather,' Ken declares from the front of the line. 'How's everyone doing?'

What he means is: how is *Nora* coping with the heightened pace he's setting? If it wasn't already obvious, the fact that he turns and specifically looks at her reveals his intentions.

She unfastens and lowers her pack to the ground, trying to limit her panting. 'I'm great! Could go even faster if you'd get your legs moving quicker.'

She doesn't know where the jibe has come from, but it has Charlie in hysterics.

Ken frowns. 'Why don't we just take advantage of the stream and rest our legs, and then we can get moving again? It's nearly 10 a.m., so we should push on for another three hours before stopping for food.'

Who put him in charge?

'I tell you what,' Charlie says, 'some of the things I was hallucinating last night... I mean, real crazy shit, you know. I swear at one point I saw a nun chasing after a demon with a crucifix. And my God, the hunger I'm feeling today is insatiable.' He opens his pack and pulls out a chocolate bar which he opens and tucks into.

Bruce crosses to Nora, and speaks quietly. 'Are you sure you're okay? Nobody is going to think any less of you if you need more than five minutes.'

She shakes her head and raises a thumb. 'I'm fine.'

Does he not realise how strong you are?

'According to the map,' Ken says, stepping forwards, 'there's a steep incline coming up soon, but after we make it past that, it should be a steady decline leading all the way to tonight's campsite. Reckon we should make it by sundown.'

Something snaps in the trees ahead, but only Nora turns to look, certain that something or someone is watching them. Her first thought is that Brynjar and Inga are suddenly going to appear, having taken another detour to... errm... *examine* each other's bodies, but neither emerge from the woods.

Another rustling sound, but still the others continue oblivious. The last time she thought they were
totally isolated was right before Snake and Weasel
came along Dead Man's Passage, and they're the last
people she wants to appear now.

Save yourself.

She turns and looks into the bushes behind her.
She thought the voice she could hear was in her head,
but now she's sure it was someone whispering. She
strains to hear any more, but it's hard with the others
so loud.

The Bracelet of Utlvyidedi will protect you.

She bolts up, certain the voice came from within
the trees. She leaves her pack where it is, but begins to
circle the small clearing, eyes darting between trees,
trying to find the source of the whispering.

Bruce steps forward and tries to reach for her arm,
but she shrugs it off. 'Nora, what's going on? You've got
that look in your eyes again.'

She continues to scout, ignoring the concerned
murmurs coming from the others. Why can't they
hear the voice?

'Nora, please sit down,' Bruce calls to her, anxiety
dripping from every syllable.

She ignores him, anxiety building in her gut. It was

her mum's admission to hearing voices that first spiked her dad's concern. But Nora's mum was much older when she lost the plot. Why is this happening to her now?

Bruce steps into her path, darting his head about, trying to force eye contact. 'Nora, please, just take a few breaths. Everything is going to be okay.'

She ignores him but the glint of something metallic from Ken's pack catches her eye. She doesn't hesitate in stooping and pulling the gun out, pointing it wildly at the trees.

'Come out, whoever you are!'

Ken and Charlie take uneasy steps backwards as Nora waves the gun around, yelling incoherently at the trees. Bruce raises his hands, palms out in a calming manner.

'Nora, please just listen to my voice: there is nobody in the bushes. You're perfectly safe.'

She looks from the overgrowth to Bruce and back again. 'Can't you hear them?'

They don't understand what is happening to you.

She turns the gun on Bruce and he flinches, but she keeps the barrel trained on his chest. She circles the group until they're standing together. Charlie and Ken raise their hands as well, as fear robs them of their voices.

'I'm not going mad,' she tells them. 'The trees, they're... they're talking to me.'

'I believe you, Nora,' Bruce says with a calmness he's not feeling. 'Just put the gun down, and we will all go and flush out whoever is making these noises. Okay?'

Kill them, Nora. Kill them all.

'No, I won't kill anyone for you. Do you hear me?'

She points the gun at the trees where she heard the last whisper and squeezes the trigger. Bruce, Ken and Charlie fall to their knees, keeping their hands pointed skywards. The sound of the gun firing seems to echo around the trees encircling them.

Kill them, Nora.

She shakes her head. She won't let any harm come to anyone else.

Without a second's thought, she tears forwards into the welcoming darkness of the trees.

44

JESS

April 2023, Rockston, Maine, USA

It can't be!

My lips part but I can't form the word. I've spent thirty years thinking and talking about her, but now that she is standing in front of me, her face thinner and more wrinkled than I've seen in the photographs, and her nest of brown curls covered by the dark grey hood, I can't bring myself to utter her name. She's like a ghostly apparition, and for all I know this could be some intense dream, but it's one I never want to wake from.

It's only when DeWalt presses the tip of the knife into my skin that I realise I am very much awake and that my mum is slowly stepping towards us.

'I am the bearer of Utlvyidedi,' she says, her accent still tinged with Lancashire notes.

DeWalt shifts behind me, as he stares at her, forcing me to twist slightly. I'd love to know what's going on behind those eyes of hers. Does she even know who I am? She's staring so blankly that I can't be sure.

'I see you've finally learned how to pronounce it correctly,' DeWalt sneers.

They've met before, and I see now that Sheriff Whitaker was telling the truth when he said DeWalt used to be part of this group; this community. And that means he is the one who has been pulling all the strings here: sending the article; convincing me that these people had murdered her; all so he could manipulate himself into the position where she has no choice but to give him the bracelet in order to save my life.

I'm so angry that I just want to lash out at him, but his grip is too firm, and the knifepoint perilously close to tearing open my throat. I need to bide my time. For now.

'You know I can't remove the bracelet, Isaac. It

only comes free when the bearer passes away. You should let this young lady go.'

My brows knot at her choice of words. *Young lady?* Why not say 'let my daughter go'? Unless she's just trying to keep sentiment out of the discussion.

'The bracelet is my birth right, and they stole it from me to give it to you. I don't care what has to happen, but it's my turn to benefit from its healing properties.'

'You're ill, Isaac, I can see that, but the bracelet can't help you. *We* can. It is good that you've returned in your hour of need, but you don't need to do this. Let us offer you palliative care, and we may just be able to extend your remaining time.'

He pushes me in front of him, and the pressure in my neck is so great that I yelp.

Where the hell is Bruce?

'It's too late for all that. I've been given every treatment available, and there's nothing more they can do. There's only one thing that can save me now. Hand it over.'

She stops moving towards us, now only a metre or so in front of me. She extends her arm, and the cloak falls back from her wrist and I see a small metal bangle hanging from it. I don't understand the significance of the bracelet. It looks like a piece of cheap tat that can be bought at any market in the UK. Is that really all he is after? I don't understand why he would go to all this effort for that tiny thing.

'I can't remove it, Isaac, and you know that. Let the girl go, and you have my word that we will do what we can to help you. You know we have access to medicines that the rest of the country doesn't. Let us try, and you have my word that no harm will come to you.'

She is avoiding my gaze, focused solely on De-Walt, and for the briefest moment I feel his arm slacken, the strain of standing finally getting to him. As quick as I can, I drive my head backwards into his face, his nose crunching on impact, and then swiftly slip both my hands beneath his arm, and pull it and the knife away from me. He offers little resistance, and I'm able to duck away, while two hooded figures immediately grapple with his arms and kick the blade to safety. I waste no time, rushing over to Mum and throwing my arms around her. She doesn't smell as I remember, and despite my squeezing, she doesn't reciprocate my embrace. I have so many questions – where has she been all this time? Why didn't she return home? Why didn't she tell me she was okay? – but I just want her to hold me and tell me everything will be okay, like she used to.

'Show's over, ladies and gentlemen,' the sheriff

declares loudly to the crowd of onlookers. 'We have a celebration due to start, so please all now make your way to the town square for the official opening, and I'll be along in due course.'

There's no argument, and the group dressed as frontiersmen slowly disperse into the darkness, leaving me, Bruce, Mum, the sheriff and a restrained DeWalt in the car park of the motel. I let go of Mum as Bruce approaches and we share a hug of relief.

'Can you take Isaac to the hospital, and I'll follow in a few minutes?'

The two men restraining Isaac put his arms over their shoulders and lead him away. His face is crumpled in pain, and although I should be furious that he was threatening my life only moments before, I am overcome by the same sadness I feel whenever I meet someone who knows death lurks nearby.

The sheriff turns next to Nora, and whispers something into her ear. She nods, and moves off silently in the direction of my motel room. Bruce and I proceed to follow, but the sheriff steps into our path.

'Can you give me a minute?' he asks, and so I watch on as Mum disappears behind the motel room door. 'I'm sure you must have a million questions, but can I ask you to go easy on her? Yes, the woman you just met is your birth mother, but... she doesn't know it. The woman formerly known as Nora Grogan arrived in Rockston thirty years ago in a very bad state. She'd wandered off the AT and must have fallen somewhere along the way as she'd cracked open her skull and was bleeding heavily. We treated her, and when she came to, she had no recollection of her name or where she'd come from.' He removes his hat and stares down at the ground. 'Because she was wearing the Bracelet of Utlvyidedi, I felt like she was a gift sent to us by the gods, and so we took her in to our community.' He looks back up at the two of us. 'Her name is Ruth and she has been taking care of us for three decades.'

'Her name is Nora Grogan,' I snap back, my anger now simmering below the surface, 'and she is my mum. You've lied to her for thirty years, you son of a bitch.'

He accepts the reprimand without comment. 'For a long time I didn't know her true identity, and by the time I did, she was already settled and blossoming. Do you know she's a qualified doctor now? She meant what she said about trying to help Isaac. She is one of the strongest and most caring people I have *ever* known. And I just want you to think about that before you go in that room and rip the rug from beneath her feet.'

'What do you mean?'

'Ruth doesn't know anything of her previous life. She doesn't know she has a daughter, nor that she had a life before she arrived in our town. She is settled here and if you disclose the truth to her, you're going to bring all of that crashing down.'

Is this guy serious? He wants me not to tell her the truth?

I look to Bruce, and shake my head in disbelief.

The sheriff is about to speak again, but I've heard enough. There's only one person I want to talk to, and so I head for the motel room, but as I near the door, my chest tightens. I've spent countless hours thinking about what I would say to her if we ever met, but now that I have the chance my mind is blank.

In many ways, it's a relief to hear that she didn't choose not to return home, rather that the choice was taken away from her. But it hurts that our maternal bond wasn't strong enough to keep her centred. She forgot all about me, and that's a real mind fuck.

I can hear her pacing as I near the door, and I take a final glance back at Bruce. The sheriff has moved away and is heading back towards the town centre. Bruce simply smiles and nods encouragingly. I can't imagine what must be going through his mind right now. Relief that his old friend is alive and well? Or regret that he never thought to come searching for her here?

I push the door open with my foot, and step inside. She stops pacing and looks at me, her eyes shining, but skin pinched in fear at the temples. She opens her mouth to speak, but no words emerge.

I can't hold back, and I swallow the distance between us, throwing my arms around her shoulders, and burying my face in the rough fibre of the cloak she's wearing. I want her to know that I don't blame her, and that I never stopped believing I would find her one day. Maybe she can read my mind, because I feel her stroking the back of my head in the same way she did when I was a child and was upset. It's the subtlest of movement, and yet it is so familiar that I break into a sob, all my questions temporarily sated. It's only when she kisses the top of my head and presses her cheek to the same spot that I feel her own warm tears. Sheriff Whitaker is right: as overwhelming as this situation is for me, it must be even worse for her; learning she isn't who she thought must be mind-blowing.

'I love you, Mum,' I whisper, because they're the only words I've longed to say for all these years.

She separates us and takes a long look at my face, and I want to say there's a hint of recognition behind her eyes, but I don't know if that's just because I want to believe it so much.

'It sounds so strange hearing someone call me that,' she says, her voice strained. 'Shocked doesn't begin to cover it.' She laughs gently, and my heart fills fit to burst. 'And look at what a beautiful young lady you are.'

She's desperately trying to hold back her tears, and tucks a stray hair behind my ear.

'If I'd known...' she begins to say, before the words die on her tongue.

There's something so heart-breaking seeing a parent cry, and I can't choke my own tears back, wiping my eyes with the back of my hand.

'I don't blame you,' I tell her evenly, and I really mean it.

As painful as it is to accept that she forgot about me, I can see the three-inch scar that runs just above her left ear, where presumably she sustained the head injury Sheriff Whitaker mentioned. This isn't her fault.

'I can't believe you're really here,' I say, reaching out and taking her hand in mine in case she slips away again.

'Is it just you? Do you have any brothers or sisters?'

I shake my head. 'No, it's only me.'

'And your... your father?'

'He passed almost twenty years ago. He never stopped loving you.'

A hand shoots to her mouth. 'So you've been on your own since you were...?'

'Sixteen,' I confirm with an empathetic smile. 'But Bruce has been like a surrogate mum and dad to me. He's a good man.'

She frowns at the name.

'Do you remember anything about how you got here? Do you remember hiking with Bruce, Charlie and Ken?'

There's no recognition at any of the names, and I'm tempted to call Bruce in to see whether seeing his face will prompt something, but when I move to the door, he's no longer in the car park.

'I am going to go and make my appearance at the festival,' she says, collecting some tissue from the bathroom and dabbing at her eyes. 'Would you look at the state of me? I'd like to talk more afterwards, if you're going to stay for a few days?'

What if her being here in this community is what's keeping a block on her memory?

My eyes fall on the rental, and instinct takes over.

'I'll give you a lift,' I volunteer, and before she can

argue, I herd her towards the car, and bundle her inside, locking the doors once I'm behind the wheel. Abducting my own mother is probably one of the craziest things I've ever done, but I don't want her staying here for any longer than is necessary. They've stolen thirty years of her life, and it's time we fought back. After starting the engine, I head out of town.

45

JESS

April 2023, Rockston, Maine, USA

'You need to take me back,' Mum repeats, as I keep one eye on the dimly lit road and the other on trying to call Bruce again.

He isn't answering, and I know I should have told him what I was planning before forcing Mum into the car, but I didn't want him to try to talk me out of it. But he needs to know now, so he can get out of Rockston before anyone realises where we've gone. I've no idea where I'm going to take her, as I doubt she has a passport, and it's going to be a challenge convincing the

British embassy that she's my long-lost mother. We'll just have to deal with that once we get there, and she's safe.

'Please take me back to Rockston.'

I ignore her request and hit redial on the phone, but it rings out again.

Where is Bruce?

'They lied to you for thirty years, Mum. Do you realise that? Thirty years when you should have been back home in Brighton with me and Dad. Doesn't that anger you?'

I turn to look at her, but she's staring out of the window, unable to meet my gaze.

'This is for the best. I'm sure once we get you back to the UK and you see and hear familiar things, your memory will start to return and you can get your life back on track.'

'You don't understand,' she says quietly, shaking her head. 'The Bracelet of Utlvyidedi has to stay in the Appalachians. You don't realise how much danger you're putting my people in.'

'Your people? The same people who lied to you about who you are; who never told you that your family was frantically worried about you; who allowed the world to believe you were dead so that they could keep you prisoner?'

'That's not what it's like. I'm not a prisoner; I have an important role here.'

'You have an important role to me too!'

I don't mean to snap at her, but my frustration at her lack of care for me is growing. I know it wasn't her fault that she never came back, but why isn't she acknowledging the fact that I've been forced to live without her love and guidance? Had she come home, I've no doubt that I wouldn't have married and divorced the wrong man; I'm certain I wouldn't be scrabbling around for any old shitty job just to pay my overpriced rent.

'The bearer of the Bracelet of Utlvyidedi cannot leave the country.'

'Says who? Those same people who've been lying about everything else? It's just a crappy piece of metal.'

'No, you don't understand, Jess. It's so much more than that.'

I try dialling Bruce again, but there's still no answer, so I place the phone between my legs, and programme the satnav for Bangor. I'll have to get a hotel room near the airport while I wait for Bruce to catch up with us.

'Mum, it's a metal bracelet. If it means that much to you, I'll buy you a replacement. Okay?'

'You don't understand.'

'Well, explain it to me then. We've got a couple of hours until we reach Bangor, so convince me why it's so important.'

'It's,' she begins, but then lets out a sigh. 'It brings our community valuable resources. Okay? Because of the bracelet, we have access to foods and minerals that we wouldn't otherwise have. It is because of this bracelet that we're able to live in peace.'

I can't help but think how much it sounds as though she's part of the cult that DeWalt spoke of. He claimed Whitaker was the cult leader and I was prepared to ignore his claim, but this doesn't sound like the logic of a person living in the real world.

'You genuinely believe that thing brings good fortune? Why don't you use it to play the lottery numbers then? Think about how well off you'd all be with millions sat in your bank accounts.'

'It isn't that kind of good fortune the bracelet provides. It's... it's difficult to put into words. It's a kind of magic, and I know how lame that must sound to you, but it is what it is.'

I can vaguely recall stories Grandad would tell me about my grandmother losing touch with reality because she believed in fortune tellers and the like. I wonder if he ever knew Mum hadn't fallen so far from the tree.

We continue driving, but I keep my eyes glued to my mirrors, checking for signs that we're being tailed. Once Sheriff Whitaker learns what I've done, I can imagine he'll notify other law enforcement agencies to try to stop me getting Mum back to England. That's assuming he hasn't already.

'I'm sorry that you don't understand, but I really must insist you take me back to my town and friends,' she says with an intonation I remember from those times I was misbehaving.

I think about the story DeWalt told me about his friend Jonny being brainwashed by the cult, but given DeWalt's earlier admission, it seems more likely that Jonny tried to break him free. But the only conclusion I can draw is that Mum is suffering the effects of some kind of brainwashing. Tell a lie often enough and it begins to sound like the truth. I need a way to break her conditioning.

I can't give up on the prospect that my real mum is still inside there somewhere, and I just need to find a way to get her to the surface. I tell her stories from before she left for the hike; how she hated Pancake Day because she couldn't toss them properly; how she would sing in the shower, and dance around the kitchen while listening to the radio, when she thought nobody was watching. I tell her about her parents and how she became estranged from her own mum when her mental health deteriorated. I remind her about the last Christmas she was at home and how she mixed up the mustard and custard powder much to Dad's hilarity. I watch her as I tell each of these anecdotes, and she smiles in all the right places, but I can't tell if any of them are ringing any bells in her head.

I don't know enough about amnesia to know if telling her stories about the past is a help or a hindrance. I hope the former, but am also aware that I'm battling against thirty years' worth of new memories that have been plastered over the top. I'm waiting for that light bulb moment when it all slots into place and she realises who I am and how much she's missed me. But I'm fighting a losing battle and each failed attempt to connect is shattering my heart further.

It's actually a relief when I feel my phone vibrating between my legs and see Bruce's name on the screen.

'Finally,' I say, slipping the phone between my ear and shoulder. 'Listen, I've got Mum and we're heading for—'

'Jess, it's Sheriff Randy Whitaker.'

I momentarily lose my grip of the wheel. 'Where's Bruce? Why are you calling on his phone?'

My imagination sparks with images of Bruce being apprehended by a lynch mob, and them threatening to kill him because of what I've done. I try to shake the images away, but my pulse is racing with paranoia.

'Is your mom okay?'

I glance over to her. 'She's fine. Where's Bruce?'

'I don't know how to put this delicately, but your friend – Bruce – is in a bad way. Isaac DeWalt escaped custody and... I don't know exactly what happened, but Bruce is in a bad way. We need your mom back here.'

'Let me speak to Bruce; for all I know you could have stolen his phone.'

'He's at the local hospital, and if he doesn't get treatment soon, he's not going to make it. I need your mom here. *He* needs your mom.'

'I don't believe you. Put him on the phone.'

I hear him sigh, and the line goes dead, but he phones back within a couple of minutes.

'J-Jess?' I hear Bruce gasp.

'Bruce? What's going on? Are you okay?'

He groans and I wince at the sound of his pain.

'Happy now?' Whitaker says pointedly, returning to the line. 'Your friend will die without your mom's help. You need to bring her back here *now*.'

I don't know how much Mum has heard, but I can see the anxious lines in her forehead. 'What is it? What's going on?'

I hang up the call, and drop the phone back into my lap, before turning to face her. 'That was your cult leader. He wants me to take you back.'

'Is that what you really think Rockston is? A cult? We are a community of likeminded people who have chosen to live in the mountains where the air is clean and everything we need is provided by nature. If you ask me, those that choose to work jobs they hate for a government that openly lies to them are the ones who need their heads examining.'

'Whitaker said Bruce is in trouble.'

'Bruce? That's your friend who was with you, right?'

I want to tell her that he's actually *her* friend, but I hold back. Every bone in my body is telling me that Whitaker is lying, and that he's using Bruce to get me to drive Mum back, but there's a voice in my head questioning this stance.

What if Bruce really is in trouble?

It isn't even a decision I have to make. There are no other car headlights in sight, and so I slow the car and perform a U-turn. I can only hope we're not too late.

46

JESS

April 2023, near Rockston, Maine, USA

The Rockston celebrations are in full swing as the town centre looms into view. Mum warns me that most of the roads through town are closed off because of the festival, and steers me round back roads until we arrive at what looks like a white detached residence on the corner of a street. It's about the size of a standard GP practice back home, but has a big wooden sign on the front lawn identifying it as Rockston hospital. The only car parked in front of the property is Sheriff Whitaker's cruiser, so I pull up behind and try to ignore the trail of blood droplets leading from the vehicle to the front door of the hospital.

Mum is first out of the car, and doesn't wait for me, before hurrying up to and in through the large white door. She's already pulling on scrubs and being briefed by a young man whose scrubs are covered in splashes of blood-red stains. Sheriff Whitaker is standing beside them both, and he is delicately holding Mum's hand.

There's no sign of Bruce.

I can't lose him. He never asked for the job of taking care of me, but he embraced it with both hands and I can't remember much about my life before he was a part of it. I should phone Paolo and warn him, but I don't want to worry him unnecessarily and I don't even know exactly what's happened to Bruce.

A door at the far end of the room opens, from which a young woman in a face mask emerges, and over her shoulder I see Bruce spread out on an operating table. I don't think twice, racing along the corridor and in through the door. I stop when I see how pale his face looks. There are small pieces of tape over his eyes to keep him from opening them, and a range of tubes poking out of his arms. There are gauze bandages over a wound in his side, but they're doing little to stem the flow of blood. He is so pale and helpless.

This is all my fault!

Had I not come on this ridiculous quest then he wouldn't have followed me over here. His life wouldn't be hanging in the balance. I should have searched for him before abducting Mum. I was worried he'd try to talk me out of the action, but I shouldn't have left him behind.

I reach for his hand, wanting to tell him how sorry I am, but I feel two hands on my shoulders and somebody pulls me backwards and out of the room. When I turn to check who it is, I see Mum's eyes staring back at me above the face mask and beneath the surgical cap.

'You can't be in there,' she says evenly. 'We need to keep the operating room free of germs. Your friend has lost a lot of blood, and I'm going to need to get him stitched up, but he's in a bad way.'

'Can you help him?'

She narrows her eyes. 'There might be something we can give him to help, but before I do, I need you to make me a promise.'

'Anything. Just help him. Please.'

She fixes me with a firm stare. 'This is my home,

and I cannot leave it behind. You have to promise me you'll let me stay here.'

And there it is: a choice between saving Bruce and saving my mum. It isn't a choice I even need to think about.

'Do whatever you need to do.'

'Are you sure?'

I nod as my vision is blurred by tears.

'Very well. There is a medicine we have here, which is full of iron, and has been handed down by generations within these mountains. It's his only chance, but if it works, he should make a full recovery.'

I think about what Bruce told me about the medicine that supposedly saved Mum's life thirty years ago. He didn't hesitate to accept the offer, but never understood the cost. What if it was that medicine that upset her mental health and led her to this point? Can I inflict the same curse on him?

'W-what's in the medicine?'

She glances over to where I now see Sheriff Whitaker eavesdropping, and he gently shakes his head.

'I can't tell you that, Jess,' she says. 'It is a well-protected secret, but without it, your friend has less of a chance of survival. He needs a blood transfusion, but we don't have any blood on site here, and the nearest hospital that does is several hours away.'

'Why wouldn't you have donated blood? What kind of hospital is this?'

'People in Rockston don't tend to get particularly ill; it's one of the benefits of living here. There are the occasional broken bones and accidents with farming machinery, but that's about all we have to deal with.'

The young man in blood-spattered scrubs comes across and tells her it's time to go in.

'Tell me what you want me to do, Jess.'

'Do whatever it takes to save his life, and we will leave this town and never look back.'

She nods, and heads inside, leaving me gawping at the door, and praying she's as skilled as she claims. I want to be in there to make sure she's doing everything she can for Bruce, but deep down I want to believe that she will have his best interests at heart.

I can see blood spatter on Sheriff Whitaker's shirt, and stomp over to demand answers about why Bruce is in this condition. He leads me to a bench outside just beyond the entrance. In the near distance, I can hear the sound of live music carried on the air. The town festivities must be fully underway by now.

'Thank you for bringing her back to me,' he says once we're seated.

And that's when I see it: the way he was prepared to lie to keep her safe; the urgency in his voice when he realised I'd taken her; the way he held on to her hand moments earlier. She is more than just a friend to him.

'You didn't really leave me much choice,' I say, my breath escaping in a thin cloud of steam as the cool night air takes hold. 'The two of you are an item?'

He smiles coyly. 'I didn't realise it at the time, but I fell in love with your mother the moment she wandered into our town, desperate for help. We became friends at first, and I loved her joie de vivre. She really embraced living amongst us, and learning about the traditions of Utlvyidedi. Of course, as I'm sure you can imagine, she didn't feel worthy enough to carry the responsibility it brings, but that in itself made her more worthy than the likes of Isaac DeWalt.'

'Where is DeWalt now? You said he escaped custody.'

The sheriff looks down at his feet. 'We were transporting him here, ready for your mom to take a look at his bloodwork and see what we could do, but the rest in the car ride must have helped him recover his energy. He was able to force the car off the road, and tore off into the night. Unfortunately he found your friend wandering near the motel, and jumped him, demanding to know where you and your mom were. This must have been shortly after the pair of you had driven off. A fight ensued and when we found Bruce, he'd been stabbed and DeWalt was threatening to stab him again. I had to put him down. He died right there in the car park.'

I can't escape how neatly tied everything will now be for him if Bruce doesn't recover. DeWalt was the only proof I had that Mum has been brainwashed, and Bruce is the only other person on my side who's seen that Mum is still alive. I've never felt so alone. All it would take is for Sheriff Whitaker to kill me now, and nobody would ever know Mum is alive and well.

'It took me years to pluck up the courage to ask your mom out for dinner,' he says, bringing his eyes back up to mine. 'She's like no other woman I've ever met. I really wish we hadn't had to meet in this way.'

'Why did you never tell her who she really is?'

He lets out a pained sigh. 'Because I'm a selfish idiot who was terrified I'd lose her.'

The honesty is unexpected.

'I should have told her the day I first saw the reports about her disappearance. It was about a year after she'd arrived, and she was finally starting to embrace the bracelet and what it means, and I'm ashamed to say that I chose not to tell her. And it was because I was in love with her, and still very much am.'

So I grew up without a mother because of this man's selfish actions.

I want to scream out how unfair it is, but it won't change what has happened.

'Words can't describe how sorry I am.'

'And if she wants to come back to the UK with me?'

'Nobody is keeping her here prisoner.'

'What about that stupid bloody bracelet? She said she can't go home with it on.'

He lets out an elongated sigh. 'There is a way it can be removed and passed on if necessary, but if I'm honest with you, I don't think your mom has any intention of leaving here.'

'That's because you've brainwashed her, and once—'

'Excuse me? Brainwashed? Heck no. This town is not some cult that keeps people prisoner by threats or lies.'

'Oh, no, but you expect them to believe in some magical bracelet?'

'It's not... there's more to it than that. I don't expect you to understand or condone, but maybe if you gave us a chance, you'd see that your mom wound up exactly where she should be. Here she's respected, cherished by so many, and makes a genuine positive difference to all of our lives.'

'And in return she has to give up who she really is.'

'With all due respect, I think your mom didn't know who she was before she came here.'

I stand, my anger finally giving way.

'Wait, please,' he pleads. 'I'm sorry, I didn't mean to upset you. You're the daughter of the woman I adore, and I was really hoping we might become friends at some point. If you give me a chance, I swear you'll see that I have nothing but the best intentions for your mom.'

But I've heard enough of his lies, and so I head back inside the hospital, grateful when he doesn't follow. I find a seat in the waiting room, and drop down. I'm not going anywhere until Bruce is awake, and if he doesn't recover, I'm going to bring every law enforcement agency and television news network to this town and reveal all their dark secrets.

It's been a long day, and despite my best efforts to fight it, exhaustion eventually takes control, and my heavy eyes close.

47

JESS

April 2023, Rockston, Maine, USA

I'm woken by the sound of a mobile beeping to say the battery is perilously low. Bright sunshine is streaming in through the window behind my head, and for a moment I have no idea where I am. And then it all hits me like a locomotive.

I jump to my feet, stalking towards the operating theatre, but as I move to push the door open, I find that it is locked. I can't see in through the round frosted glass window, and so I bang my hands against the door, calling out Bruce's name.

There's no answer, so I go off in search of any member of staff who can tell me where he is, and where my mum has gone. A growing sense of dread consumes me. My phone beeps again, and it's a frustrating reminder that in all the time I spent with her last night, I didn't once take her picture. I have no evidence that she's still alive.

What if they've killed Bruce and she's gone into hiding again?

The walls inside the building all look freshly painted, and there isn't a single sign to direct me to any specific locations.

Is this even a hospital?

I make my way back past the waiting room, and am relieved when I'm able to push open the main door and see the rental parked where I left it last night. There's no sign of the sheriff's cruiser. Racing over to the car, I open the boot, planning to search inside my bag for my charging cable, but then remember my bag is in the boot of Bruce's rental. Along with my passport.

I close my eyes and focus on my breathing. Panicking is not the solution. I just need to choose my next steps wisely, and pragmatically.

'Excuse me, are you Jess?'

I start at the woman's voice. She is dressed in a

pale blue nurse's uniform with a thin cardigan wrapped around her shoulders.

'Um, yes, I'm Jess.'

'Thank God,' she says, plastering on a relieved smile. 'I was supposed to wait with you until you woke up, but I had to go out the back to use the restroom, and when I returned you were gone. Anyway, I'm supposed to tell you that your friend – Bruce, isn't it? – that he's been transferred to the Whitaker house to aid his recovery.'

'He's okay, then? He made it through the surgery?'

'Oh, yes, as I understand it, everything went well and he's recuperating. The hospital isn't the most comfortable and so the sheriff said he'd put him up for a few nights.'

I've heard enough, and once she's given me directions, I drive over there. A small picket fence surrounds an enormous front lawn, leading up to a detached house twice the size of the one I grew up in. There is a decked porch out the front with a swing seat and shuttered windows. I park on the street in case I need to make a quick escape, and head up to the front door.

Mum meets me behind the screen door. 'Welcome to my home,' she says, as she pushes the door open, and allows me to enter.

The hallway is bright and airy, and smells of freshly baked cookies. It's like something out of *The Stepford Wives* movie.

'Would you like some tea?' she asks, and I nod as I stifle a yawn. 'Bruce is resting upstairs, but is already on the way to recovering. I expect he should be fit to travel again in a day or so. I've made up the spare bedroom for you so you can be nearby.'

The scar above her left ear seems more noticeable with all the sunshine beaming through the tall windows in the kitchen. She fills and places the kettle on the stove, before passing me a cookie jar.

'They're freshly made,' she says encouragingly, and so I take one and bite down into the soft and gooey texture.

'You used to hate baking,' I tell her when I've swallowed. 'Actually, all forms of cooking in general.'

She smiles at this. 'Did I? Well, I love cooking now, and baking. There's something magical about ingredients coming together to form something different, and better in many ways. Take that cookie, for instance. On their own, the chocolate chips are delicious and sweet; flour, eggs and butter on their own are not so delicious. But when you combine them in just the right quantities...' She smiles again.

'So is that what happens in Rockston? You take

people from all different places to make a better whole?'

'Something like that.'

'Is it okay for me to go and see Bruce?'

She nods. 'Absolutely. If you go up the stairs, he's in the first room on the left. Please tell him I'll bring him some tea when it's ready.'

I leave her dropping tea bags into a china pot, and make my way up the wide wooden staircase. There are art prints in frames leading all the way to the top of the staircase, and the final frame contains a black and white image of Mum and Sheriff Whitaker sharing a joke as they run through a field of flowers. It breaks my heart that she looks so happy in this life that omits me.

Bruce is gently snoring as I poke my head around the door, but a floorboard creaks and stirs him awake.

'How are you feeling?'

'Honestly? Like I've been stabbed, but it's better to be able to feel something, you know?'

'The sheriff said Isaac DeWalt stabbed you.'

'Yeah, my own stupid fault for not getting out of the way when the sheriff warned me to. Thank God he was on hand to get me to the hospital.'

I perch on the side of the bed. 'It's funny, when I woke up this morning and couldn't find you, I actually allowed myself to believe they might have bumped you off and left you in an unmarked grave.'

He chuckles, before wincing with the effort. 'I do wish I knew where you get your overactive imagination from. I'm fine, and your mum and Randy have been nothing but welcoming.'

'So you're buying this John Lennon "let's all live in peace" crap?'

'Do you know what? I think I'm starting to. From what they've said, there's virtually no crime here, there's a real sense of community spirit, and very little illness. What it lacks in big city convenience it more than makes up for with sociability.'

'Jeez, don't tell me you drunk the Kool-Aid too. Next you'll be telling me you believe in fairies and orbs.'

'Not at all. I'd miss Brighton too much if I lived here. All I was saying is I can see the appeal.'

'The sheriff reckons Mum won't come back with us, and in fact she made me promise I'd let her stay to save your life.'

'Well, I, for one, am glad you made that bargain. I guess a bit of my good sense rubbed off on you too.'

I give his leg a squeeze through the blanket. 'I'm not sure I would have made it to thirty-five without you. And I don't think I've ever formally thanked you for everything you've done for me, but I really do appreciate you and Paolo.'

'It has been my honour, and although I've no right to, I do think of you as my little girl.'

I'm about to speak again, but he raises his hand to interrupt.

'Which is why I feel confident in telling you that you ought to stick around here for a while longer.'

'In Rockston? Are you insane?'

'You came here looking to find out what happened to your mum, and now you've found her, but if you head home, you'll never learn what her life has been like for the last thirty years.'

'I can't just move to Rockston.'

'Why not?'

'Because I have a life in Brighton.'

'Do you? I'm sorry to speak out of turn here, Jess, but there's nothing tying you to Brighton. No job, evicted from your flat, and likely having to live with a middle-aged man who should know better and his younger Hispanic lover.'

'But I have you and Ashley.'

'And we'll remain there waiting for you to visit. You need to start living your life, Jess. You've been trapped by the shadow of your mum's disappearance, but for the first time that shadow is no longer there.

Ashley's going to have her hands full with a new-born imminently, and you're still young enough to start over.'

'She's not willing to move back, so why should I be the one to make all the effort?'

'Your mum has a new life here and no real reason to dig up what went before. No amount of effort and therapy can replace what you've both lost. But the fates have aligned in your favour, and there is no real reason why you shouldn't move here for a bit and use the time you have to get to know your mum for who she is now.'

'But what if she doesn't want me to stay?'

'Have you asked her? You were so hell-bent in getting her away from here you didn't once stop to question what she wanted. Put yourself in her shoes for a moment. You wake up one day and someone tells you that the last thirty years of your life has been based on a lie, and that you're in fact someone else with a whole other life you can't remember. I don't know where I would even begin to start processing that. Take me, for example, I spent the first thirty or so years of my life pretending to be someone I wasn't, because I was scared to explore who I really was. But since allowing myself to embrace my true self, I've found happiness and that I'm far more capable than I ever gave myself credit for. Don't deny yourself the chance of happiness.'

I want to argue that he's wrong and that I can't just start my life over, but then Mum comes in, carrying a tray with teacups, and I remember how three days ago I would have given anything in the world just to be able to tell her I love her. In this place, my dream has become a reality, and cutting my nose off to spite my face (my dad's favourite expression) doesn't benefit anyone.

EPILOGUE
JESS

July 2023, Rockston, Maine, USA

The cursor swirls on the screen while the call waits to connect. When it does, and I'm met with the most precious pair of eyes, my heart feels fit to burst.

'Oh my God, Ashley, he is absolutely gorgeous!' I gush, staring at my first godson as he gurns up at the camera.

'I know, right? I mean, I know all babies are meant to be cute, but he's on another level, isn't he? But then I'm biased.'

'I don't see any sign of bias there,' I concur. 'He is going to be an absolute heartbreaker one day.'

The screen temporarily goes blank as Ashley flips the camera on her phone, and I catch Roy's arm as he carries baby Archie out of shot.

'And how is Hove's most glamorous mum coping?'

'I don't know, but I'll let you know if I bump into her. Personally, I'm doing better since he came out of the Neonatal ICU. They're really pleased with the weight he's gaining, and it looks like we're nearing the edge of the woods. We should be able to bring him home soon. Speaking of which, are you ever going to come home?'

I can't believe it's been three months since that last-minute dash to the airport ended with me finding Mum here in the Appalachian Mountains. If Ashley hadn't been so heavily pregnant when I told her of my discovery, I'm sure she wouldn't have hesitated to jump on a plane and join me over here. I hadn't re-alised just how much I've missed her beautiful smile and pragmatic reasoning.

'Actually, that was part of the reason I wanted to speak to you,' I say, trying to remember the words I've rehearsed too many times to count. 'I've been thinking that I might stay a bit longer.'

I inwardly curse as the words slip out; they're not nearly as decisive as I'd intended. I'd meant to say I've decided to stay indefinitely because... well, because I like it here. I never knew air could smell so clean, and even when it rains here, there is a freshness to the raindrops like nothing I've ever experienced; it feels like the ground is being cleaned and prepared for nature to thrive. That phrase 'there's something in the water' is overused, but here it feels like there might actually be something in the water. I've never felt so healthy. I've even started running, which is a sentence I never imagined I'd ever say. Every morning, I rise with the sun, and I'm completing daily 5K runs, and double that at the weekends. I've never had such energy.

Of course, Mum's healthy cooking is probably partly responsible for that. I can remember hating vegetables as a child, but had they been prepared as they are now, I'd have probably given up meat sooner. Cheese is still a vice, but the only one I can genuinely think of. I can remember nights, when I'd had a bad day, where I'd drink until I passed out, yet I've not had anything alcoholic since arriving in Maine.

'Longer?' Ashley echoes, bringing my attention back to the conversation.

'Yeah. Mum's memory still hasn't fully returned, but every now and then she'll have a light bulb moment where something flashes before her eyes. I've got her writing them down so we can try and piece together a timeline of sorts. I don't want to abandon her and undo all the progress she's making.'

'And living together is working out okay?'

I look around the guestroom I've called mine for the last three months. I rearranged the furniture after Mum and Randy said I could stay for as long as I wanted, and it's all I need: a bed, a desk from which I can write, and a bookshelf of classics that I'm slowly making my way through.

'Actually, yeah, living together is brilliant. Mum and Randy are out most of the day, and then we come together for dinner and Mum and I stay up late chatting.' I smile. 'I genuinely couldn't be happier.'

'I'm pleased for you,' Ashley says, but her expression doesn't match the sentiment. 'But you *are* going to come back for Archie's christening, aren't you?'

'Wouldn't miss it!'

'Good,' she says, and actually sounds relieved. 'Daisy might finally stop asking me when she's going to see you again.'

I know she doesn't mean to make me feel bad, but the guilt at not being able to spend time with my god-daughter is eating me up inside. We've been chatting on Zoom every week, but I know it's not the same.

With a new sibling to contend with, she probably needs me more now than ever.

'You can tell Daisy that I *cannot* wait to see her, and am going to spoil her rotten. Tell her I'm going to take her to Hamley's and let her abuse my credit card with reckless abandon.'

'I will pass on the message, but I should warn you she has very expensive tastes, just like her Auntie Jess.'

I've been writing freelance for a travel website in my spare time, and have earned enough to settle my debts. I keep trying to buy things here, but Mum won't let me put my hand in my pocket. I guess I'm not the only one suffering with guilt.

'Will your mum be coming to the christening too?' Ashley asks next, and I don't know how to answer.

I haven't told Ashley why Mum believes she can never leave the US, because Ashley is even more cynical than I am when it comes to all this Trail Magic stuff.

'I'll have to check and let you know,' I say, to avoid the subject again. 'Has Bruce been in to see baby Archie yet?'

'So many times that I think the hospital are considering giving him his own dedicated parking space.'

She laughs. 'He told me you've started writing a book?'

I was hoping to surprise Ashley with this news. I've actually written more than half the book, and the feelers I've put out with agents suggests it should find a publisher when it's ready. I haven't yet broached the subject with Mum; I'm not sure how she'll feel about me telling her story. My hope is that it will help her remember more, and give her something to cling to. That's why I've got her writing those flashes of memory, but only time will tell if she agrees to it being published.

'Well, you always told me I should write a book one day.'

'I'm pleased to hear you're finally listening to me. Is your mum about? I'd love to introduce her to Archie.'

'Um, no, she's out at the moment, but I'll make sure she's here when we next catch up so you can say hello.'

'Shoot, I'm going to have to go. Roy is shouting something about needing a fresh baby-grow. I'll firm up church dates for the christening and let you know.'

'Perfect! Take care of yourself and give Daisy a big kiss and cuddle from me.'

The call ends, and I lower the lid of the laptop,

stand and head down to the porch. There isn't a cloud in the brilliantly blue sky, and somewhere there is a bird whistling a tune. Despite my refusal to believe in the idea of Trail Magic, there is something inexplicably magical about this town, and the bond that exists between a mother and daughter.

ACKNOWLEDGEMENTS

Words cannot begin to express how grateful I am to you for reading *One Wrong Turn*. I hope you enjoyed it (and go and tell all your friends just how much they should also read it). Please do get in touch via the channels below and let me know what you thought about it.

On 22 June 2022, my brilliant agent, Emily Glenister, tweeted: "I want a chilling, speculative thriller set in the Appalachian Mountains. There. I've said it. #MSWL". At the time I was drafting a number of ideas to pitch to her as our next project. When I read the tweet, I had to Google exactly where the Appalachian Mountains were, and became enthralled by the trail that runs from Georgia, all the way up to Maine. Within a couple of days, I had the basis for this story where a journalist goes hunting for her missing mother within those mountains, and when I pitched it to Emily she told me to write the book. Cue obsessive research, reading, and watching viral TikTok videos, and mentally I was fully immersed in the area. On 31 July (a mere 39 days after the original tweet), I sent the first draft of the book that would become *One Wrong Turn*. So, but for that tweet, this book wouldn't exist!

It has gone through multiple revisions since then, with both my agent Emily, and my brilliant editor Emily Yau at Boldwood Books, offering valuable insights on strengthening character backstories and driving the pace of the story. And I am so proud of what the story has become.

Thanks also to the full Boldwood Books team who all contribute to the finished product, and do so with such contagious enthusiasm. I really feel I've landed on my feet with a publisher as commercially switched on as Boldwood Books are. And I love that they want me to write more than one book a year, as writing is my favourite thing in the world.

As always, thank you also to my best friend Dr Parashar Ramanuj who never shies away from the awkward medical questions I ask him. Thank you also to Alex Shaw and Paul Grzegorzek – authors and dear friends – who are happy to listen to me moan and whinge about the pitfalls of the publishing industry, offering words of encouragement along the way.

My children are an inspiration to me every day,

and as they continue to grow so quickly, I am eternally grateful that I get to play such an important role in their development. They continue to show one another affection, patience and kindness, and make being their dad that bit easier. I'd like to thank my own parents and my parents-in-law for continuing to offer words of encouragement when I'm struggling to engage with my muse.

It goes without saying that I wouldn't be the writer I am today without the loving support of my beautiful wife and soulmate Hannah. She keeps everything else in my life ticking over so that I can give what's left to my writing. She never questions my method or the endless hours daydreaming while I'm working through plot holes, and for that I am eternally grateful.

And thanks must also go to YOU for buying and reading *One Wrong Turn*. Please do post a review to wherever you purchased the book from so that other readers can be enticed to give it a try. It takes less than two minutes to share your opinion, and I ask you do me this small kindness.

I am active on Facebook, Twitter, and Instagram, so please do stop by with any messages, observations, or questions. Hearing from readers of my books truly brightens my days and encourages me to keep writing, so don't be a stranger. I promise I *will* respond to every message and comment.

Stephen (a.k.a. M. A. Hunter)

https://twitter.com/stephenedger

https://www.facebook.com/AuthorMAHunter

https://www.instagram.com/stef.edger/

https://www.bookbub.com/authors/stephen-edger

https://www.goodreads.com/author/show/4973250.
Stephen_Edger

ABOUT THE AUTHOR

M.A. Hunter is the pen name of Stephen Edger, the bestselling author of psychological and crime thrillers, including the Kate Matthews series. Born in the north-east of England, he now lives in Southampton where many of his stories are set.

Sign up to M. A. Hunter's mailing list here for news, competitions and updates on future books.

Visit M. A. Hunter's website: stephenedger.com/m-a-hunter
Follow M. A. Hunter on social media

ALSO BY M. A. HUNTER

The Boat Party

One Wrong Turn

THE

Murder

LIST

THE MURDER LIST IS A NEWSLETTER DEDICATED TO SPINE-CHILLING FICTION AND GRIPPING PAGE-TURNERS!

SIGN UP TO MAKE SURE YOU'RE ON OUR HIT LIST FOR EXCLUSIVE DEALS, AUTHOR CONTENT, AND COMPETITIONS.

SIGN UP TO OUR NEWSLETTER

BIT.LY/THEMURDERLISTNEWS

Boldwood

Boldwood Books is an award-winning fiction publishing company seeking out the best stories from around the world.

Find out more at www.boldwoodbooks.com

Join our reader community for brilliant books, competitions and offers!

Follow us
@BoldwoodBooks
@TheBoldBookClub

Sign up to our weekly deals newsletter

https://bit.ly/BoldwoodBNewsletter

www.ingramcontent.com/pod-product-compliance
Lightning Source LLC
Chambersburg PA
CBHW010657100726
47900CB00010B/2698